The Last Odinian

By Alec Arbogast

Ink Smith Publishing
www.ink-smith.com
© 2017 by Alec Arbogast. All rights reserved

All rights reserved. This book or any portion thereof may not be reproduced or used in any manner whatsoever without the express written permission of the publisher except for the use of brief quotations in a book review.

Printed in the U.S.A

The final approval for this literary material is granted by the author.

All characters appearing in this work are fictitious. Any resemblance to real persons, living or dead, is purely coincidental.

ISBN: 978-1-947578-01-2

Ink Smith Publishing
710 S. Myrtle Ave Suite 209
Monrovia, CA, 91016

This book is dedicated to Maureen, Robert, and Dane,
whose guidance, support, love, and wisdom are unrelenting

"The boundaries which divide life from death are at best shadowy and vague. Who shall say where the one ends, and where the other begins?"
–Edgar Allan Poe

Prologue
The Ritual

I twisted and struggled and pulled, pulled hard, but it was no use. I wasn't strong enough and was rapidly growing weaker. All that cut through the dense canvas bag covering my head was the occasional slice of sunlight through the trees. I felt cool blades of grass brush my ankles. The unkempt vegetation had been steadily growing since the woods began.

Two hands were rooted firmly under my armpits. I could tell each one belonged to a different person by the way I was being yanked back and forth, like a trophy being carried by two competitors wanting a bigger share of the prize. They had been pulling me up an increasing terrain for what could have been minutes or hours, it was impossible to tell.

My throat felt stripped and raw from my previous attempts to scream for help. My larynx had to fight for even the most minute utterance, and the pain that incurred from even the slightest jiggle was immense. I figured I had been battered one too many times in the neck, leaving my voice box broken. All I could manage was a moan like a dying seal as I was dragged towards an unknown fate.

My assailants didn't speak to each other, or to me. They hadn't said a word. The sound of breathing and grunting came from every direction. The only noise I could distinguish from inside my burlap prison, aside from the rustling of leaves, was the solid stamping of feet. Feet. How many were there? It was impossible to tell. I focused on the scent of pine and dirt, and tried to steady my breathing, but each slow breath only magnified the pain in my chest.

After some time, the terrain began to even out. I inhaled, disregarding the inevitable searing pain in my rib cage that followed. The earthy smells were still abundant, but were slowly becoming enveloped by another scent. Like the taste of blood—tangy and slightly metallic.

I breathed in one more agonizing time. A foul second layer of this mysterious new scent greeted me. It smelled like I was approaching a dead carcass.

For a moment, the pitter-patter of feet ceased and I was no longer moving. I heard the sound of an old wooden door pivoting on rusty hinges just a few feet ahead, and felt the hands under my arms tighten as I was jerked forward again. The hint of sunlight that had been tickling my retinas disappeared and my world was plunged further into darkness.

The softness of the ground below ended and my feet found cold, hard stone. My center of gravity shifted and, with a cycle of dragging and falling, I blindly stumbled down a stairwell.

The sound of footsteps echoed off the nearby walls, as I was dragged into some sort of catacomb. The stench from before became nearly unbearable, and there was a dampness to it. I was underground.

The stone floor leveled off and I could make out little wavering circles of light drifting by on either side. The warm crackle of flames licked at my ears and shoulders. Where were they taking me, and what did they want with me? Another helpless little groan was all I could muster, paired with two swift but clumsy kicks left and right. They didn't let my flailing disrupt their pace. Whoever they were, they were wearing garbs that flowed back and forth as they walked. The fabric brushed against my bare shins as they escorted me to their destination.

Robes? Could this be some sort of demonic cult? I didn't know. All I knew was that my ability to breathe within the scratchy canvas bag was deteriorating as the oxygen thinned. We were going deeper and deeper down the narrow tunnel. I began gasping for air, my lips puckering, my chest constricting around the remaining air in my lungs.

The strange hands loosened slightly and pulled me to a stop. Footsteps echoed and rattled as the other figures dispersed to my left and right. All I could see were two ominous balls of light in front of me, and I could feel the warmth from other torches bouncing off the walls to the sides. I gulped in air, and once my lungs were satisfied with the new supply, I tried to slow my breathing. My heartbeat eased from a gyrating thrum in my throat, to a quick pulsing.

Breathe in, breathe out, I told myself. I could do nothing more.

For a moment, all was still. The tormenting silence in which they stood yielded to the faint din of a rat shuffling along the floor beside me. I could even discern the sound of its tail dragging on the stone. We were too far into the tunnel for any exterior noises to devise a way in. No more wind, no rustling tree branches. No more birds, squirrels or crickets. Just a suffocating silence.

A horrendous shriek pierced my ears. They must have been carrying another prisoner with them the entire time. At first, I couldn't tell what direction her voice came from. Her screams filled the stone box and refracted off each wall with a jarring intensity. I was able to pinpoint the woman's location after the reverberations died down, and the girl's initial scream turned into softer whimpers.

I looked to the left and saw a blurry, flailing motion in front of torchlight. Why had the girl been silent until now? Had she been drugged, and was only now waking?

"What are you doing with me?" the girl pleaded.

"Crying, into the world I came.

No grave shall there be, to bear my name."

A wall of voices surrounded us, drowning out the girl's screams. Chanting in unison just inches away, the two men holding me nearly ruptured my eardrums with the timbre of their voices.

"The earth, the wind, the rain, the fire.

My life's design, to build a pyre.

The embers of my soul shall kiss the sky.

Return to earth and let me die."

A seething silence followed. The rusty scent that reminded me of death continued to grow. I felt as though I would throw up at any minute, although my mind was too foggy to determine whether my nausea had been caused by the disgusting smell, the lack of oxygen in the chamber, or from the brutal beating they gave me before shoving me in the back of their van.

I attempted to lick my lips and felt my tongue catch between them. They were rough, like two strips of sandpaper, and my tongue felt dry and thick. I smacked it against the roof of my mouth over and over again, trying

3

to coax some spit out of my glands. It was no use.

My heart felt like it could seize up at any second; a pervasive dizziness forced me to close my eyes. Then the screams started again, in tandem with the chanting.

"Crying into the world I came."

The girl's shrieks became more prominent as they dragged her to the center of the chamber, just beneath the two torches in front of me.

"No grave shall there be, to bear my name."

The girl's cries began to sound slightly muffled, but did not desist.

"The earth, the wind, the rain, the fire."

I detected movement directly ahead, discerning the outline of a struggle.

"My life's design, to build a pyre."

I heard the faint shimmering slice of metal on metal, like a dagger being unsheathed. Then, the tearing of cloth. The voices swelled in strength.

"The embers of my soul shall kiss the sky."

The girl's cries sounded guttural now, riddled with raw, quivering tones of desperation.

"Return to earth, and let me die."

As soon as the last syllable in the twisted incantation was uttered, the girl fell silent. Her final haunting shouts of protest echoed through the chamber. Once again, a blanket of silence unfolded across the room. I felt a large hand fumbling at the back of my neck and winced as the sack was pulled off my head.

The first thing my gaze fell upon was the fresh corpse of a young woman, probably no older than her early twenties. She was tied to an upright wooden stake, her hands bound behind her. Her blouse was splayed in two, and jagged strands of it were strewn beneath her feet. Between her breasts and down the soft of her stomach was a rough pagan-like symbol, carved flesh deep into her body.

Blood was seeping out of the wounds and trickling down her abdomen to her white skirt, which was now patterned with thick, red droplets. The pallet of ravaged skin on the girl's torso was not severe enough to have been the cause of her death, but a more surgical, precise gash along her throat was.

Surrounding the body of the victim were men in long black robes with hoods covering their faces. All I could see were their frigid, emotionless eyes floating in the darkness of their hoods. They were all staring apprehensively at the lifeless figure, as if they knew something was coming, but didn't know for sure what that something was.

One of the hooded figures closest to the body held the murder weapon in his fist. A long, scalloped dagger shone under the torches, saturated with blood and bits of filleted flesh. Behind the gruesome image was a sort of shrine, upon which, were propped a couple of ancient looking relics. One of them was an ornate cross that had meticulous etchings carved on its thick, stone body.

My ability to see under the dim and flickering light of the torches was impaired, but I could tell the cross was archaic; it looked like it could have been crafted during the dark ages. To the left of the cross was a more peculiar relic. It was a knight, thoroughly plated in armor, upon a formidable horse sculpted in mid-gallop. The beast was titanic in stature, positively dwarfing the man upon it. The knight had a unique looking sword in his hand that contained little geometrical adornments along its shaft.

I looked to the left and right. My veiled guesses had been relatively accurate; I was in some sort of underground tomb. Along the surrounding stone walls were large rectangular cutouts, and in each space were caskets large enough to fit human bodies.

Who built this catacomb of death? A chill descended upon me when I considered there may be an empty casket waiting for me.

An undercurrent of grunts and murmurs spread amongst the robed men. As they whispered, I began to feel a bud of pressure in my ears. At first, it was so subtle that I barely took note, but it rapidly developed into a virulent gust, as if my whole body was being yanked forward by an unseen force. The men around must have felt it too, briskly falling into silence around me. The stench I had managed to forget during the murderous event was growing even stronger, like my nose was buried inside the gut of a dead man.

At once the torches began to quiver, their flames dancing and sputtering. An icy gale burst into the tomb and threatened to blanket us in total, suffocating darkness. I could not only feel the change in pressure, but could hear the whistle of air as it stampeded from behind us and propelled towards the center of the room.

All around me, I saw the ghostly silhouettes of the men in the lingering light stumble forward and collapse under the pressure; their robes flailing and twirling madly. There was a swooshing noise followed by a deafening crack. The torches wavered and died, enveloping the tomb in a terrific blackness.

I couldn't see a thing. My unsteady breathing and a deep throbbing in my head was all I could focus on. Soft curls of air brushed my shoulders as the two men who still held me tightly exhaled. I felt something squirm over my foot, a rag of coarse hair massaging my ankle, and kicked. I heard a rat squeal and scurry away.

The utter silence caused a frenzied panic to pervade my mind. The hairs on the back of my neck stabbed like needles. I realized something else was in the room with us. A devious presence had crept into the chamber; something that seethed with malice, and simmered with hatred. I could taste it; that same metallic scent that stung my nostrils earlier now fell upon my tongue.

The fingers of a new fear poked at my mind while the torches reignited all around me. Everyone's focus hastily gathered to the center of the room, where, looming behind the body of the dead girl, was a ghostly figure.

The fear in the room was palpable; everyone's eyes locked upon the figure. When it exhaled, two tendrils of air shot out of its nostrils and bathed me in a frosty embrace.

"Bring her to me." Its menacing timber, which was

disproportionately large for its body, rattled the chamber. The two men clutching me with trembling hands, clambered forward.

"We..." one of them stammered. "We lost the child back in the forest, my lord."

Chapter One
The Man in the Road

His fingers danced across the grooves of his jacket, the corduroy, soft and plush against his skin. Fingering the seams of an outer pocket, he brandished a box of cigarettes and pulled one out. Before raising it to his face with a shaking hand he paused, realizing his lips were still kissing a lit cigarette. He stared for a long moment at the little paper box in his hand and thumbed a tattered corner. The familiar logo, "Golden Light Cigarettes," seemed to dance under the warmth of the dim fluorescent light, and the image of a lighthouse printed on the front of the box swayed in the shadows.

A gruff voice broke the silence.

"Hey mister uh, Koh-nig, was it?" Waking from his trance, he fumbled for the pocket of his jacket and buried the cigarettes inside.

"Koenig," he said, out of the corner of his mouth that the cigarette wasn't occupying. "Pronounced Kay-nig." He had a commanding voice. One that wasn't particularly deep or refined, but had a gravelly tone that never shook or stuttered. He turned to face the officer behind him. "Although Edward will do just fine. Easier to pronounce."

"Koenig, that's exotic. What is that, Swedish? Dutch?" Sheriff Grady asked. He was a tall man with a rough complexion and a receding hairline accentuated by the grey hair that he slicked back. With a stern face that was likely aged beyond its years, he looked like a man who had seen a great deal of action. But the softness in his midsection suggested that it had probably been awhile.

"German, actually." Koenig faked a smile. "Although, I do have a lot of Swedish and a little Dutch in me, along with a smatter of blood from of the rest of Europe. Pretty good guesses." Grady extended an arm toward him and he obliged. The man's rough and calloused hand was certainly not that of a pencil pusher. Koenig could tell that Grady was a man accustomed to taking charge and getting results rather than frittering away with small talk.

"Well guessing the correct continent is close enough for me," he chuckled. "Welcome to Pinemist Bay, mister uh, Koenig, pleasure to meet you. I'm Sheriff Robert Grady." Grady had a harsh, scratchy bark for a voice, and he heaved when he spoke; like his lungs had to work hard to get anything out.

Let's just get on with it. I've had a long night, Koenig thought to himself, faking a smile at the sheriff.

"Nice to meet you Sheriff Grady. This is a lovely town," he said.

"Aw, well, thank you. One of my assistants said there was an outsider who had requested to speak with me, said you needed some refuge from that downpour, and that you had somethin' to report to me." Grady barked as he led Koenig into his office; the wooden door creaking as it opened. Everything in Pinemist Bay seemed sprawled out, disjointed, and eerily quiet. If anything broke the silence, even a small sound like Grady's office door, it didn't just graze the ear, it pierced it.

Following Sheriff Grady into the room, Koenig heard footsteps echo down the hall to the right, and the low grumble of voices as the late-night staff floated around the station. The crew was sparse tonight.

"Come on in, sit down. Make yourself at home. That corduroy coat must just soak up the rain," Grady chuckled.

"This helps." Koenig nodded, propping his drenched umbrella against the chair as he sat down. Grady walked around his large oak desk and let out a sigh as he seated himself. Koenig heard the clacking of footsteps approach the door and he heard it moan once again, sending a little shiver down his spine.

"Anything I can get for you Sheriff?" a woman's voice asked. Koenig turned to see Grady's secretary holding the door open and leaning inquisitively towards them. She appeared to be in her mid-thirties and had thick glasses on her face. Her hair was a red that nearly matched the burgundy colored blouse beneath. Koenig could tell that her eyes were hazel, but under the shadows cast by the dull hallway lights, they glowed a much darker, sultry shade of green. Koenig found himself lost in her eyes. This woman had a gentle, simple beauty that captivated him unrelentingly.

"Get this gentleman a coffee, Darlene. He needs something to warm up his bones," Grady said. "How do you take it, Edward?"

"Black with a sugar cube, please," Koenig said, and then looked away so as not to make the woman feel uneasy by what was becoming a prolonged stare. He took a long drag of his cigarette and stamped it out in the visitor's ashtray. The only light in the room came from a desk lamp beside Sheriff Grady, which caused a mosaic of shadows to bounce across the room. Underneath the lamp was the sheriff's own ashtray, upon which was propped a slowly burning cigar. The smoke trailing from its tip looked ghostly under the light.

"And for you, sir?" she inquired.

"Black, if you will," Grady said, while ushering her away with a wave of his hand. When the door closed behind her, the air inside the room grew still and quiet. It was as if Grady's office was a giant vacuum, siphoning out all the chatter of the station. Through an open window to the sheriff's left, a breeze was stirring behind the pines. The scent of rain and earth tickled Koenig's nostrils.

Leaning back in his chair, the sheriff's eyes fixated on Koenig.

"Well, Edward, on behalf of the entire county of Pinemist Bay I'd like to thank you for making the trip up to our quaint little town. We're a pretty good stretch from Chicago." Grady tapped his fingers on the desk. "I trust the trip went alright?" He lifted his hand and motioned briefly at Koenig's head, where a bruise blossomed like an aging purple lily. "What's that on your forehead?"

****

The wind howled menacingly and rain slapped the windshield of his car. The wipers moved like a pair of frail, bony arms of a drowning man, waving frantically for survival.

Koenig had never been a nervous driver. Climbing up this steep mountain road on any other day would have been like a regular trip to the lake. Today, however, there was something menacing in the air. For the past several miles, the road was largely fixed on the edge of an ever-climbing mountain, and Koenig could barely see the valley below through the torrents of rain and wind, and a curtain of fog that blemished the mountains. To the highest peak ahead, he had a hard time making anything out. *How can that be? How can there be such dense fog with this much wind and rain?*

The dashboard of his restored '76 Mustang glowed ominously as night began to fall. Beside the instrument cluster, the hands of the clock read 7:06.

How do I get myself tangled up in these situations? Koenig thought, and slapped the wheel. *Oh god Edward, you're in it now and there's no going back, not with Dalla's voice screaming inside my head.*

As the car lurched around a curve on the edge of the precipice, a raw, gyrating pain assaulted his head. He slammed on the brakes and centered the wheel as the ponderous car began to over-steer. It was happening again.

Ever since he left home earlier that morning, he had been having bizarre seizure-like episodes where his vision would blur and a violent, pulsating pressure would encompass his head. The sensation was so great that he needed to pull over every time it occurred and wait out the storm. The feeling would arise out of nowhere, and during the occurrence, his four-year-old daughter's voice would inexplicably echo in his mind.

As if in a dream, she called to him, beckoning him towards Pinemist Bay. "*Daddy,*" Dalla said, and as she spoke, a searing pain shot up his spine and resonated in his skull. "*Come find us in Pinemist Bay. Mommy and I need you...*" Her voice, and the overwhelming sensation in his head, attenuated and his vision stabilized. He rubbed his temples, surprised to find them damp with sweat, and rolled his eyes to the left. He took an edgy, trembling breath.

The edge of the cliff was not a foot from his left tire. If he so much as opened the door and stepped out, he would be a dead man. Peering downwards, he could clearly see the bottom of the chasm far below. The terrain was riddled with pine trees that looked like flakes of pepper from such a height. He shook his head, rallied his nerves, and eased back onto the road.

As he continued up, the ground began to level out. The path slowly diverged from the side of the cliff into the meat of the mountain and became unforgivingly windy. The pine trees now closed in overhead and the world suddenly seemed smaller.

Without having seen a single signpost or marker, Koenig had no idea where he was. He could have been twenty miles up the mountain, or sixty. There was no concept of time in this no man's land, no indication that time even existed, except for the slowly moving hands on the clock atop the dashboard.

Koenig had switched off the radio near the bottom of the canyon when the reception had become too spotty. This was the first time in a while he had been truly alone with his thoughts, which, in the current state of things, was not good. He rubbed his tired eyes as the big eight-cylinder engine roared under the hood, catapulting him ever onward into the unknown. Koenig found himself stretching forward in his seat, attempting to see the sky between the blur of tree branches that passed above the car, but to no avail. The fog was too thick, and even if the air had been devoid of haze, he still would have failed to see beyond the dense pines. It made him uneasy to be encased in the dark womb of nature, and it was agitating that he couldn't make anything out beyond even the first line of trees in front of him. Rocks, boulders, shrubs, droopy branches and languid trees; everything appeared abruptly and then flowed past, disappearing into the darkness behind. Then, something unexpected came into view.

At first, Koenig couldn't tell what it was in front of him. There was a small white flash and an object appeared directly ahead, too small to be a tree or a signpost, and too narrow and upright to be a deer. Koenig squinted, then slammed on the brakes and cranked the steering wheel. For a mere moment, the object came into view under the Mustang's powerful fog lamps and Koenig thought he saw the pinkish-yellow of skin. His brain was unable to process more before the big, heavy car lost control and, with a piercing screech from the tires, careened off the road. He felt the lap restraint constrict against his legs as he was lurched upward, and then the shoulder harness bit into his torso as he was thrust forward with ferocious momentum. Koenig's head met the steering wheel with a crunch.

All went still.

With some effort and a long groan, Koenig slowly lifted his head. The engine rumbled in front of him. *Good. At least the motor is still running,* he thought. He immediately touched his hand to his forehead and winced from the pain. No wetness, though—no blood. Just a sharp bump. *I knew I should have put the damn airbag back in after I restored this thing,* he shook his head. The only airbag Koenig did put back in after the restoration project was the one on the passenger's side, for when his little girl rode along. Letting out a sigh of relief, Koenig looked into the rear-view mirror of the car and unbuckled his seat belt. The fog behind was churning in ghostly circles.

"What the fuck was that?" he grunted to himself. The muggy air was too thick for him to make anything out. Normally, Koenig would have immediately gotten out of his car and inspected it up and down for body damage or a popped tire. Something was holding him inside though; a fear or dread that he couldn't shake. It was like the feeling he got as a child when he walked by a mirror in his house and saw something in the reflection that didn't belong there. Some abhorrent shape would appear and then vanish, or something might dart by the corner of his bedpost in the reflection. But every time young Koenig's eyes returned to the mirror, whatever he saw would be gone. He continued to gaze into the rear-view mirror, his stare unwavering.

Come on Edward, you're 33 years old, shake it off. He didn't dare peel his eyes off the mirror. *Whatever was back there, you're probably in no danger,* he comforted himself. The fog behind the car that had been tumbling from the commotion was finally settling down and beginning to thin out. Koenig saw a figure slowly materialize in the road. It was a human being. At least, it looked like one from his vantage point.

Koenig rubbed his eyes with cold, sweaty fingers, half believing the figure in the road would be gone when he looked again. It remained. He was sure now that the figure was human; a man, standing, but slightly hunched over. Koenig was curious, but apprehensive. Feeling a tremulous chill sink deep into his bones, he stepped out of the vehicle.

The man in the road remained motionless, facing slightly away, as if he was transfixed by something, during Koenig's slow approach. As far as Koenig knew, the man hadn't moved a muscle since Koenig narrowly avoided hitting him with his car. He couldn't even tell if the man was breathing. The man just stood there, looming like a statue in a graveyard. As he approached, and the thinning layer of fog between them dissipated, Koenig saw that the man was naked.

"Hey man, sorry about that." Koenig startled himself when he realized his voice was shaking. "I, uh, I didn't see you standing there...I almost hit you." The man remained still. Making sure there was a comfortable distance between them, Koenig walked around to meet him face to face.

The man was old and sinewy. His bald head coruscated as rain drizzled down his cheeks to his shoulders. Goose bumps were poised all over his old, saggy flesh. Koenig cleared his throat.

"You're sopping wet old man, what are you doing out here?" Koenig pulled his jacket off and turned it around to wrap the old man in it. Right as the jacket was about to embrace him, the old man came to life and burst into a frenzied rambling. Startled, Koenig stumbled backwards and nearly lost his footing on the drenched road. The old man was speaking at a blisteringly fast pace, and Koenig couldn't understand what he was saying through the ramshackle phrases. He couldn't tell if the man even knew where he was.

Koenig wiped his eyes with a soaked and trembling hand, and watched as the old man's head began to shake violently. The ramblings eased and he slowly lifted his head to look into Koenig's eyes, but with the violent tremors the man was experiencing, it was impossible to establish eye contact.

"Edward...Koenig," the old man spat between inane grunts. Koenig felt the air escape his lungs and he clutched his chest with an unsteady hand.

How the fuck does he know who I am?

Koenig's heart was hammering against the wall of his sternum, and he began to feel dizzy. *I must be dreaming; I have to be.* The old man's jaw started to open and close repeatedly, as if he was struggling to find his own tongue.

"What...what did you say?" The words came out this time, but were soft enough that a gentle breeze could whisk them away. The old man did not seem to hear Koenig, and he didn't reply. His ramblings slowly subsided, but his head continued to spasm violently.

"Edward...Koenig. You must...listen to me." The old man fought with every word, as if it pained him to speak.

"I don't understand!" Koenig interrupted. "How do you know who I am? I've never met you before in my life. This must be some kind of dream..." His eyes stayed on the old man's face. Although he desired to, Koenig could not bring himself to return to his car and leave the man to the elements, not before hearing what he had to say.

"There is not...much time, and they are listening...always listening." The wind started to whine between the trees. Behind the old man, the pines began to wave their arms and sway from side to side. The gale strengthened, carrying a stench that crawled into Koenig's nostrils and made him cringe. It was similar to the foul smell of something dead and decaying, accompanied by a rusty metallic scent; like a big rain-soaked nail buried in the flesh of a wet dog. Koenig looked around nervously; the fog surrounding them was lifting.

"You are here, now...so what is set in motion cannot be undone," the old man said. "But, maybe you can still vanquish him..."

"Vanquish who?" Koenig asked, feeling the hairs on the back of his neck stiffen. The old man's head wobbled from side to side, as if he was scanning the nearby woods for someone, or something.

"When did you last speak...to your family?" His focus returned to Koenig.

"Right before I left," Koenig said after a brief pause. "What do they have to do with any of this? My wife and daughter are in Chicago."

"Listen to me...do not let the Vucari find you. If you walk the year, true darkness will reveal itself to you."

Do not let the Vucari find you; if you walk the year, true darkness will reveal itself to you. Koenig was trying to memorize the old man's instructions, even though he was nothing but baffled by the entire situation.

"Will you...remember that, Edward?" the old man begged.

"Yes. Who are you?" Koenig thought this was the most pertinent question.

"All in time, Edward." The old man's head momentarily stopped moving and his cracked mouth upturned into a grin that looked sincere but tortured. Koenig entertained a twinge of compassion, even appreciation, for the old man.

"Now, you must leave at once...return to your car and continue to Pinemist Bay, and remember what I have told you."

Koenig took a long last look at the old man, desperately craving to pursue the many questions in his mind. Then, he turned toward the side of the road and slowly walked to his car. Deep in thought, he climbed in and took a long breath to steady his nerves. He cradled the shifter in his palm. Before clicking it into reverse, Koenig looked into the rear-view mirror, still worried about the old man alone on the road. But the old man, and the fog, were gone.

****

Koenig watched a trail of steam escape from Grady's mug and swell under the warm light of the desk lamp. He felt the heat from his own cup in his hands and, feeling somewhat more relaxed, let out a sigh.

"Well, Edward, it's not too often that we have outsiders around here, given that we're so isolated. We're a simple, but kind folk. So…why is it that you stopped by my station before headin' into town?" Grady asked.

The sign for the sheriff's department had been the second one Koenig came upon after leaving the old man. He had driven further up the winding road until it leveled out, when the ominous glow of the "Welcome to Pinemist Bay County" sign materialized. It had been partially overtaken by foliage, but Koenig could still make out the image of a shimmering bay cradled under a nest of pine-covered mountains. A few hundred yards later another sign reflected in his headlights, "Pinemist Bay County Sheriff's Department." It was an old printed sign lit up from underneath by two powerful halogen lamps.

He had rushed in to the sheriff's department because he needed to inform the authorities about his bizarre encounter on the road. Koenig was half assuming that the old man may have been one of the escaped crazies from a local asylum, and half assuming that what he saw was a figment of his imagination. Altitude sickness was known to cause hallucinations.

Now, sitting in the sheriff's office, Koenig had wanted to tell him about the old man in the road, even if just to restate the events and confirm his sanity. But he couldn't bring himself to do it. He was well aware of how crazy his story would sound, and more importantly, he didn't know or trust anyone in this isolated town. It didn't help that the sheriff's demeanor was rubbing him the wrong way. Something intangible about Grady put Koenig off.

"I wanted to come in and warm up," Koenig said, biting his lower lip. "My eyes were getting pretty weary after tackling that windy canyon road. I figured maybe you'd have some coffee on!" He raised the mug for emphasis, hoping the sheriff would believe him and move on.

"We've got the best brew in all of Pinemist Bay County here at the station! We get it from Blackrock Café in town; be sure to visit there during your stay if you're a fan of coffee!" the sheriff said. "So what is it that you do, if you don't mind my askin'?" Grady leaned back in his chair and rocked it from side to side with his feet.

"Corporate analyst for a pharmaceutical company based in Chicago." Koenig hadn't thought of his job since starting up the road to Pinemist Bay. His mind had become a convoluted mess ever since his daughter's troubling messages began, and the old man in the road had escalated it.

"Ooh we got a pill pusher in our little town, run for the hills." Grady's coarse voice let out a laugh, and he raised a gimpy hand. *Grady thinks himself a comedian. Sad thing is, in a county with 7,536 people, he may be the town funny-man.*

"So what's the name of the company you work for?" Grady asked, returning to his line of questioning.

"Hammond and Wilkes, LLC," Koenig stated. "You've probably heard the name, we're the supplier for about half of the drugs along the west coast. We've got a large distribution network in California."

"No, no," Grady said, shaking his head firmly. "I've never heard of that company. But, and don't take this the wrong way, mister, here in Pinemist Bay, we take a firm stance against drugs of any kind. You see, we believe there are other ways, safer and better ways, to connect with our spiritual side." Grady's voice grew louder and his eyes widened.

"And we don't cover up our flaws, our God given traits, with some synthetic, phony-baloney, mind trickin' voodoo substances." Grady hit the desk, knocking his cigar off the ashtray. At first, he just stared at it, as if he had surprised himself with his outburst. Then, clearing his throat, he gingerly picked the cigar up by its butt and placed it back on the ashtray, leaving behind a charcoal colored smudge on the desk.

"Anyways, Edward, what was the purpose of your comin' here?" He changed the subject. Feeling even more uncomfortable in the man's presence, Koenig shifted in his seat.

"Well, I rarely take real vacations and I thought to myself, why take another boat out on Lake Michigan, or stay in town and check into another hotel in the Chicago Loop? Why not go somewhere you have never been? And I remembered how my father had come through here very briefly on his way up to Vancouver for business. He had told me that the Cascade Mountains really helped him to relax. He mentioned this place in particular."

What he said was only partly true, his father did travel to Pinemist Bay once when Koenig was a teenager. George Koenig was frequently out of town for work, but after the fateful trip to Vancouver, he was never the same. He returned a changed man, a broken man. George kept to himself far more than usual after visiting Pinemist Bay, and developed a debilitating drinking problem that worsened through Koenig's teenage years.

Koenig began to find it hard to live with his father after that, but he and his mother stood by George's side and attempted to maintain a degree of normalcy in their lives. George continued to harbor a deepening depression, but over time, he divulged some details of the fateful business trip that changed his life. Whenever he spoke of his journey up the Pacific Northwest to Canada, which he only ever did when he was drunk, he would whisper it to young Koenig—a warning.

"I want you to promise me something, Eddie. When you grow up and move out of the house and explore the world, which you will do someday, it's the way of life, promise me you will keep your wits about you if you go to Pinemist Bay. It is a dangerous old port town. Somebody may try and take you there, or to convince your family to go, but don't let them. Remember what I'm telling you. Can you promise me that, Eddie?"

He remembered nodding in reply and thinking to himself that he would likely never travel that far from their hometown of Rochelle, Illinois. Through the years, however, Koenig's mild curiosity about Pinemist Bay developed into a hunger. He starkly remembered watching his father's casket being lowered into a grave at the Rochelle Public Cemetery, and thinking to himself that, one day, he would discover what it was in Pinemist Bay that broke the strongest man in his life.

Before he even made it out of Illinois, he met his future wife, Eveline. They settled down in the burgeoning Chicago Loop and had a beautiful daughter together. The mysterious old port town sat on the back burner for a while after that. The image of the deflated man that it turned his father into did not. It became inhumed in his psyche indefinitely.

"Well, Sheriff Grady, it's been great meeting you, but it's been a very long night and I'd like to change out of these wet clothes and get some rest." Grady glanced at the clock on the wall and stood up.

"Yes, Edward, I completely understand. It is a long drive all the way up here from the airport." Grady chuckled as he leaned over his desk and took Koenig's hand in another firm shake. "Thanks for stoppin' by," he said. Koenig could smell a mixture of cigar smoke and coffee on the sheriff's breath, but another scent lingered equivocally behind them; like an afterthought in a writer's mind. Whiskey.

As Koenig stood and leaned over Grady's desk, a light scintillated off something behind it. He hadn't noticed from where he was sitting, but the lower drawer of the sheriff's desk was half open, and inside lay a half-full bottle of amber liquid: "Mt. Hood Single Malt Whiskey."

Taking care not to look too long, Koenig's eyes met the sheriff's again, but too late. Grady glanced down inquisitively for what might have caught Koenig's eye. He couldn't tell if the sheriff noticed that his drawer of debauchery was open, but a momentary look of unease painted Grady's face. He cleared his throat, looking back at Koenig. The sheriff's grasp on Koenig's hand tightened more forcefully now, and he pulled him closer.

"Thanks for stopping by," he repeated, this time with a labored intensity behind his eyes. "I like to know what goes on in my town, ya know, keep a close watch." Grady's eyes were slimmer now, as if he was studying Koenig. "I'm the jurisdiction around here, and nothin' gets past me. Anyone that comes in, anyone that goes out, I'm aware of it. I've got eyes everywhere."

His tone changed to a more conversational one and his grip loosened. Koenig could feel cool air kiss his sweaty hand. "So anything you need, you just let me know." Grady grinned. It was an ugly, self-serving grin that revealed only one or two teeth in the middle. Mustering a smile, Koenig pulled his hand away.

"Thank you for your hospitality, Sheriff Grady. I'll be sure to let you know if I need anything."

Grady rounded his desk, his big belly grazing the edge, and led Koenig out of his office.

"My assistant Darlene will show you out." Koenig had forgotten about Darlene. He looked to his left and there she was, sitting unassumingly in her booth to the left of Grady's office. He motioned to her in an awkward gesture and she smiled back.

"Would you like her to show you around town, Mr. Koenig?" Grady asked. "It's a pretty small place, but I bet you must feel like a fish out of water."

"Oh no, no that's fine," Koenig said, thinking of his wife, Eveline, and how their situation was already delicate. "I'm sure I'll get along just fine by myself, thank you."

"Alright mister. Well, you can stay at the Pinemist Hotel. It's the only lodging around here for outsiders," Grady said. "And they're plenty accommodating. I had better get back to my work." With that, Grady's door moaned shut, leaving nothing but a frosty silence between Koenig and the girl.

"Let me walk you out, Mr. Koenig." Darlene maneuvered out from behind her desk. Koenig fought hard not to stare. They slowly made their way down the halls of the sheriff's department to the soundtrack of their own echoing footsteps. The building was nearly empty now.

"So, how long do you plan on being here, Mr. Koenig?" she inquired.

"Please, uh, call me Edward. I'm not really sure how long I'll be here, I just wanted to get away," he said.

"So, have you heard of the disappearances?" she asked, with a softer voice now.

"Disappearances?" *Did a senile old man happen to go missing recently?* He looked over at Darlene. The equanimity of her facial expression didn't mask the fear beneath it.

"They're saying that it's not safe to go out at night, at least, not until the situation is figured out." She looked around cautiously as if she didn't trust someone who might be lingering in earshot. "That's one of the reasons we're all here at the department right now. Normally things here shut down at around eight or nine o'clock. Everybody's working overtime trying to figure out what's happening in Pinemist Bay. Things like this haven't happened in a peaceful town like ours in quite some time."

Maybe that's why Grady seemed so suspicious of me. They rounded a corner and continued down a long hallway, which led to the station's entrance. About halfway down the hall, a janitor was meticulously mopping along the grooves of the tile floor. He slowly lifted his head as they walked by, but it was difficult to see his face through the shadows cast by his baseball cap. All Koenig could make out was a toothless smile following them as they walked by.

Koenig yearned to know more about the mysterious disappearances, but he couldn't bring himself to ask Darlene. *Why is she telling me all of this?*

"Well, Mr. Koenig – Edward." She was blushing. "It was nice meeting you."

"You too, Darlene." He couldn't think of what to say. "Uh, thanks for the coffee."

"My pleasure, I hope you find the hotel all right." He began down the steps and opened his umbrella, already getting pelted by unsavory slices of rain. "And be mindful of the lights in there. That building is old, and the wiring is pretty bad." And then she said with a hint of emphasis, "In the darkness, you may not know if someone's coming for you."

    Koenig paused mid-step upon hearing Darlene's advice and thought of what the old man had said. 'Do not let the Vucari find you.' Was he being paranoid, or was there some kind of connection? Could she be hinting about the same danger the old man warned him about? He pivoted to face the doorway, but she was gone.

Chapter Two
The Hotel

The town of Pinemist Bay was nestled on a series of small hills that reached up into the mountains to the east, and tapered off into the bay to the west. It couldn't have been more than a mile long in any direction. Most of the shops and businesses were located on Main Street, which zig-zagged down the center of the town and then forked off in either direction along the bay. It was a laid back, rural town. Everything about Pinemist Bay was the exact opposite of Chicago.

Koenig stretched forward until his nose was almost touching the windshield of his car in a fruitless attempt to read the street sign in front of him. The rain made it difficult to see almost anything. This far northwest, the rainfall was never sparse, and in the dark pit of night, it was an impenetrable wall of water. Unable to decipher the words on the sign, Koenig inched his car further down the road.

Unsurprisingly, the streets of Pinemist Bay were entirely deserted. Koenig surmised that the town was like the mountains that engulfed it, a desolate and lonely place. He imagined that the residents were always either sleeping, or hiding behind their window shades and complaining about their neighbor's lawn that was getting too high, or groaning that the general store never carried the items they needed. *A desolate town that capitalizes on trivial matters because there's never anything to do or talk about,* Koenig thought to himself.

As the Mustang crested another hill, the dim lights of a tiny town blinked at him behind a sheet of rain. Lampposts positioned at every half block scintillated through the darkness. They were the only objects on the road that Koenig could firmly distinguish, the buildings behind them just a tenebrous backdrop. Main Street was a bit brighter. Lights in the upper floors glowed warmly, and a few storefronts were still glowing.

I'm assuming that the hotel is on Main, Koenig thought. *I should have at least gotten directions from that beautiful Darlene girl.*

He turned onto Main Street, passing a building with a large vertical neon sign that loomed above, reading 'Seaside Diner.' The sign glowed warmly in the night, and made the slivers of rain falling around it shine electric green and blue before vanishing to the darkness below.

Beside the diner was a hulking white, colonial style building. It had blue window shutters that climbed four stories high and met a black shingled roof. Koenig squinted to see that the building wrapped around the block and continued up the next street. Pulling the big muscle car closer to the front door, he saw an old vanilla colored placard. Underneath, a lamp bathed the old sign in just enough light to be legible in the torrent.

Pinemist Hotel
Established in 1804
Historic Landmark

    Lurching the car into a rough U-turn, he parked curbside in front of the door. He stepped out of the vehicle and snatched his suitcase from the backseat. Taking the steps three at a time, he bounded under the shelter of a low awning that stretched the entire length of the hotel. The front door was a worn shade of green and made of some type of wood that didn't age well. Cracks and grooves ran from its base to its heart, where they splayed out in all directions. Koenig opened the door and stepped inside.

    The lobby of the Pinemist Hotel was an ornate and eclectic mixture of trinkets and artifacts. Across its breadth, it housed enough velvet-upholstered chairs and sofas to seat a battalion of men. To the left was the reception desk, and mirroring it was the lounging area. The ceiling stretched far overhead and much of the structural framework looked like it was pulled from the hull of a wooden ship.

    Probably a salvage job from a vessel that crashed into shore during a storm. Koenig thought to himself. *That's probably all that it does here…storm.*

    Shaking his head in amazement at the night he'd had, Koenig stepped into the lobby. Uneven floorboards beneath his feet moaned in protest as he walked across the room. He stopped to examine an old brass diver's helmet that was propped next to a gas burning fireplace.   To Koenig, the lobby appeared reasonably well maintained. Dying embers were crackling in the hearth and he could easily see his reflection in the diver's helmet. Somebody was thorough in the up-keep.

    The curvature of the helmet created a fish-eye sort of effect in the reflection, and Koenig stopped for a moment to study his distorted face in the image. He looked somehow changed. Tired for sure, but it wasn't the fatigue in his face that caught Koenig off guard. The reflection staring back at him looked…older.

    As he leaned towards the helmet, something stirred over his shoulder.

    "That's part of an old diving set from the 1800s," a girl's voice said. Alarmed, Koenig turned to face the stranger. It was a young woman, probably no older than 26. Her hair was long and dark, and pulled back in a braid. She was adjusting her glasses and staring at Koenig through the thick lenses.

    "They used to use those around here, believe it or not," she continued. "Off of Blackrock Peak, back in, like, the 1890s. There was a legend that a cluster of pirate ships sank near Blackrock carrying stolen cargo. Gold, emeralds, sapphire, art, you name it. The citizens of Pinemist Bay searched on and off for treasure for two decades until the operation costs outweighed the potential for findings. Of course, in those days the suits were really complicated to use, and the technology was so bad they probably only went diving like ten or twenty minutes at a time." The girl was no longer looking at Koenig, the old diver's helmet had a sway on her. "...and the waves are always choppy in these parts. They say they lost one or two divers down there, suit and all. Is that where the term diver down comes from?"

"Uh, I don't think so," Koenig responded. He couldn't tell if she had heard him, but the tenacious girl continued.

"Plenty of ships pass down here from British Colombia, but I don't believe for a second that any pirates came near here." He took a step toward her.

"Are you the check-in girl?" he asked, sounding more impatient than he meant to.

"That's me," she replied, while absentmindedly twirling her clump of hair with a finger. She was wearing an outfit that belonged in Amish country; a dark grey skirt that reached below her knees, black stockings beneath, and a raven colored blouse on top with uneven, lumpy white seams that were certainly hand-stitched. The entire outfit looked handcrafted, except for the worn and tattered penny loafers that she was clacking together like Dorothy in Oz. All that was missing from her uniform was a big white bonnet on her head, and Koenig thought she would have made a beautiful puritan bride-to-be.

"I'd like to check in please," Koenig said.

"Oh, of course, sir," she said as she swiveled around, her loafers clacking over to the back of the counter.

"How long will your stay be mister..."

"Koenig, Edward Koenig. That's K-O-E-N-I-G." He rapped his fingers on the counter. *Maybe I should just go home. Why the fuck am I here?* "I'm not sure how long I'll be here, I'm, um, visiting friends." He wanted to avoid unnecessary conversation. According to her facial expression she didn't believe him, but after a slow nod, she continued filling out the paperwork. He wondered how rare it was for an outsider to come to Pinemist Bay, and if everyone here knew each other, like one tightly-knit fucked-up community.

Too much isolation is never a good thing, he thought sourly.

"Sorry about the babbling," she said bashfully. "I can get carried away, and it's rare we have outsiders here. New ears to pick."

"What's your name?" Koenig asked.

"Sally Schubert."

"Don't worry about it, Sally. I'm interested to hear about the history of this place, I've just had a very long day." He realized that sometimes he wasn't considerate of people, but right now, anyone other than his family was irrelevant. Sally's apology was indicative that he had come across cold again. He didn't care. The encounter with the old man still burned in his mind like a blowtorch, and he hoped he would see things more clearly after a good night's rest.

"No worries." She stepped into the back room and then reappeared with a weighty brass key. "You can stay in room 254. Just sign here please. There are no noise ordinances in the building, but a decent number of the rooms are occupied by citizens of Pinemist Bay, and some of them can get cranky," she stated, her tone flat.

"Fair enough," Koenig said with a smile. He ran a hand through hair still wet with rain, and wiped it off on his coat. He noticed a little pamphlet kiosk on the desk. "I'll take this map too, are you running the desk all night?"

She nodded. "I'm the night watchman, or watchwoman. I've got a little cot in the back since, well, we rarely get guests here." She motioned to the office behind her.

"Alright then, to your post." He saluted comically, as if she was a deckhand and he, her captain. Grabbing the room key, he turned and walked towards a set of double-sided stairs, glancing one more time at the diver's helmet before turning the corner.

Pinemist Bay is a weird little place, he mused.

The creaky wooden floors in the lobby gave way to a blood red carpet that continued down a lengthy hallway. On the western side of the building, the hallway was a straight shot from one end to the other.

Around the northwest corner, the hotel became a labyrinth of little corridors and cutouts. Between the two sides, was a set of stairs that reached to the third and fourth floors.

Koenig followed the door numbers around the northwest corner, occasionally hearing little signs of life from inside the rooms. Someone in room 276 was watching television, a couple was arguing in 269, and room 260 was open just a crack. Nothing audible emanated from that room, however. He arrived at 254 after what felt like the fifth or sixth bend in the hall.

The click of the key sounded amplified as it slid into the lock. Besides the low din from the rooms, few sounds swelled through the hallway, and the dated red carpet consumed many of them. Pausing before he opened the door, Koenig realized that for the first time in probably eight or nine hours, he couldn't hear the pitter-patter of rain. He turned the key, hearing the clack of the tumblers echo off the walls around him, and entered.

His room was small, traditional and eerily senescent. To the immediate right of the door was the bathroom, furnished with an old, crumbling yellow wallpaper. Further into the room was a mini closet with a few coat hangers, which were gently clattering together over the central air vent that blew from below. The main room consisted of a mid-sized bed to the right and a small wooden stationary in front of it with a plush antique chair. A reasonably sized window was situated just opposite Koenig, and rain drummed upon it incessantly. Muted streetlights glowed in the distance and a few neon signs shined through the storm, illuminating the room in splotched patches.

Koenig set his suitcase down next to the table and slid his coat off. It was holding in a substantial amount of rainwater and felt cumbersome as he propped it on the coat rack. Taking a deep breath, he slowly unbuttoned his shirt and repeated aloud what the old man had said to him: "Do not let the Vucari find you."

Shaking his head in disbelief, Koenig walked over to the desk and picked up the receiver of an old rotary phone. The desire to touch base with his wife and daughter was strengthening, especially after what the old man had said. The old device responded to every input from his finger with solid mechanical clunks as he dialed his home phone number. He placed the receiver against his head, cringing slightly from the odd smell that emanated from it. The scent reminded him of an old abandoned house, containing furniture laden with dust from years of neglect. If the act of aging had its own scent, this receiver embodied it. He wondered if everything in Pinemist Bay was like the hotel; rustic and old, but pulsing with dormant energy.

After a few seconds, there was a dial tone and the connection began to ring through on the other side. Koenig held his breath while the phone buzzed in his ear. Each unanswered ring reminding him that his wife should be home, and should pick up the phone. At last, he heard his own automated voice message speak its lines. Clearing his voice and trying not to sound shaky, Koenig spoke into the telephone.

"Hey babe, uh, it's me. Listen, I'm up at a hotel here in Pinemist Bay...I know, I made it really far...listen, I just wanted to check in on Dalla and you. It's getting late and maybe you're asleep already. I hope you tucked Dalla in and gave her a kiss for me...I'm pretty tired so I'm gonna pass out now but I'll call you in the morning. In case you want to reach me, the number here is 503-555-1871...I love you." He fumbled the receiver back onto its post.

Is Eveline at the store? he thought. *Is she having one of her long, therapeutic baths and doesn't want to traipse water through the house? It's too early for her to be asleep...Is she just ignoring me? I can't say I blame her.*

Koenig collapsed on the bed and sighed. The nerves in his neck that had felt like two pinched hoses through the night were already loosening up. He looked down and saw his heart beating through the shallow breaths that his lungs allowed.

Considering one more time what the man in the road, as well as Darlene, had said, Koenig stood up and checked each room to see if the lights were in working order. First, the bathroom. With one click, the vivid yellow wallpaper shone brightly under the vanity light. It worked. Then, the main room. *The fixtures in the Pinemist Hotel certainly are ancient.* With one solid clunk of the old switch, light filled the room. The chandelier was an ornate decoration. Its lightbulbs were housed in elegant glass boxes that were cradled by angular steel arms. It looked like it belonged in Victorian-era London.

As Koenig took a step toward the bed, the lights flickered off and back on. The falter was rapid enough that a well-timed blink would have missed it. He paused for a moment, staring up at the ceiling. The lights flashed one more time a minute later, but stayed off for a few seconds this time. Koenig's blood stanched. A chill cascaded from his lower back up to his neck and shot down each arm, reaching his fingers and then dissipating until all he could feel was his heartbeat pulsing beneath his fingernails.

Inhaling sharply, he shook off the feeling. *Fucking old wiring. Darlene warned me about it.*

He slid under the covers and listened to the continuous flutter of rain on the window. The diner next door threw brash drops of neon light on the ceiling, creating a moody mosaic of colors that calmed his nerves. Finally, a dark shroud of sleep enveloped him.

Chapter Three
Eveline and Dalla

There she was. The sun's early rays warmed the field, while roosters cawed from atop an old red barn on the horizon, singing the dawn into life. A gentle breeze stirred down the heart of the valley. There was Eveline, right in the middle of it all. Her ash-blonde hair was the first thing to shine under the light of the dawn. The smile on her face looked perfect as it always did, and her gentle facial features accentuated it further. From her pointy upturned nose to her wide-set blue eyes that, to him, were deeper than a galaxy, Koenig wouldn't have changed a thing. How long had it been since he had seen her? He couldn't remember. He didn't care either. Her outstretched arms were all his tired mind wanted to focus on.

Koenig collapsed into her embrace and found it hard to summon words. A cool breeze sifted through her hair, pushing little golden strands into his cheeks with a gentle caress. Her lips drew close to his ear and she whispered,

"Edward, I've missed you..." He couldn't respond. He wasn't sure if it was because he was holding back tears, or if he had become simply catatonic upon seeing her, but words weren't coming out. He just held onto her tighter.

"Mommy, who's that?" A little face leaned out from behind Eveline. It was his beautiful four-year-old daughter Dalla. Dalla looked more like her mother, and Koenig was happy that she did. Eveline was a vision, and with similar beauty, he believed Dalla would not be wanting for anything in her life. While he preferred that Eveline be the one whose features pass onto their children, Koenig wasn't by any means unattractive. Thick dark hair covered his head, and he had strong, masculine facial features perched underneath a low set brow.

The only features on Dalla's face that were inherited from Koenig were his steely eyes. The soft features of her face were a disparity to the piercing set of blue-grey pupils that lay in the center.

"It's daddy," Eveline said softly. Koenig took his daughter in his arms and hoisted her onto his hip. "Dalla, baby, how are you?" The tears he had been choking on were unabashedly running down his cheeks.

"It's felt like a year," he said, looking back at Eveline.

"For all of us," she said, taking his hand in her own and leading him down a path to the edge of the cornfield. Relieved to be reunited with his family, Koenig followed his wife up toward the rustic old barn, his daughter bouncing up and down on his side.

The air was crisp and placid, and every slow inhale rejuvenated his body. Peaking over the lip of the valley, the sun had intensified, and bathed the three of them in a serene warmth. Dalla raised a pudgy little hand over her eyes, shielding the sun while humming a nursery rhyme under her breath.

The house was nestled at the foot of the valley wall, directly under the shade of a large oak tree. Facing them was a set of white barn doors, one of them slightly ajar. Eveline led them past the barn doors to the side of the old building, pulling open a bug-screen and unlocking the main door. With an abstract and oddly distant smile, she unhooked Dalla's arms from around Koenig's neck and pulled her off of him.

Inside was a small living space that was attached to the aft section of the barn. It consisted of a small kitchen with white and moss-green checkered tile, and a dilapidated farmhouse sink that was kissed with ruddy streaks of rust. Beyond the kitchen lay a tiny living room with two musty old chairs and an antique television set with rabbit ears sticking out of the top.

"Stay here, darling," she said as she turned on the kitchen light. "Mommy and daddy will be back soon." She walked to the kitchen counter and pulled something out of a drawer. As soon as the warm fluorescent light gleamed on the item, Koenig was able to recognize it. Dalla's coloring book.

On the cover was a gleeful clown dressed in an apple red costume balancing on a unicycle, with a beach ball teetering on his nose. Just the sight of the book struck a vehement chord in Koenig's mind.

"Mommy? Where are you going?" An uneasy voice called from behind Eveline.

"Don't worry baby, just sit down and play with your coloring book." Eveline barely finished the sentence before pulling the door shut.

"Baby," Koenig said, staring at the door as she swept his hand up again and pulled him around the back of the barn. "We can't leave Dalla like that."

"Don't worry, Edward, she'll be fine. She's got everything she needs in there," Eveline said, turning to face Koenig. "And I've finally got everything I need right here." She stopped for a moment and wrapped her arms around him. Before he could say another word in protest, her tongue was in his mouth. She squeezed tightly around his waist and explored with her hands, giving his balls a gentle squeeze.

"Babe, what are we doing? We can't just leave Dalla in there by herself. It's not right." She placed a finger on his lips to silence him.

"Edward, stop worrying about everybody else for once and focus on me," she said coyly. "Do you trust me?"

"Yes," he said automatically. Through seven years of marriage, he did, but this was different. Everything seemed…off. She pulled at his hand once more and continued to lead him further behind the house. The wall of the valley tapered off into another path just behind the barn. The foliage became dense and oppressively close. Why was she leading him into the forest while they left their only child alone in the house? He couldn't tell what was pulling at him harder, the soft but firm hand gripping his, or the smile she flashed at him intermittently. It was disarming.

Koenig could hear the sound of running water and saw something glistening ahead. In this lush, dreamy forest lay a clearing surrounded by a shallow stream. Eveline pulled her hand away from Koenig's as they jumped over a narrow section of the creek. Without saying a word, she pivoted and pulled Koenig down onto the soft earth in a fiery embrace.

Chapter Four
The Seaside Diner

    The rain stopped sometime in the dead of night. By late morning, the sky was congested with clouds, and Pinemist Bay was covered in a thick layer of mist. After sleeping still as a cadaver through the night, a rapping on his hotel room door roused Koenig. With more than a few groans of protest from his joints, Koenig stumbled out of bed and glanced at the alarm clock on the side table. It was 9:27 AM. As if the long night of sleep hadn't interrupted his train of thought, he awoke to find the agitation over his wife and daughter still consumed him. But they could wait another minute. Half asleep, he walked to the door and looked into the peephole.
    Facing him through the doorway was a crisp black tuxedo. Its lapels were broad and flat, and it had meticulous stitching all the way to the cuffs. Despite the distorting effect of the peephole, Koenig could tell that the quality of the fabric was exquisite. The classy tuxedo was in excellent condition, but looked retro, like it was wrenched out of the 1800s.
    Attached to the suit was a sight so horrific that Koenig questioned whether or not he was still dreaming. Standing in the hallway was a man with old, but severe, burns that marred over half of his face. His forehead was the texture of a leather hide left in the sun too long, and his left eye had sunken into one of the grooves of his face. His other eye was largely intact and was sporting a monocle. Koenig squinted to confirm that this was true; the man actually had on a monocle.
    Underneath his left eye was an empty cavern that used to be a jaw. Little strings of tendon connected his upper cheekbone to his lower mandible, and they vibrated like harp strings when he breathed. The mystery guest's hair was slicked back and his expression resembled that of either impatience or confusion. Koenig rubbed the sleep out of his eyes and squinted once more at the peephole, hoping the terrifying man might evaporate and prove a figment of his imagination. *More evidence that Pinemist Bay is a weird little place.* He swallowed hard.
    "Who is it?" Koenig inquired, not letting his eyes leave the enigmatic sight.
    "It is Kendric. Is Ms. Nylund in?" The strings of tendon stretched like flesh bungees as he talked.
    "No one by the name of Nylund here," Koenig said. The man looked towards the floor, and after a brief pause his creepy gaze settled back on the door's peephole, as if he could see Koenig through it. He knew this

was impossible, but couldn't shake the feeling the man could see him.

"Can I come in and verify that?" the man asked in a monotone voice. Taken aback by the inquiry, Koenig shook his head. *This weird fucking stranger thinks he is going to come in here, into my private hotel room? Not a chance. This guy has some nerve.*

"Absolutely not," he said in a firm voice. "Listen, if this is an urgent matter, I'm sure you can ask the girl at the front desk for assistance. She is perfectly adequate at her job."

The cold, unsettling face continued to look into the peephole for a haunting moment. Then the mysterious man turned and walked down the hall, disappearing from the small oval of vision the peephole allowed. Koenig leaned up against the door until his forehead began to burn. He wanted to see if the man would pass by again. He didn't. He opened the door and peeked down each end of the hall. Not a soul was there, just a desolate hallway with an ugly red carpet. Brushing off a feeling of dread, Koenig retreated back into his room making sure the door latched behind him.

Concern for his wife and daughter was no longer brimming, but pouring over the sides of his mind, Koenig felt dread at the idea of picking the phone up again. *What if Eveline doesn't answer? What then?* He stepped back into his hotel room, sat down at the stationary and stared hard at the telephone for several minutes, all the while mulling over what the old man had said the previous night.

He was reduced now to nervous habits and found himself compulsively grinding his teeth. The grating sound it produced actually slowed his mind, allowed him to think a little more clearly. Koenig went for the receiver, and with a click and a scoop, it was in his hand. He cleared his throat and pulled it toward his face. Before the receiver reached his mouth, he placed it on the desk and stood up.

In a brisk manner, Koenig walked over to the bathroom and flipped on the light. He flung a splash of cold water on his face and looked up at the mirror, breathing in deeply. The man staring back at him looked exactly like the man in the old diver's mask the night before, aged. His eyes followed the curvature of his own face and traced the wrinkles in his forehead, which looked exaggerated by the way he was furrowing his eyebrows. *Call your wife.*

Giving himself a quick half nod, Koenig left the yellow bathroom and approached the receiver again, picking it up this time without hesitation and dialing in the phone number with a sturdy hand. For all he knew, that old man, Darlene, everything that transpired the night before may have just been a coincidence. A dream. *A nightmare.*

Ring, ring. *Come on baby, please pick up. It's almost 12:00 your time.* Ring, ring. Whether he believed the events of the previous night actually transpired, Koenig harbored a fear for his family and couldn't shake the feeling. He didn't travel very often. He had made sure he wouldn't be a nomadic father after having grown up with one himself, but whenever he did go out of town, he and wife always communicated frequently. *At least until the first slip up.* Ring, ring. *Is she fucking someone to spite me? Did she pack up hastily last night and take off with Dalla?* Ring, Ring. *No, we are past* that. Eveline and I have been through some trying times, but we are past that.

The two final rings echoed and he heard his own robotic sounding voicemail again. He heard himself say, "You have reached the Koenig residence. We can't come to the phone right now but we'd love to hear from you. Please leave your name, number and message after the tone." He threw the receiver down, watching it tumble over the switch hook and clatter upon the table. And then a thought came to him. The previous night, Dalla had communicated with him through her mind, like she somehow latched onto his brain waves to send him a message. If she could talk to him from afar, why couldn't he do the same?

He sat down and shut his eyes, rocking back and forth in the chair. *Dalla, can you hear me?* Nothing. He tried furiously to concentrate, but on what? He had no idea how his four-year-old girl had the ability to communicate long-distance without the help of telephone wires like everyone else. *Dalla, are you there? It's daddy, baby. Can you hear me?* A vacuous silence.

Searching deep within the recesses of his mind, Koenig found an inner strength and clung to it with all his might. He forced himself to stand up, leave the room, forget the telephone, and forget about the fact that, for now, communication with his daughter seemed to be one-way.

The lobby of the hotel looked charming in the morning hours. Ribbons of light cascaded down from the ceiling and reflected off the diver's helmet, as well as various other ornaments throughout the lobby. A young man had replaced Sally at the front desk and was busy assisting a few other guests. *I guess they do occasionally get visitors...* Koenig approached the young man, almost pushing an old lady aside in the process.

"Excuse me, sorry. I was just rudely awakened by another guest in the hotel, his name was Kendric. Can you make sure he stays away from my room from now on?" Koenig was not about to take chances with strangers in Pinemist Bay, especially with someone oozing a minatory vibe like Kendric. The young concierge had a puzzled look on his face.

"Sir, I'm not supposed to give out this information, but we do not have a resident or guest with the name Kendric. I personally know the client list by heart, including you, Mr. Koenig."

"How do you know who I am?" Koenig asked the boy. "I just checked in last night."

"You are the only person staying here that I haven't met in person, and also the first guest in almost a week, aside from the Waldens." He motioned to the family that was standing off to the side. The mother and father both had an impatient look on their faces. The children were staring nervously at the disgruntled, ill-mannered guest. Koenig nodded briefly at Mr. Walden and turned to face the clerk, reading his name tag before continuing.

"I'm sorry, Stewart, sometimes I come on a little strong, but this man is easily recognizable. He had burns all over his face and he wore a nice suit."

"As far as I know, Mr. Koenig, no one with burns on their face has been in the hotel all morning."

"You're sure?" he asked. Stewart nodded.

"How about a Nylund? He asked for someone named Ms. Nylund."

"Nope, sorry sir." Koenig took a conceding step backwards and held a hand toward the Walden family in an apologetic gesture.

"Enjoy your morning guys, sorry," he said.

****

The large green door of the Pinemist Hotel swung open and, like giant floodlights inside a cave, daylight assaulted Koenig. The smell of salt water caressed his nostrils and he could hear the gentle crash of waves just a few blocks away. Suffocated by a humid fog that rolled in soon after the rain had ended, the town had a demure, silent quality to it, and appeared even more isolated than before. It was like a microcosm of the real world that had been isolated for so long, it breathed its own unique life into itself.

Quaint little shops lined Main Street in either direction and a small park lay across the street from the hotel. Nearby, a few people were dithering about the town. Some walked alone, a couple was holding hands, with the wife occasionally stopping to peer into shop windows and point at something she fancied. As they continued further down Main Street their bodies turned into inky silhouettes that slowly evaporated into the mist.

Strolling down the hotel's walkway towards Main Street, Koenig noticed that his Mustang was waiting by the curb where he left it. He had even managed to park the vehicle pretty well during his careless scramble on such a crazy night. *One stroke of fortune since coming up here. Wouldn't have been surprised if it had been towed.* He paused for a moment and breathed in deep, the thoughts in his overactive mind turning from his family to the growing hunger in his stomach.

To the immediate right was last night's glimmering beacon of neon, the Seaside Diner. In contrast to its appearance before, the sign looked soft and muted in the morning fog. Stopping at the diner seemed like a good idea to Koenig. He didn't know what to think of the occurrences since his arrival, he wasn't even sure the situation had fully sunken in yet, but one thing was certain in his mind: he needed to follow the old man's words down this rabbit hole and see where it led. The diner might be a good place to start. He needed to satiate his hunger, and there might be locals at the diner with information about the area who could steer him in the right direction.

The Seaside Diner was a squat, rectangular building with windows running its entire length. The base of the building was outfitted in retro chrome panels that scintillated in the murky air. Emanating from each window, a warm light turned the diner into a ghostly object that diffused light into the haze.

Koenig walked alongside the diner and found himself coaxed up the stairs by the aroma of fresh coffee. He opened the door and entered. Roy Orbison was crooning on the radio about a lost love, the warble of his voice reverberating off of the walls. Lining the left end of the diner was a long bar equipped with an espresso machine, a soda dispenser, and a four-pot coffee brewer that was billowing steam out of its servers.

There was a single line of tables between the bar and the lengthy column of booths that were stacked against the window. The diner had a sterile appearance, with a clean white tile floor and beige colored walls. Unlike the Pinemist Hotel, the Seaside Diner didn't have a brooding, sinister energy, it just felt like another building. Koenig wandered up to the middle section of the bar and sat down. Almost as soon as he had sat down and placed his forearms on the countertop, a sprightly waitress approached.

"Hello stranger!" she said with a smile on her face and a smack of gum in her mouth. Her hair was dark and curly, and she wore far too much mascara for a single person. Her name tag said Jenny.

"Good morning," Koenig said and watched as she poured a cup of steaming hot coffee into his mug. *I* will *have coffee, thanks.*

"What can I getcha?" she asked, while chomping on her gum like a grass-grazing cow.

Koenig considered her request. "I'll take a couple of poached eggs with a side of sausage, and maybe some hash browns."

"Will do mister, uh…"

"Koenig," he replied.

"I'll have that out in a minute Mr. Kenning," Jenny said, the smile on her face unwavering. "We pride ourselves on bein' quicker than a mare set loose from a stable." Koenig looked around the diner, taking note of the sparse clientele. Jenny seemed to notice his tacit argument. "You should see how fast those plates go a-flyin' when rush hour hits!" she exclaimed. "Thursday mornings are just a lil' more relaxed. In fact, it's just me and Billy back there today."

She pointed at the service window behind her. Billy was hard at work over the stove cooking up a meal for one of the few other patrons, his face mostly covered by steam. He gave Koenig a brief smile and nod, and Koenig returned the gesture. Still beaming, Jenny held out her hand, "I'm Jenny by the way, Jenny Wilbur." Koenig shook her hand and mustered up a friendly countenance.

"Nice to meet you, Jenny." She curtsied, turned away and began making her rounds.

Koenig scanned the diner. There were only three other people there aside from himself. An older lady was sitting in a booth directly behind him, her mouth wrestling with a runny string of eggs that dangled from her fork. Sitting in a booth towards the end of the diner was a man hunched over a mug of coffee. To his left was a third patron who had his elbow propped on an old jukebox. He leafed through the selection, finally settling on a short waltz by Ray Noble's Orchestra, and when that was over, the silky voice of Bobby Darin suffused the diner. Darin was singing about a distant lover to whom he yearned to return, but an ocean lay between them.

Koenig slumped over his coffee cup, thinking about how he's whisked himself away to this desolate port town all because a voice in his head that was ostensibly that of his daughter told him she was here and she was in danger. But whether his family were somewhere in Pinemist Bay, or they were back at home safe and sound, just like Darin's lover in the song, Koenig felt like there was an ocean between them.

He sighed and, swiveling on his barstool, looked towards the window. Condensation was spreading along the frame and slowly creeping inwards, partially obscuring the world outside. The simple fixture dangling over the booth spewed a cynosure of light that pierced the dim world outside, like a lighthouse hovering over a misty bay. Gazing out at the mysterious seaside town in which he felt trapped, Koenig's mind started to wander.

Should I just pay for one more night at the hotel and drive back down the canyon? I could drive through Tillamook and then east to Portland International, and look for outgoing flights back to Chicago. Might be a five-hour drive to the airport if the weather doesn't turn to shit. Eveline and Dalla may be in trouble. I need to get back home and check on them, or I can tough it out here and figure out what the old man in the road was talking about. Or maybe I dreamt up the whole scenario and I'm losing my mind...

Koenig's mind was a slalom of emotions and thoughts, swirling in relentless circles to the point of exhaustion. He took a sip of the piping hot coffee Jenny had given him, hoping something bitter and strong would focus his mind. Before he put the mug down, the sprightly waitress had reappeared and placed his breakfast in front of him.

"See Mr. Kenning!" she said. "Fastest diner west of Helena!"

"That's impressive Jenny," he replied. "It's Koenig, by the way."

"Oh, I'm so sorry mister!" she blushed. "You've got a really unique name. I swear I've heard it somewhere around here..." She stared off in thought for a moment and Koenig, digging into his eggs, began to inquire about Pinemist Bay.

"So how long have you lived here, Jenny?" he asked.

"I've been here for a little while now," she exclaimed. The gum in her mouth had to have lost its flavor by now, especially with the way she was chomping on it. "When I was a child I moved here with my foster family. I don't remember life before Pinemist Bay."

"So, you probably know all the ins and outs of this place, huh?" he inquired. "Maybe you could tell me a bit about Pinemist Bay."

"Well, I may not be the best person to come to, but I know a thing or two about this place for sure, Mr. Kenning, and there's been some odd things happenin' lately." Jenny's voice became quieter than a church mouse, and she glanced at the other patrons uneasily. Her continuous smile had disappeared and been replaced with a timid, apprehensive look, as if she had said something she shouldn't have.

"What are some of the weird things that have been happening around here, Jenny?" Koenig whispered back, dying to gain some insight on the mysterious town.

"Well," she hesitated. "I don't know if I should be talkin' about anything like that right now, Mr. Kenning," she whispered, while darting concerned glances towards the other customers.

Koenig complied, not wanting to get the girl into any trouble.

He didn't know what was going on at Pinemist Bay, or what the townsfolk were capable of. "Sorry, I didn't mean to stir up any trouble,

Jenny. I was just wondering if you had ever heard of a phrase, 'walking the year?'" Jenny's eyes became wide as saucers and she trembled. It was a small shudder that went from her shoulders to her neck, almost unnoticeable, but Koenig picked up on it.

"No I haven't heard of that," she spat. "Alright, Mr. Kenning, your bill is $8.87. The coffee is on us." Jenny handed him the ticket, looking uneasy. He stared back for a long moment, wondering if he should pursue his line of questioning. Based on her laconic reaction, his inquiries were certainly leading somewhere.

"Thanks," he said as he thumbed through a wad of bills. "Listen, I'm new to town, obviously, and I think my wife and daughter might be in some trouble. I know this sounds like an odd request, but I need to learn more about what is happening in Pinemist Bay. Would you be able to help me out Jenny, just help me figure out what's happening and if my family may be involved? We can meet somewhere more discreet if need be."

Jenny mulled the request over for a minute, tapping an anxious finger on the bar.

"You sure are a desperate man, Mr. Kenning, aren't ya?" After a sigh, she continued, "Sure, I'll help you out with what I know, but it's not much."

"Thank you, Jenny." Koenig's relief was evident in his voice. *I knew it was a good idea to come in here.*

She disappeared in the back for a moment and turned up the volume on the restaurant's speakers. Bobby Darin suddenly sounded like he had been handed a megaphone. The gentleman in control of the jukebox was apparently only aware of music that was over three decades old, and he seemed to be enjoying the classics, too; bobbing his head to the beat, tapping his foot against the machine, and occasionally hollering along to the music as if he was the only person there.

When Jenny returned, her breathing was shallow and there was a slight rattle in her voice. "It started a couple months ago." She spoke softly, and even though he was leaning over the bar, Koenig nearly had to read her lips. "People started disappearing again."

"Again?" Koenig interrupted.

"It happens every once in a while, maybe a few years in between each group of incidents. Several people from Pinemist County go missin'. Sometimes they turn up, usually within a few days if they do, and sometimes they don't turn up at all," she said.

"In what condition are they when they do resurface?"

"It depends." Jenny looked left to right cautiously. Koenig glanced over her shoulder. Billy was tackling a hefty pile of dishes. Plates clanged together in the sink, sending suds flying over Billy's shoulder. "Sometimes they turn up alive, but brain-dead, catatonic," she continued. "Sometimes they're found in town, dead as a doorknocker, up in the mountains, in the woods, or in the outskirts of town…in their own homes…"

Tears were swimming behind Jenny's eyes. "Some of the locals are curious about these disappearances, or live in fear because of 'em. Others don't bother with any of it, and others still aren't even aware anything's goin' on. But nobody knows what it's all about. The people of Pinemist Bay have been yearwalkin' since near when this area was settled, and there's talk that it's got somethin' to do with that."

"Yearwalking?" Koenig blurted. *The old man said, 'if you walk the year, true darkness will reveal itself to you.' Could this be what he was talking about?*

"I've heard that mentioned before, what is it?" He had to fight to keep his voice low. *She mentioned people returned in a catatonic state. Could my father have had something to do with this?*

"It's an old ritual, pagan or some such. People still do it from time to time around these parts, but not nearly as often as they used to."

"But what is it!"

"I can't talk anymore, mister," Jenny said, wiping her eyes and leaving an ashy trail of makeup down her cheeks. "I've gotta do my rounds. And you need to get a move on, for both our sakes." As soon as the last word had escaped her mouth, Jenny was strolling across the diner towards the seated gentleman; a steaming pitcher of coffee in her hand.

Koenig saw her lips moving as she gestured with her coffee pot to the man, who was still hunched over his coffee like someone with a debilitating case of narcolepsy. It looked as though he was hiding from someone. Koenig watched the man's head move from side to side, and then wave Jenny away without as much as a glance.

Koenig looked down at the coffee cup in front of him, feeling the steam kiss his chin. He watched Jenny pass by, the smile that had been painted on her face when he arrived was far gone and replaced with a look of dread. Her mascara-smeared eyes darted in Koenig's direction and she disappeared into the kitchen.

Koenig took the mug in his hand and threw his head back for another long sip of coffee. Before the hot liquid had entered his throat, he caught movement in the backsplash mirror of the bar. Somebody was standing behind him.

"Enjoying your stay mister...Koenig, was it?" He swiveled on his stool and nearly soaked the bar in coffee and phlegm. It was Kendric. He was standing behind Koenig with his suit coat slung on his arm.

Seeing him in plain sight was an abhorrently different experience than through the peephole of his hotel room. Light and shadow played across Kendric's mutilated face like a symphony of horror as he stood under the bar lights. Koenig forced the coffee down his throat and exhaled. Like a boxer caught off guard, he didn't know whether to swing a punch or duck for cover. For a moment he just stared at the decrepit man, and the man stared right back, his one working eye fixed on Koenig. Words came to him at last, and he steadied his voice.

"That's really none of your business, Kendric," he said. "But yes, I'm having a fine time. Did you ever find that Nylund person?"

"Ms. Nylund is no longer a concern of mine," Kendric said with a tranquil, yet haunting voice. "I have other matters to tend to. How is your family, sir?" Kendric's snake of an upper lip coiled into a crooked smile. "I assume you're a married man?" The question felt like a giant splinter, driving deep into Koenig's mind and setting off all his nerves at once.

"Listen Kendric, I don't know who you are." He found himself pointing at the man with a finger that was shaking out of either anger or fear. "I don't know what you think you know about me, but you had better stay away. I know the sheriff and I won't hesitate to march up to the station and tell him you've been harassing me."

"What's the harm in asking an outsider how he is enjoying his visit?" The congealed flesh on Kendric's jaw danced to life with each syllable, and when he finished talking, it lumped and sagged like strips of burnt rubber oozing off a tire. Koenig hesitated for only a moment.

"I don't think you heard me clearly," he said, standing up. "Stay out of my way." With the turn of his heel, he was heading towards the door. It took all his might not to look over his shoulder, but he managed it. As he reached out to grab the doorknob, a thin whisper grazed his ear.

"The old man cannot protect you." Softer than an afterthought, the words came and went. *How does he know about the old man?* He whipped his body around, turning so fast that he almost lost his balance. He saw the old lady slurping down the remains of her egg. The other patron was still tapping his foot against the jukebox. Kendric was nowhere to be seen.

Chapter Five
Safe Haven

The Pinemist Bay Public Library was in a stack of buildings near the mouth of the valley, southwest of the Sheriff's Station. Isolated from the town by a couple of miles, the library was part of a collection of businesses known as Safe Haven. It adopted the moniker by earlier residents of Pinemist Bay who would take advantage of the terrain when the ocean would spit rogue waves onto the harbor.

Safe Haven was an exterior limb of Pinemist Bay that could be accessed by using a road called Wanderer's Way, which climbed up the southern corner of the suburbs and ended in the detached sub-section of the town. Koenig's Mustang growled as it climbed the gradual slope of Wanderer's Way, then settled into a purr as he slowed down and pulled over. He flicked on the cabin light and checked the little map again. Wanderer's Way led straight to the library.

Koenig reached into the soft outer pocket of his jacket and tugged on the cigarette box. Smoking had long been a crutch of his. Eveline, being the responsible wife she was, couldn't stand them. He would occasionally sneak a smoke when she wasn't around, or even tip-toe out to their deck on the wind-whipped Chicago mornings while she lay in bed, and take a few long drags, watching the sun peak over the buildings and coruscate over Lake Michigan.

When she did catch the smoke on his breath, Eveline was never pleased. She would lecture Koenig, "You have a daughter now, and you need to set a proper example. You need to be there for her when she turns eighteen, when she moves out of the house, finds her love and starts a life of her own. If you keep smoking, it's not gonna happen." She always ended her lecture in the same way, "You just need to be there, Edward," she would say, pointing at him with a stiff finger.

Then she would take one deep breath, compose herself, and no more would be spoken on the subject. Eveline was a woman of dignity, Koenig loved that about her. She never dragged problems out and certainly never let their daughter Dalla hear their heated discussions, which had grown more frequent of late.

Koenig rested his forehead on the heel of his palm. Thinking about his wife and daughter made him crave a smoke more than ever. Images of how he betrayed them had been hovering around the periphery of his mind since he left home. Having decimated Eveline's trust yet again, he got himself booted out of the house. *She needs time. Maybe we both do.*

Koenig turned the carton over a few times in his hand, following a fold that ran down the side of the box with his finger. With a tenuous grasp, he pulled a cigarette to his mouth and exhumed a small pack of matches from another pocket. He struck hard on the rough strip and watched the flame suck in its first breath of oxygen. Cupping his hands together, he lifted the match to his face until it caught and then tossed it out the car window.

He sat there with the big muscle car still situated in the middle of the road, and felt a warm, sweeping current of emotion take hold. A memory came to him. A memory that he had strongly coveted, one that was immensely precious to him. It hadn't graced his mind for a couple of years.

He saw a girl leaning against an old red Datsun at the only drive-in movie theater in Rochelle. Her hair was wild and long, and flowed down to the middle of her back. She had on jean shorts and knee-high leather boots, with one propped on the rear bumper of the car, the mud-caked soles smearing the chrome surface.

The image faded away before it fully materialized. He began to cry, something he hadn't done in years. Perhaps he was crying because of the overwhelming feeling that he had shattered the family again, which was hitting him now in full force. Or perhaps in this quiet moment, he was finally able to decompress from all that had happened since the previous night. The past fourteen hours or so had seriously jarred his mind. A doubtful slice of his usually stoic conscience believed he had gone crazy.

Koenig took a long pull of his cigarette. He was sucking so hard on the butt that it was already down to a nub. He looked to the left. Dense forest lay just beyond the road. A mess of shrubs, shadows, and thickets blocked everything from view.

The elevation he had gained over Pinemist Bay became apparent when he turned his head to the south. To the east, through valley air laden with a chalky mist, Koenig could see a mountain range looming overhead. Some of the peaks were so prominent that they must have belonged to the Cascades. He had assumed that Pinemist Bay was near the perimeter of the Cascade Range, but didn't know the town was right at the foot of the geographical Goliath.

Spanning the entire upper portion of his windshield was a particularly tall and wide mountain. It had several sharp peaks and, reaching to what must have been at least twelve thousand feet above sea level, was nearly devoid of vegetation.

Adjacent to the soaring peak were more subdued hills and cliffs that meandered into the visible horizon and out of sight. The entrance of the area constituting the majority of Pinemist County was nestled somewhere between them. Towards the bay on either side lay a pair of gentler sloped mountains, these ones more densely populated with pines and vegetation than the soaring peaks ahead. Koenig could see several shingled roofs and smokestacks poking out through the trees on the hill to the right. He wondered how many people dwelled in the vast sprawl of mountain forests surrounding the port town.

The intense heat of the lit cigarette had nearly reached the filter and was licking at Koenig's forefingers, rousing him from his reverie. He tossed the butt out his driver side window, wiped a swathe of tears off his cheeks, and continued up the road. *Be strong, Edward. You owe your family that much.*

The road leveled off as the car approached Safe Haven. Several lampposts diffused light from the compound, their feeble glow gently stretching towards Koenig. Safe Haven was massive. Its entirety covered the span of roughly two football fields. He pulled his car between two buildings and stopped in front of a gargantuan generator that he assumed powered the entire compound. He didn't bother parking in a designated spot. Safe Haven appeared deserted and he couldn't imagine anyone would tow him.

Koenig stepped out of his car and surveyed the area. Squaring off the parking lot was a large rectangular building, or what looked like several buildings connected at the joints to form one continuous loop of concrete. It was drab and argentine, and almost blended into the bleak haze that surrounded it. The facility appeared eerily untouched, as if the citizens had forgotten Safe Haven existed, or simply didn't bother with the mild commute. This made for an atmosphere of utter placidity that unnerved Koenig.

As he lingered in the parking lot, he entertained a curious sensation. Something was watching him. He could feel its veiled pulse, as if a sniper was perched out of sight on one of the roofs, eyeing his every move. It was not a comforting feeling that he was now more or less isolated from the main community by an abandoned stretch of road. Still, he was at Safe Haven for a reason. It was imperative that he learn more about yearwalking. The library may be the first piece in Pinemist Bay's macabre puzzle, and he needed to begin fumbling it together.

Taking a closer look at the various installations, Koenig surmised that Safe Haven was a repurposed facility. Everything was too coldly ergonomic in design, too bleak to have been meant as a public-use building. He glanced at the long concrete structure. Towards the center of the building was a set of stairs with a landing and a single door. A raven-shaded plaque stated, Pinemist Bay Public Library. From aesthetics alone, the building could have been a storage facility or a warehouse—not very inviting.

With a brisk turn of his key he locked the Mustang, crossed the parking lot, and perched a foot on the first step of the library stairs. He fished for the little map in his jacket pocket one more time to acknowledge that this was indeed Safe Haven. He was in the right spot. Without a shred of delicacy, he stuffed the paper back in his pocket and opened the front door.

A treacherously lengthy hallway greeted Koenig. There were no markings or indicators of which direction to go, save for a single door several yards away that disrupted the eerie congruence of the hallway. The carpet and walls were a blanched mauve, the same color of a sun-bleached plum.

Several paces from the front entrance, the sweet, musty scent of old books caressed his nostrils. He approached the lonely door and pulled, the egregious sound of its unexercised hinges piercing his ears as it opened. Generously sized bookcases occupied the vast space of the library. Glancing up, Koenig saw a wide second story landing along the far wall. It was a hell of an installation.

"Hello?" he called out, hearing nothing in reply except his own echo reverberating through the labyrinth of bookshelves. With legs that felt heavy with trepidation, Koenig stepped further inside the library. Peering left to right, he called out one more time, "Is anybody here?"

Silence.

With no front desk, no signage, and no clerk, Koenig found himself dithering among the bookcases. Cartography, world maps, scientific journals. He meandered through the disconsolate building's many sections until coming upon a hard-right turn leading to a portion of the library that was well-lit, with a window spanning the entire length of the outer wall. A light rain was falling now and had begun to mop up the muggy air.

Koenig continued through myriads of books, moving past fiction and towards history. Inhumed deeply within the library, the silence assaulted him. He could hear his heart beating on his chest like a metronome of dread. On either side of the cramped bookcases was a straightaway that looked as long as an airport hangar.

Walking down an aisle labeled, *Mythology*, Koenig thumbed through the books until he found a few promising possibilities: *Norse Mythology*, *Scandinavian Folklore*, and *A Study of Swedish, Norwegian and Finnish Cultures*. Just as he went to pull the old books off the shelf, he felt a warm river of air graze his neck.

"Anything I can help you find, dearie?" The voice nearly caused him to propel into the bookcase in a fit of surprise. He craned his neck. Hunched over his shoulder was a little old lady with wispy hair and ripples of aged skin that stretched across her face.

"I'm so sorry, dearie," she rasped, while licking her thin, dry lips. "I didn't mean to frighten you." Koenig was unsure how to react to the old woman. As she looked at him, or rather towards him, he noticed that her eyes were quivering and her head rattled slightly, reminding him of the old man in the road. He assumed she was in her early 80s; perhaps her vision was diminished. But she had managed to find him amidst the maze of books, so if her vision wasn't keen, one of her other senses must have been. Either way, something about her wasn't right. *Is anybody in Pinemist Bay normal?*

"Oh, uh, don't worry about it. I just didn't know anyone else was here, that's all," he assured her. "So, you're the librarian?"

"That's me," the old lady croaked. "I'm the old groundskeeper of this establishment. If this was a church, I'd be the minister." Koenig faked a chuckle and nodded, replacing his gaze on the books in his hand.

"Oh I don't get too many visitors up here," the librarian continued. "It's nice to see a fresh face. Especially one as handsome and earnest as yours, young man."

"Oh. Thank you," he said, conquering the challenge of looking at the woman's face without seeing the spectral old man in the road. "How long have you lived in Pinemist Bay?"

"Oh dearie, I've been here awhile." Her onyx eyes, mapped with ruddy veins, wandered to the ceiling and lingered there for a moment. "You know, I can't recall how long it has been, but it was before this building had any books in it, that's for sure. This facility used to be a big empty hangar that we used as a high point when the tide would blow over the beach. It used to get so far up that parts of Main Street had to be rebuilt several times. But we have precautions against that now." Her wrinkled face upturned to a smile. "What's your name, dearie?"

"Uh, I'm Edward." She seemed to be waiting for more. "Koenig," he grunted, reluctantly.

Her eyes scuttled towards the floor. "Now that means King in German. Do you have a middle name, dearie?" she inquired.

"Um, it's Tuija."

The old lady looked at him. In an ephemeral flash, her eyes focused intensely on his, her gaze spearing through his cranium. "I was wondering if there was any northern ancestry in your blood," she said, breaking eye contact once more. "You look a little more Swedish than German. Tuija is a Swedish name."

Koenig didn't know where she was going with her curious line of questioning, meanwhile thoughts of Dalla and Eveline seeped in; thoughts of how Eveline hadn't answered the phone or called him back. Koenig was growing impatient. "That's very keen," he remarked. "My father's mother was largely of Swedish descent. My mother's side is mainly Irish, though."

She considered him for a minute. "Hmm. That name has got some power behind it, young man." *Okay, this old woman is a little off her rocker.* His signal for bowing out of the conversation was a clumsy pawing at all three of the folklore books, after which he stood up and tepidly glanced back down at the librarian.

"Well miss, uh…"

"Just call me Doris," she replied.

"Thanks for your help, I hope you have a good day now."

Normally, he wasn't so aggressively anti-social, but with all that Koenig had on his mind he couldn't help taking the brisk route away from idle chatter. Meanwhile, the feeling in his stomach, like it was turning itself inside and out, grew larger. His indefinable curiosity towards the place, that same sensation that kept Pinemist Bay alive in his mind well after his father's passing, was metastasizing from his gut to his brain. He was seared in half emotionally; the angel on one shoulder wary of the dangerous situation he was in, while the devil on the other dragged him onwards to an unknown conclusion.

He found a cozy nook right by the window, which ceaselessly dripped with a heavy northwestern rain. The deluge fluctuated between tender splashes that snaked down the window in rivulets, and a thick coat of water that reminded Koenig of the sprayers in an automatic carwash. Obscurity was not an issue now and, looking out at the world, Koenig could see into the thick forest a hundred yards to the south. The sound of the drumming rain amplified his yearning for a warm cup of coffee, and with a stroke of his hand, his lips were folded over another cigarette. *It's not coffee, but it'll do.*

As the first lines of smoke wafted into his eyes and tapered away, Koenig hoisted the big volume entitled, *Scandinavian Folklore,* off the stack and centered it in front of himself. The book was archaic. It had a gnarled leather wrapped cover that had developed little divots of age, spots where it had been grasped too many times by an excited reader. Dead center along the left and right sides were faded bruises in which Koenig could nearly make out the imprints of generations of fingers. Along these lines the leather was cracked and stripped, like an old tanned hide draped over a fence on an abandoned plot of land.

The front cover had an etching of what looked like an elegant elf with her arms outstretched toward a naked man. The man was wrapped in chains and had a gaping hole in his throat. Behind these figures was a man of monolithic proportions wielding a spear, the handle of which was laden with ornamentation.

Opening the book and leafing through the first pages was like wrenching open a time vault trimmed with dust and decay, but brimming with secrets. Between cracked lines of old text were dozens of illustrations of fantastic environments and items of mythological origin. It looked like a Tolkien compendium. As he turned the pages, Koenig breathed in the idiosyncratic fusty scent adorned by aged books, and it reminded him of his childhood; of when his mother Irene would take him to the library and read to him for hours on end.

Glancing at the table of contents, Koenig pinpointed a section entitled: 'Folk Beliefs and Rituals from the Dark Ages Onward.' He thumbed through a chunk of the prodigious book. Among the first pages in the 'Rituals' section were topics ranging from trolls fighting wolves, and enchanted sets of kitchenware taking over households, to old stone wells harboring dark secrets. Koenig browsed further until he came upon a chapter titled 'Heathen Scandinavian Practices.' Koenig spotted the two words now adhered to the fabric of his mind, 'Year walk.' He read on, his heart gyrating in anticipation.

Yearwalking and Other Divinations

The practice of Yearwalking, known as Årsgång (Osh-Gong) in Swedish, like many Northern European and Pagan rituals, remains something of a mystery. It is collectively perplexing to historians because, despite dating back to the early Dark Ages, ca. 7th century, there is very little known documentation on this peculiar divination. Although evidence points towards Eastern European influences on Scandinavian culture, it is believed that Årsgång was developed in Sweden, or perhaps Norway.

Records indicate that yearwalking persisted throughout these two countries, with a concentration taking place in the southern countryside of Sweden, where it persisted until the mid-1800s. What is known of yearwalking can be equated to a Scandinavian version of a 'spiritual journey.'

To initiate a yearwalk, the participant, or walker, must first

41

enclose themselves in a dark room with no windows or other outlets to the world, probably their living room or basement, for the duration of one whole day. During this time, they must refrain from consuming food or interacting with other people. The purpose of this is to assist the walker in disassociating themselves from the physical world.

At precisely midnight, the walker emerges from their dwelling and travels to their village's church. Upon reaching the church, the walker must then move in three counterclockwise circles around the building followed immediately by blowing into the keyhole of the main entrance with their mouth. This act is said to eliminate the walker's spiritual connection to Catholicism for a short while.

Just as his mind began to sink into the reading, Koenig felt a presence behind him. Doris had returned and was glancing over his shoulder.

"Hello there," he said. "You have got to stop sneaking up on me like that, Doris."

"Oh, I'm sorry, dearie. I'm just a curious old bag. It looks like Mr. Koenig is interested in the subject of yearwalking," she said, intrigued.

"Uh, yes," he said and glanced back at the book. "Do you know something about it?"

"Oh dearie, at my age you know at least something about everything." Her head was still chattering upon her frame like a dashboard bobble-head on a dirt road. "Yearwalking is a fascinating subject, isn't it?"

"Yes, very. While you're here why don't you sit down and tell me what you know of it?" he asked. "I'd love your insight."

"Oh alright, then," she said, and slowly took a seat opposite him. He thought he could hear the rattling of her old bones as she moved. How then, had she managed to wander up behind him unbeknownst twice?

"Ooh that fog is starting to lift. And what rain!" she exclaimed. "My oh my, we have some peculiar weather up here at Alistair's Brigand."

"Yeah it is pretty dreary. What is Alistair's Brigand?" he asked. Doris was staring out the window, looking as though she was eyeing something specific, but when Koenig glanced in the perceived direction all he could see were the damp pines that crested the forest. As her gaze sauntered back to the table, Doris's eyes unfocused once more.

"Oh, I'm sorry, Edward. Sometimes I use the old name when I talk about Pinemist Bay. You see, this place didn't used to be Pinemist Bay at all. That name came about sometime towards the beginning of the century. The original name was Alistair's Brigand, named after the man who first settled the port," she stated.

"And it was way back in 1848 when the old bay first became inhabited, don't you know? At first it was a tiny little settlement, only a couple hundred sea-faring men who saw potential in it as a trade port between Canada and California. If I recall correctly, most of them came up during the California Gold Rush."

"Interesting," Koenig said.

"The history of Pinemist Bay is quite interesting indeed, Mr. Koenig. Albeit, somewhat tragic, but certainly interesting."

"What kinds of unfortunate events have happened here, Doris? You of all people must know," he begged.

"Well dearie, my mind isn't what it used to be and time has escaped me again. I don't have too much longer to spend on idle chit-chat, even if it is with a handsome young man such as yourself. We were discussing the act of yearwalking." She had effectively killed Koenig's question.

There certainly are subjects that the citizens of Pinemist Bay don't like to touch.

"What was it that you wanted to know, dearie?"

"Well, I was wondering exactly what happens after one blows into the keyhole of their local church." Doris stared vacuously for a minute, as if debating what her response should be. In a similar way to the old man in the road, Koenig could feel a peculiar energy pulsating from her, but he couldn't put his finger on what it was.

"Well, there is much speculation and debate on what happens after that, as very little is documented on the subject. It is known that long ago, to the tune of several hundred years, that folks from Eastern Europe, Slavic folk, brought much of their own culture to Scandinavia during a massive migration. They might have even introduced the belief system known today as paganism during this shift. The two cultures, with their rich histories, mingled and before long, their own rituals and customs blended into one. Somehow, kiddo, the Scandinavian practice of Årsgång became connected with various Slavic traditions, and the two cultures' spiritual worlds conflated into one.

"What is most commonly accepted is this, after blowing into the keyhole, the walker, as they're called, opens himself up to this spiritual world. He enters a sort of ghostly plane where he is very much still in this world, but he's in an altered version of it.

"You could think of it as another dimension within our own, but that's not precisely what it is. It is a dark place brimming with powers of an evil nature, dearie. These powers are quite harmful to the walker, as are the many beasts that are said to roam his path. Plus, he has temporarily disconnected his spirit from God and all things holy. As I said dearie, yearwalking came about in the Middle Ages when paganism was spreading throughout Europe, and dismissing God was in fashion.

"This world that the walker enters is colloquially referred to as Drugoy Mir, which is an old Russian term that means Otherworld. In Drugoy Mir, it's said the walker can encounter any number of creatures from Scandinavian and Slavic folklore; some of them good, and some of them evil. There is one spirit that superstitious folk rarely dare speak of, *His* evil is so great." Doris was almost whispering now, but she put a glaring emphasis on the word: his.

"Who is he?" Koenig asked.

"I cannot speak of Him now, dearie," she said, with a voice as cold as a winter wind. "So, once the walker blows into the keyhole he must fend off these spirits, should they assail him.

"If he succeeds, the walker is said to be granted with glimpses, or visions, of the future, most commonly documented to be a taste of what will come the following year. This is where the term 'yearwalk' comes from, dearie. You walk to see into the coming year."

Koenig nodded. "Thanks for all this information, Doris, you are a lifesaver. How do you know so much about this subject?"

"I've been around for a while, dearie." As she spoke, her capricious expression changed once more. "Well, my time is up. I have some errands to tend to." She stood up slowly and gazed down at Koenig. "Pinemist Bay can look a little gloomy to an outsider, but it really is a magical place. It's especially pretty up at Blackrock Peak," she said, intermittently nodding her head as she spoke.

"There is this quaint little lodge overlooking the rocks with a wondrous view of the bay. If you can, I'd make time to go over there and give that lodge a visit. You just might find what you're searching for." Without another utterance, but a lengthy emphatic stare, she slowly turned and hobbled away.

****

He exited the building, becoming submerged in a whipping frenzy of rain. Cold blots splashed on his skin and leaked into tendrils of water that descended his spine in icy patterns. In his scattered mind, he realized he forgot his umbrella back at the hotel. He threw his arm above his head, attempting to block some of the rain with his sleeve, and quickly scuttled over to the Mustang; the tawdry vehicle shimmering against a dull backdrop of concrete buildings and a cinereous sky.

He fumbled his car key out of a soggy corduroy pocket and plunged it into the lock. Before ducking into the car, he took one last glance at the enigmatic structure from which he had just left. The library was a massive prostrate figure, squatting low and stretching the breadth of the lot. The far end of the building was barely visible in the torrent, it's angular corner cutting a hard line against the mounting darkness. Koenig squinted.

A shape hovered beside the far end of the building. It was soft and animate, tilting from side to side, and as the wind picked up, Koenig thought he saw the shape billow and expand. He extracted the key from the lock and knelt beside the Mustang, partially obscured by its long hood. The mysterious shape receded behind the building and out of sight.

Koenig looked up. Lightning licked across the sky, a brilliant harbinger for a gathering storm. He didn't know what he saw, only that he had felt the glaring eyes of an unseen observer since he arrived in Safe Haven. Stirred by an unbridled curiosity, he rose from behind the car and, hugging the building closely, shuffled to the spot where the shape had lurked. With tremulous fingers curling around the edge of the building, he slowly peered around the corner.

Behind the facility lay a thick copse of trees. Gazing through the foliage, Koenig could barely discern the shapes of buildings looming on the other side, revealing a continuation of Safe Haven. As he stared through the menacing sway of the forest, Koenig thought he saw a large mobile shape drifting. It popped in and out of sight behind a sea of pine needles that were shivering on their branches.

He broke into a low gallop and was swallowed by the darkness of the forest. All around him, the tapping of raindrops sounded as the body of trees moved together in a soothing rhythm. He trundled through sopping wet vegetation, never taking his gaze away from the collection of buildings ahead. The shadowy figure he was pursuing appeared again, moving out of the forest directly ahead. Standing upright and moving deftly, he was sure it was a person now.

He waited at the edge of the trees for a moment. Although the figure hadn't glanced back, he was uncertain whether they knew he was tailing them. He followed carefully, ducking out of the woods and edging toward the structures. A chunky stone walkway bled out from under the grass and led up to a street lined with old buildings that had a majestic appearance. Koenig peered at the singular collection of buildings.

The dignified old structures were losing a long and silent struggle with the voracious forest. A canopy of vines veiled the gables above; the tall grass, like jagged, green teeth, munched on the buildings, inching their way above the lower windows in their conquest to devour. Along the streets had sprouted saplings, who raised their sword-like arms to the receding structures, eager to join the fight and deliver the final blow.

Far different from the architecture of anything Koenig had seen in Pinemist Bay, the building closest to him was composed of what looked like sandstone, and had a brilliant turret that was tall enough to overcome the creeping foliage and oversee a stretch of the woods. The figure he was tailing brushed past the tall grass and whisked into the front door. Koenig managed to get a more discerning look at the figure this time, noting that they had on some sort of heavy garment that trailed behind them. A cloak perhaps.

The grim eeriness of the town's abandoned outlying structures captivated Koenig, but he couldn't allow the digression to last. He moved up the stairs of the first building, flashing glances at its windows, but unable to see anything besides darkness inside. He moved to the front door and slowly pulled it open, thankful that the senescent hinges were noiseless. He peered inside the old building.

Whatever was bathed in the slivers of light created by the windows was all he could see; the rest was shrouded in darkness. Fragments of dust hung on the air above old documents that littered a desk under the window. Hoping that something on the desk could help him decipher the mysteries of Safe Haven, he tip-toed inside the room and approached the window sill to the left. Strings of spider webs were strewn upon an old light fixture on the desk. He considered attempting to turn it on, but to avoid drawing unwanted attention to himself, he grabbed the top document off a stack and held it under the light of the window.

It was a copy of an archaic obituary, with the detailed depiction of a man's face in the top left. It was a side-profile drawing, and to Koenig, the man resembled Charles Darwin, with a bald head, blunt nose, and a scraggly beard.

Sheldon Voight Ambrose
1818 – 1887

Doctor Sheldon Voight Ambrose, hailing from the borough of Liverpool, England, esteemed physician and theoretical scientist, was found dead in his home on the rainy evening of the twenty-third day of October, the year 1887. While there is some mystery regarding the cause of death, it is certain that Ambrose suffered from severe malnourishment during the fortnight leading up to his passing, and according to several members of the quaint town of Alistair's Brigand, suffered from increasing mental hysteria. In the weeks before his death, Ambrose had locked himself away in his home located in Pinemist Bay's outlying community known as Safe Haven. Insight from community members concerned about the aged doctor's health shows that he had lost a tenuous battle with sanity, with some townsfolk claiming that he would shout incoherent phrases at them, including drivel about his daughter Alyssa, and 'the man of shadow.'

A veiled murmur tore Koenig's attention from the news clipping. It was an ethereal, fluctuating noise that came from above. He drew back from the light of the window and listened intently. Two indistinct voices floated through the old floorboards; their sound, toneless and rounded. He slowly made his way across the dim room, delicately following the sounds as they bounced off the walls around him.

What are you doing here, Edward? You have no idea who these people are, or what they're capable of.

He trailed the voices to a circular room with a spiral staircase. Segmented windows provided a bleak luminescence into the stairway. Koenig stood at the base of the turret. The voices were more prominent now, but still inscrutable, and the architecture of the turret layered them with a warbling moan that further masked them.

He ascended the staircase slowly, succumbing to a terrific burning in his knees. With every revolution around the structure, the mysterious voices gained clarity. It was two men speaking in laconic grunts and murmurs. He made one final turn around the turret and halted at the top floor landing. Upon the landing was a tall figure dressed in a dark cloak. He was facing away from Koenig, his hood covering his head.

"Where's the girl?" the man hidden from sight asked.

"We still haven't found her," the man nearest Koenig said.

"We must work quickly then, Wilson. The secondary target is in his possession as we speak. He is most impatient."

"We will find her," the man nearest Koenig assured. Koenig leaned forward on his toes, attempting to get a glimpse of the other man, but a stabbing creak of the floorboard resounded from the pressure. The nearest figure whirled about in an instant and Koenig thrust himself backward in an instinctual reaction, nearly tumbling down the stairwell in the process.

Without daring to glance back, he propelled himself down the spiral at a dizzying rate, the stairway turning into a mosaic of light and dark patches as he leapt into the foyer and blew through the front door. Bounding down the stairs, he made his way to the shelter of the trees. He dove into a thicket, the rainy leaves licking his face, and made himself as quiet and as prostrate as he could.

Several seconds later the two cloaked figures emerged from the building and scampered down the stairs. They dithered about in the street for a moment, then stalked toward each other in a calculated fashion. They exchanged words, but Koenig could hear nothing over the soft din of rain on the leaves. All he knew was that one of them was named Wilson, which was of no meaning to him. After the exchange, the two enigmatic figures drifted apart and disappeared into the woods, silent as specters.

Chapter Six
Betrayal

Her unbundled hair brushed her clavicle and settled beneath her rib cage. Watching it unfold, he realized he had forgotten how long it was. Her expression was awash with a mellow coolness, the equanimity of her stare betrayed only by a slight blush in her cheeks. She was on top of him.

Rays of light strained through the trees in the background and set her pale hair on fire in a varnish of wavering gold. Eveline's eyes were fixed on Koenig's for a timeless moment, and while he was lost in her stare, he felt a silvery clarity that he hadn't experienced in some time. He knew what he wanted, the only thing that his heart desired, and it was right in front of him.

With a girlish smirk on her face she leaned forward and entered his mouth, aggressively caressing his tongue with her own. Her hands meandered from his chest to his abdomen, a cascade of nerves firing off in response. Never before had he felt such a fiery passion for his wife. The clearing in which they lay dissolved, and his comprehension of time and space faded. They were the only two objects in his universe, their bodies colliding and combusting into one. And then she drew away again, and the world flooded back into existence.

Eveline teased him by pulling down a sleeve of her blouse, revealing just the bumpy tip of a nipple. His heart pulsing in tight clusters, Koenig reached towards her desperately and she pushed his arms to the ground. Her fingers crawled up her right shoulder and she pulled the remaining sleeve down, unveiling her large, sloping breasts.

More assertively this time, he outstretched both arms and firmly cupped her peaks, barely able to contain their volume in his hands. Eveline protracted her shoulder blades, accentuating the structure of her clavicle bone and exposing the soft lines of her muscles.

Her breath had a feverish heat to it as she worked her way down his torso with her lips, slowly unbuttoning his shirt and pecking his skin at each step. With the ease of a seasoned lover, she unbuttoned his slacks and took him in her mouth, embracing him in a succulent kiss. Had he been on his feet, his knees would have buckled.

The midday sun poked out over the trees, coruscating off Eveline's hair and glimmering on Koenig's chest. Beads of sweat trickled down his brow, but he didn't bother to wipe them off. His hands were clutching her head, his grip tightening vehemently as she worked him with her tongue. Breathing became difficult, and his gasps grew coarse and hitched.

Laying against the cool earth, Koenig's eyes meandered across a cloudless sky. The tall grass surrounding them waned in the breeze, slowly enveloping and then releasing their bodies like a capricious Venus flytrap. His mind had been a whirlwind lately. Thoughts would jettison down and thrash about, only to sink further into his subconscious and disappear like lagan detached from its buoy. The feeling was peculiar, but was readily shelved by the realness of Eveline. Letting loose all his inner qualms, he concentrated on nothing but the sensation.

Her tongue poked, tickled and caressed, while her mouth engulfed him. The tide of his pleasure was rising rapidly, threatening to swallow the pier. Koenig sat up, bits of earth hugging the sweat on his back, and playfully fingered the grooves of her spine. His hand travelled outward, passed over the bump of her shoulder, and then glided down the length of her arm where their hands met and folded together.

He stayed there for a minute gazing at the surrounding forest. Around the lip of the valley only a few hundred yards away was their daughter. She hadn't crossed his mind in what felt like a stretch of time and, for a short ping of a moment, concern for her encompassed him. The fleeting shred of dignity in his mind begged him to dig his heels into the ground and flee from his wife, to run back to the old red barn and bring his daughter under the security of his bastion.

That part of him didn't trust Eveline, or whoever the phantom version of her that lay before him was. The woman before him looked and felt like Eveline. He was well acquainted with her on an intimate level, but in the visceral depths of his mind, he felt it was not her. Eveline wouldn't lure him from their child, abandoning her in some unfamiliar place.

The overwhelming rush of pleasure trickled from his center and bloomed toward his glutes and thighs. He laid back down as the tide blew over. Gripping his wife's hand with white knuckle intensity, he succumbed to the storm of passion and then fell limp as the sensation subsided. He stared at the sky, not thinking, just breathing.

Dalla. Koenig pushed himself up again, his head no longer clouded by his baser instincts. He looked down at his wife to tell her that he felt ashamed, and that he was going to go check on their daughter. Before he was able to utter one syllable, he noticed that her soft ashen hair was gone, and he was staring at raven black locks that flowed off his thigh and splayed out on the ground.

Disbelieving, Koenig sealed his eyes shut and then opened them, peering down again as her head slowly surfaced from his groin. First her sharp nose came into view. Then her angular jaw line. Her pallid green eyes fell on his.

It wasn't Eveline at all. It was the girl he had most recently been unfaithful with. Reality flooded back, like curtains drawn on his ignorant conscience. His wide-eyed gaze locked onto her face, her lips snaking into a jagged smile beneath cold eyes that unfailingly stared back at him. She was savoring the look of puzzlement in his eyes.

Incredulous, he grabbed her by the shoulders and threw her to the side. She didn't utter a word of protest. She didn't speak at all. She just lay there and watched as he clambered to his feet. He maintained as much eye contact as possible, only breaking his vision to frantically button up his pants.

Was this a dream? Hadn't he been with Eveline just moments ago? He didn't care. Dalla was the only thing on his tumultuous mind. He turned toward the forest to run, and as he pivoted, he heard the woman say, "Come back to bed, stranger."

Her voice brought a searing recollection of buried emotions to his mind. He remembered that same sultry tone caressing his ear during that fateful night.

"Eveline doesn't need to know," she went on. "It'll be our little secret."

"Fuck you!" Hearing this woman utter his wife's name brought to the situation a grave sense of validity, and solidified his incrimination. "Stay away from me, you psycho, and stay away from my family!" With that, he sprang over the creek and out of the clearing.

Chunks of green whizzed by as he dashed through the trees, cutting the most direct route he could remember back to the barn. The high sun disappeared into the exuberant patchwork of foliage above, only slicing through the thinnest clumps of leaves to light the way. Were it night, he realized, it would have been nearly impossible to make it through the depths of this forest to get back to his daughter. He leapt over a downed tree, the gnarled hull of the rotted trunk nearly clipping his foot and bringing him down.

Light began to filter in at a steadier pace and Koenig finally reached the end of the thicket. Passing through the lip of the valley, he turned the corner and the red barn came into view. With lungs heaving towards their capacity in every stride, and a heart smoldering with expended energy, he slammed into the back of the old building and fumbled his way to the entrance. *Dalla, please be here.*

He wrenched the bug-screen open and tugged on the door. It didn't give. *Fuck, it's locked!* "Dalla, I'm coming baby, hang on." Plucked from the depths of his soul, remorse began to take over. *I've failed you before, I'm not gonna fail you again, honey.*

Koenig rounded the front of the building, recalling from before that the large barn doors had been slightly askew. A quick assessment confirmed this as he noticed loose piles of hay wedged underneath each door, holding them in place. He placed himself in the space between them and gauged the size of the gap. His adult frame was unable to squeeze through, but it looked spacious enough for a small child to fit. Wedging himself between the doors, he pressed with all his might and they slowly obliged.

The inside of the barn was a disheveled muddle of hay and dust. It looked as though it had long since been abandoned. After scanning the barn house and discovering nothing but the shallow echo of his own heavy breathing bouncing off the walls, he continued to the far side of the barn. There was a door connecting the barn house to the added-on living quarters and, with a quick jerk of the handle, it gave way to the small room.

This is where Eveline and I left her. "Dalla!" he called between heaving breaths. "Are you in here?"

No reply.

Bearing the weight of panic and disconsolation, Koenig stumbled back into the barn and stood there for a moment, defeated. It was an odd but familiar feeling. Over time, he had succumbed to the belief that he was slowly dragging his family into a black hole, an abyss from which he would soon be unable to yank them free.

He had cheated on Eveline at least three or four times; his intoxication used to be so frequent that it had become hard to say exactly how many times he had betrayed her. And every time that he fucked another woman he was also betraying his baby girl. He knew he didn't deserve his family.

Now Koenig's worst fears were playing out in this macabre dream world. His wife had disappeared, morphed into a monstrous memory, and he had abandoned his four-year-old daughter. He shuffled over to a bale of hay laid crudely in front of the doorway, slumped over, and pressed his face into the heels of his hands. Staring at the mess of dirt and straw between his feet, he spotted an ostentatious object shouldered between chunks of debris. It was the tattered corner of a book.

Feeling palpitations in his heart, he brushed aside the mess. Swipe left. First, the beach ball came into view. Swipe right. The pale upturned face. After a final flick of his wrist, the unicycle was unearthed and the entire front cover of Dalla's coloring book was visible. Lying not two feet from the barn doors, it appeared to have gotten buried when Koenig had forced his way in.

Hands trembling, he reached down and gingerly scooped up the only piece of his daughter within reach, the last remnant of a severed family. He pressed the book firmly to his chest and unabashedly dissolved into tears.

"Daddy." Koenig cringed as his vision fuzzed like a dead television channel, while the muscles in his neck and shoulders seized up. Then the barn flooded back into view and he instantly regained motor control. Dalla's voice had called out to him, but she was nowhere to be seen. The strange occurrence that brought Koenig to Pinemist Bay was happening all over again. She was trying to contact him once more. *How is she doing this?*

"Dalla!" he cried out. "Dalla, where are you? Oh god, baby girl, I'm gonna find you." He squeezed through the barn doors, the setting sun dousing the field in an aureate glow. The cornfield was ablaze in a red twilight, and the mountain peaks that enveloped the valley loomed menacingly above. A cool breeze kissed the stalks of corn and strained through Koenig's hair. He stepped forward and shouted to his daughter one more time.

After a brief but agonizing moment of silence, his vision became muddled again and he felt the same insurmountable pain in his neck. He collapsed to his knees. It was as if an electrical node had clamped down on his spine and exploded his nerves.

"Daddy, I'm here," Dalla said.

"Where are you?" He winced through the sensation, rocking back and forth on his knees and cradling his head in his hands.

"Come find me, daddy." Hearing her voice, even if it was coming from inside his head, allowed him to pertinaciously clutch to some deep hope that it wasn't too late. "I'm hiding over here, past the cornfield, daddy." Even though Dalla was a precocious girl, not many four-year-olds would be able to speak as eloquently as the voice he was hearing. He knew that she couldn't either. Something was awry.

"Okay honey, I'm coming." He waited for the sensation to subside and for his vision to normalize. When it did, he sprang up off his knees and dashed into the maze of corn. Vibrant green stalks rushed past his face, and every once in a while he had to duck like a boxer, or throw up his arms to deflect an ear of corn as it whizzed past. He hadn't been forced to run in years. The swiftness of his stride and his nimble-footed grace came as a surprise. His daughter was lost, and in this moment, he felt nothing could stop him from reaching her.

Koenig could see the end of the cornfield bouncing into view and the giant canyon wall directly beyond it. With an ardent wave of his hand, he brushed through the last row of cornstalks and slammed into the rock face. The sun-drenched surface radiated a muted heat that gently kissed Koenig's cheek.

Sidling along the massive rock wall, he found himself drawn towards a warm, pulsating energy that seemed to issue from somewhere in the mountain's hull. A ghostly energy began tugging him forward. It felt like Dalla was leading him from inside his own mind, and somehow he knew he was getting closer.

"Daddy, I'm right here." Her voice now echoed with a timbre that shook Koenig's head.

"Where?" he pleaded.

"Just a little further, daddy." The tendons in his neck bulged like steel cables each time she entered his mind, and the muscles attached were on the verge of exploding under duress. "I'm in the cave," her voice boomed. As the hazy distortion covering his eyes dissolved once more, he continued along the wall, fervently gripping the coarse structure as he went.

The energy he was following intensified, and he could no longer simply feel the heat of it, he could visualize it too. Tiny embers of golden light plumed around him. They were strewn together, forming an elegant pattern that danced about him while he ran. It felt like a protective force field; a mobile safe haven, and he no longer knew if he was coming to his daughter's rescue, or if she was coming to his.

He came upon a sizable crack in the mountain's surface and pivoted to face Dalla. She was standing in the crevice and staring up at him, the mysterious golden energy encompassing them both and swirling viciously around.

"There you are, baby!" Koenig's misery dissolved as he reached down and scooped his daughter into his arms. "Why did you run away? I'm so sorry daddy left you Dalla. Never again!"

"I don't have much time, daddy." She seemed eerily composed, almost saturnine. He noticed that as she spoke to him out loud, he was unaffected physically. Only when she spoke from inside his own head, did he experience the violent seizures.

Does my daughter have some kind of telepathy, or is this all just part of a crazy dream? Dalla's grasp of the English language had been far more determinate the last time he heard her speak. Hearing her now, he was stupefied by her profound vocabulary and pronunciation.

"Is this a dream, Dalla? Are you really here?" he asked.

"It's me, daddy. I made it through to you, but they're looking for me," Dalla said. With extreme delicacy, Koenig placed his daughter back on the ground.

"Who's looking for you, Dalla?" The golden force field surrounding them started to waver and, like coils of dust caught in a gale, it began to evaporate into the air. Dalla seemed to notice, as she glanced at the shaking beads of gold above her.

"We're out of time," she said with a bizarre placidity. "Daddy, listen. The Vucari have mommy and they're looking for me. Listen to the old man, daddy, he is nice and I think we can trust him. He's waiting for you in Drugoy Mir."

"Who has mommy?" Koenig asked. "And how do you know the old man, Dalla?"

As he spoke, the outlines of Dalla's figure began to scintillate in the darkness of the crevice. She was fading like a memory, but Koenig wasn't about to let her go again. He leapt forward with great vigor and, in a ludicrous moment, his airborne body passed through Dalla's. She was becoming as hollow as a ghost. His body dove straight through hers and subsequently crashed down on the other side.

As she dissipated into nothingness, he heard the echo of her voice. "Find the house on the hill, daddy. The one with the old well and the fading cobblestone walkway."

Chapter Seven
Blackrock Peak

A cosmos of thoughts tumbled through Koenig's mind. Part of him indubitably believed that the recent events, from the old man in the road, to his daughter speaking to him in dreams, had been real. This part of him was mulling over last night's dream.

His head was drooped over a cup of strong black coffee, and his guilt-ridden mind was focused on that girl; that random bar girl he had given himself to in a night of drunken revolt. He didn't even know her name. He just remembered her tall, slender body and her sultry voice that seemed to simmer in the darkness of the hotel room. And he remembered her mischievous, nearly tempestuous smile. He had been helpless to resist.

He hadn't stayed long enough to discover what stoked the fire in the girl's eyes, and he didn't want to. Something about the innate passion she exuded was too much for him. When he was unfaithful to Eveline in the past, it had been with empty shells of women. Girls with no depth that he didn't want to get to know. This girl had been different, and that terrified him.

When Koenig came home that night, Dalla was crying violently and wouldn't let him comfort her. Hitherto, Dalla had always slept through the night without a hiccup. It was almost as though she had sensed what he had done. Eveline sensed it too and the bar girl had been the last straw for her. She had handled all of Koenig's shortcomings with grace and puissance until a few days ago, when she'd had enough.

This time, she evicted him from their home, wrenched him from their daughter, and uprooted his entire life. What was puzzling him, as he sat in the Seaside Diner watching droplets of rain speck the windows and coruscate in the muted morning sun, was how he had managed to forget the real reason why he left home. He had ably dismissed the traitorous occurrence from his mind and pushed vacuous thoughts forward to occupy the space they left. During the drive up the canyon, the affair had crossed his mind only a couple of times.

Eveline's ruling of a separation was why he had left in the first place. He had dithered about downtown Chicago in his car considering his debacle, then started the process of renting a room at a neglected, dreary little motel just off of The Loop. It was at this time when Dalla's voice inexplicably entered his mind, urging him towards Pinemist Bay.

I'm getting what I deserve. Have I finally broken our family?

He sat in the booth of the diner contemplating everything from the adulterous incident, to his discussion last night with his daughter, while some girl that was not Jenny made her rounds and refilled his cup several times. Her name tag read Epiphany.

"Hey Epiphany, where's that Jenny girl that works here?" he asked on her fifth or sixth circulation. Epiphany's sienna-dyed hair was pulled back in a bun and bounced with every step she took toward his table.

"Um, I'm not sure where she is today, sir. I was told she got sick," she said, as she poured fresh coffee in his mug. He studied her face intently. She seemed unaffected by his question, and during her response there was no waver in her inflection.

Perhaps Jenny really had fallen ill, but a tiny bud of conscience nagged at him, hoping she hadn't been harmed by the mysterious Kendric, or some other figure in the brooding and sinister town. If any harm had befallen her, he knew it was his doing. He lit up a cigarette, finished the coffee, and left.

The deluge reduced to a drizzle by late morning. Koenig stalked the streets of Pinemist Bay with his corduroy jacket fastened at the waist, and his little wrinkled map wedged in his side pocket next to his cigarettes. His destination was unknown. His two hottest leads, the house on the hill that Dalla mentioned in his dream, and Blackrock Peak, which Doris suggested he visit, were not inscribed on the map. He considered the likelihood that Doris was not aware of his mysterious predicament, but an inscrutable feeling told him she was. Either way, he did not have much to go on.

Hands inhumed in his pockets, Koenig meandered away from Main Street and towards the bay. The frigid waters shimmered under the sun as the tide lazily strolled back and forth. In the daylight, Pinemist Bay was an unassuming vessel of beauty that so effectively shadowed its intent.

A huge and senescent, but likely serviceable, fisherman's wharf lay idly at the cusp of the water, and several service buildings lined the street adjacent to the beach. Seeing the bay for the first time, Koenig entertained visions of what the aging port town used to be when it was known as Alistair's Brigand. He envisioned grandiose ships docked at a lustrous harbor, with all manner of maritime equipment scattered along the docks, and droves of properly attired and heavily mustached businessmen wrestling their sea-legs into town to inquire about the nightly rate at the Pinemist Hotel, while they waited for the next ship for Canada to dock.

Looking at the bay's dilapidated piers, the ramshackle remnants of what once was, Koenig felt a shiver crawl down his spine. At one point, Alistair's Brigand was probably a burgeoning port town, but as the mist of the mountainside slowly engulfed the town through the years, it settled right in and morphed into something mysterious and evil.

Koenig weaved his way up from the bay and into the edge of the town. A few blocks west of Main were strings of neglected two story houses, each one endowed with a long porch that nearly met the next. He walked into the first building on the street, a hobby shop called Francine's Quandary.

"Abby, don't touch that! It's probably very expensive." A woman herded her daughter away from an antique wooden frigate, drawing the girl's attention to a series of bobble heads and figurines. The shop was old and musty and, like most of the buildings in Pinemist Bay, suffered from considerable wear. Little crescent shaped windows on the south and north sides of the shop filtered brilliant streams of sunlight into the store. At the entrance was a little framed white paper.

Historic Landmark

This building, residing amidst a row of Midwestern-style duplexes on Grand Street, is an official landmark of Pinemist Bay County. Serving as a microcosm of the entire county, this establishment has entertained a colorful history over the years. During the prohibition era, American citizens would cross the border of Canada by land and sea, smuggling alcohol via massive wooden crates and oil drums. Pinemist Bay was an ideal location for smuggling liquor from British Colombia, and before long piqued the interest of society's wealthy elite.

In 1920, the accommodating cellars of many buildings throughout this neighborhood were used to temporarily store shipments of contraband from distributors in Canada. Liquors ranging from gin and rye, to brandy and Canadian whiskey, as well as imported spirits such as port and sherry were regularly in supply. Being located near the sea, and housing an array of large two-story buildings equipped with awnings and decks, Grand Street was briskly converted from a collection of independent businesses into a swell of saloons, bars, and clubs. The name Grand Street was colloquially changed by smugglers into Rumrunner's Quarry, and in 1921 began exclusively catering to the aristocratic clientele who traveled to partake in the clandestine events of the boomtown.

"Pinemist Bay has a really rich history, doesn't it?" a delicate voice said from behind. Koenig turned to see the woman smiling at him, her arms wrapped around her daughter who was shifting irritably back and forth like a child does when she's told to stand still. The little girl's eyes were fixed on Koenig as she swayed.

Their appearance was befitting of the iconic family from Little House on the Prairie; complete with long flower-printed skirts and vintage clogs with buckles on the side of each shoe. The pair starkly reminded Koenig of the Pinemist Hotel's receptionist, Sally Schubert. *This whole town is stuck in the 1700s.*

"It's true," he said, smiling. "Everywhere I go something exciting happens. What's your name?" he asked, looking down at the girl.

"Melanie Houghton," she said. "My mom calls me Mel."

"I have a daughter that's about your age, Melanie." Koenig smiled. "Do you like it here?" Melanie nodded.

"All my friends are here," she exclaimed with vehemence, her frizzy, unkempt hair partially veiling her expression. He deduced from the girl's buoyancy and charisma that she was indeed content. Perhaps his experience in Pinemist Bay was unique to him, and there lingered some scrap of normalcy in the community.

"That's good," he replied. "Friends you met in preschool?" *At least some kind of school system would be a good sign.* Melanie nodded, and then broke her mother's loose grasp and bounced away to a rack of trinkets near the store counter.

"She's really something," he said to the woman, pushing his hand toward her. "My name's Edward."

"Daphne Houghton." The tenacity of her grip was alarming, considering her supple frame. Daphne wasn't a beautiful woman. Her appeal lay in the unassuming charm of her expressions and the way she held herself, inviting yet independent. She had choppy black hair, with stout bangs and a long slim neck below. Melanie must have received her curly hair from her father.

"I don't even need to ask if you're from around here," Daphne said. "I can already tell that you're a fish out of water. Honey, you look like you've been through the wringer." Her compassion was a welcome guest. Koenig felt a swell of tears form behind his eyes, and all at once the emotional load he was carrying became all the more apparent.

"I'm not actually," he choked. "I'm from Chicago. I'm heading up to Vancouver on a business trip." The words fell out of his mouth autonomously, and a slight twinge knotted his stomach when he realized he was using his father's situation to cover up his own circumstance. It felt discourteous to the memory of his father. The memory of a man who, while poisoned by alcohol and grief, loved his family to the very end.

"And you get to visit our quaint little town on the way," Daphne said.

"Yes, as a matter of fact…" Koenig added, as he pretended to study an antique gramophone speaker. Claiming the device was authentic, the label stated the gramophone was from 1924, and was used in the 'rowdy, raucous bootleg era, in a converted bar on Rumrunner's Quarry called Alistair's Tavern.'

"Do you happen to know where Blackrock Peak is?" he asked. "I've heard it has fantastic views of the sea." Daphne stared at him inquisitively for a moment.

"Why yes, it's directly south of Pinemist Bay. You would take Anastasis Way, which you'll find two blocks east of Grand Street, all the way out of town and then some," she said, imitating with her hand the crude route he would take. "And then when you're about to round the corner on this cliff face, it's huge, you can't miss it, you take a steep, unpaved side road called Fisherman's Folly. Just continue up that road to the peak of the mountainside and voila! You're there."

"Ah, thank you so much!" Koenig sighed in relief upon knowing his next move. "That's pretty easy."

"Yes." With a look on her face that was equal parts concerned and bemused, Daphne continued, "I'm not sure why you would want to go there on a day like this though, honey. The rain is bitter cold, and the weather might hinder any good view of the ocean. Not to mention you could slip and hurt yourself. It'll be downright slick footing up there today and no one would be around to help you if something did happen."

****

    Koenig stopped for gas beside a smattering of houses that lay just beyond the outskirts of town. The wind hurled torrents of chilly northern air in his face and, when paired with heavy spats of rainfall, it made for an unforgiving cold that sank into his bones.

    Pinemist Bay was largely made up of older homes and forgotten business, but the southern section in particular reeked of rot and neglect. There was a two-story bungalow next to the gas station that suffered from an overgrowth of vines, with an exterior that was populated by divots of missing brick and loose mortar. Just beside it lay an old shed that used to be white, but had developed sickly looking spots of mauve from a varnish that had long since soured with moisture and rot.

    He fastened the fuel cap, shook a cold coating of rain from his jacket, and continued down Anastasis Way. He watched as the lights of the gas station shimmered in the rear-view mirror and then bled into a stormy mosaic of grey that was consuming Pinemist Bay. It was steadily getting darker and Koenig thought he heard a splash of thunder in the distance.

    Once outside of the town, the road became a lengthy curve hugging a patchwork of forest. Koenig hovered his foot over the brake pedal of his sports car for most of the ride, as the rainfall became substantial enough for hydroplaning to occur. The last thing he wanted was to dove-tail into the side rails and become stranded in the undeveloped outskirts of a maleficent old port town.

    To the left, waves arced and crashed with a compelling luster against a bedding of slick black rocks. Beyond the shoreline, Koenig spotted an old tugboat wrestling with the surf amidst increasingly choppy waves. As he glanced left, he noticed a large lighthouse looming to the south. The structure appeared to be roughly half of a mile out to sea, and the only way to reach it by land was a stretch of prostrate boulders that stretched out in front of a large cliff face. He presumed this was Blackrock Peak.

    As the towering hunk of rock approached, and the forest began to drive upwards to meet the massive piece of earth, Koenig saw a road sign glimmer through shades of slate and argentine. Fisherman's Folly. The dirt road jostled and lurched the car during its ascent. The heavy rainfall had moistened the earth, and he feared that his car would lose grip on the slippery mud and plummet back to the base of the hill. Keeping it in first gear, he powered his way to the summit.

    An elevated, lightly wooded bit of forest, Koenig assumed Blackrock Peak was given its name in reference to the sheer volume of large jet-black rocks that the peak overlooked. What Doris said was true, storm or no storm, it was a sight to see. Koenig parked the car, eased himself onto a muddy shelf of land, and stood centered on the cliff. The lighthouse, and the line of rocks leading to it, lay directly before him. The wet body of rocks shimmered in rays of sunlight that sliced through the leaden sky, while the lighthouse spun before him, its somber wisps of light straining to reach the land.

Koenig walked away from the edge of the cliff and into a thicket of trees, thankful for the minimal protection their arching branches provided from the rainfall. A few birds darted between the densest bits of foliage they could find, and a squirrel scampered down the trunk of an aspen tree and into a bush. There were few signs of life on this stormy day, and Koenig began to feel more isolated than ever since arriving in Pinemist Bay. A dispirited man would have fled the place days ago, but he pushed forward, with only the hopes of unraveling the mystery so that he may see his family again.

I hope Doris actually was hinting that there's something relevant to me here in Blackrock Peak. Otherwise, I'm wasting my God-damned time. Something about her struck me as wise and intuitive, like she somehow knew what I was going through. Nevertheless, the leads I'm following here are exceptionally vague.

Farther from the promontory, Koenig found himself stumbling upon the eastern end of the hill after a minute or two of exploring. At this point, the land swiftly fell into a lengthy decline, beyond which it appeared to level out again into a stretch of denser woods.

Peering down the slope and into the woodsy abyss below, Koenig heard a jarring slap of thunder, and then something else. A shriek suffused the forest. It was languid and horrific, like the wretched squall of someone under extreme duress. He pivoted and faced into the forest, uncertain what his next move should be. For a moment, all he heard was the soft sound of thousands of raindrops cascading through the surrounding foliage. After a tormenting pause, and a stillness that made his increasingly frigid joints stiff, Koenig heard another stifled shriek.

Without hesitation, he tore off into the woods in the direction of the screams. Ducking under low hanging branches and pushing his way through a patch of bushes, Koenig came upon the southern slope of Blackrock Peak. At the edge of the cliff, perched on a bed of mossy earth was a battered fisherman's shack. The queer little house appeared to have been abandoned for some time. The wood side panels had become networks of sizable cracks and blemishes that bled fungus. The roof had a palpable degree of sag from years of stress and neglect.

Galloping now to discover the origin of the cries, Koenig came upon the door of the shack with a ferocious momentum. He had to dig his heels into the spongy earth in order to stop before busting clean through the entrance.

Koenig stalked around the side of the old shanty and perched onto a slippery concrete ledge to peer into the window. Rain dinned on the old tin roof above and pummeled his face, making it difficult to see anything. The room was small, commensurate to a studio apartment in a big city, and partially shrouded in shadow. Inside the swell of darkness, Koenig could make out ghostly shapes bobbing around. He couldn't discern more until two of them moved in front of the opposite window.

Appearing identical to the two men at Safe Haven, several hooded figures in long robes moved about the room. Koenig couldn't see much, but he could hear them shuffling around in the murk. A hollowed-out whimper brought his attention to the left of the room where there was a kitchenette containing a porcelain sink, a cream-colored refrigerator, and a frail old dining table. He heard a few electrical whirs, as if something was being spooled up, and then a small circular patch of the room was illuminated in an eerie white glow. The sound had been made by a manual crank flashlight. What it illuminated in the corner of the room made his blood boil, and he had to shove his fist in his mouth to prevent crying out.

Her back was to him, but Koenig was positive that Jenny from the Seaside Diner was in the room. He saw her curly black hair bobbing in the half-light as she was held by two robed bodies, with a third standing behind them. She was struggling to break free of the mysterious figures, but he could tell she was spent. Running down either of her arms were clusters of scalloped burn marks that glistened in the dim light, and he identified a large welt on her upper back, directly between her shoulder blades.

The lone hooded figure moved beside Jenny and her captors, stopping in front of a rusted electric stove. He clicked the dial counterclockwise and stepped back again. Upon seeing this, she quivered and fought, but in vain. The robed figures were too strong.

"No, no. Please," Jenny begged, her voice coarse and ragged. Koenig wanted to yell, or to clamber in and save her, but he knew that he was outnumbered and that these strangers would only do him harm as well. Knowing full well that he could do his wife and daughter no good dead, he resigned to stand by and watch.

"I admire your resolve Miss Wilbur, but this will only turn out badly for you. Quite badly, actually," the man stated. "I can make this even more painful, and I've got all day. Just answer my questions. That is all I require."

Jenny turned her head toward the robed man. Koenig could see terror distilled in her eyes, and her pallid face contorted with pain and fear. Seeing her in this predicament brought a deft swell of tears to Koenig's eyes. His fist was still buried in his mouth, the knuckles on his hand blanching under the pressure of his jaw. *What have I done?*

"What did you tell Edward Koenig?" the man continued. "What does he know?"

"I already told you," she panted. "He stopped in the diner and was asking questions about Pinemist Bay. I just answered his questions, but I didn't tell him anything about the Vucari or the hotel, I swear." After a harrowing pause, in which the only sound was the unrelenting drum of rain upon the roof, the robed man said,

"You're withholding information, Miss Wilbur. I am disappointed."

As if heeding a tacit cue, the two men holding Jenny pushed her forward and dangled her bare arm over the stove top. One of the coils was glowing white-hot now, and she began to shriek as they pushed her arm up against it. Koenig's heart dropped into his stomach and he averted his gaze, overcome by a wave of nausea.

The mild sear of burning flesh was drowned out by guttural, gyrating ululations. Gripped by curiosity, he returned his gaze. They moved her over to the kitchen table and placed her firmly in a rickety old chair. The robed men had mesh covers under their hoods that disguised their faces even under the lustrous artificial light.

The flashlight began to lose power and started to flicker, sending the room into a dizzying frenzy of intermittent light. Jenny was caught in the center of the pulsing luminescence, and Koenig could see her tortured expressions in brilliant, harrowing flashes. He was sure he would never forget the sight.

"Look at you. You are in a tremendous amount of pain, I can tell. And those beautiful little arms of yours are going to be permanently scarred, Miss Wilbur. I can end your suffering and I can even spare your life. You just need to tell me what Edward Koenig knows about yearwalking and about *Him*."

The man emphasized the word 'him', alluding to someone that Jenny knew, and someone the robed man thought Jenny had informed Koenig of. Could it have been the old man in the road? Kendric? Koenig remembered how Jenny had suddenly turned taciturn back in the diner when the subject of yearwalking arose. Perhaps she had kept her lips sealed to protect him? Either way, this man was determined to learn the extent to which she had squealed.

Languid and pale, Jenny steadied her breathing and mustered a response. "Please, I'm not lying! He asked about yearwalking and I told him I didn't know!" Tremors of guilt coursed through Koenig's body and he clenched his fists to keep them from shaking.

"It is crucial that Koenig meets Him. Koenig has something very valuable to His cause, and we must find it. Now I don't enjoy being here in this musty old shack, soaked to my bones from this ill-mannered tempest and forced to cause you pain, but you must understand that my hands are tied Miss Wilbur, and I'm running out of options."

The man stalked to the far end of the kitchen and brandished a pair of pliers from a creaky, peeling drawer. He nodded to his two main henchmen, who obliged his tacit command, grabbing Jenny by her head and prying her mouth open. One of them curled his fingers over the teeth of her lower jaw to keep her mouth agape.

The leader stood over her and inched the rusty tool towards her mouth. Jenny squirmed and moaned in protest and just before the device latched onto her molar she bit down hard, clamping her mouth over the fingers of one of the henchmen. He let out an astonished cry and withdrew his hand. The other man struggled to maintain a grip on her head.

"You bitch!" the man howled as he clutched his hand, which was dripping with a shiny coat of blood. He then raised his uninjured hand and hit her across the face with an open palm. A deafening crack resounded through the tiny room upon flesh meeting flesh, and all the silhouetted men were watching intently now.

"Easy, brother," the leader said. "Go take a look at that hand." He motioned to the shadows and another henchman, indistinguishable from the rest, materialized into the kitchen and took the wounded man's place. They forced Jenny's mouth open again, the new assistant holding her mouth open with two hands for good measure.

"As you now know, Miss Wilbur, we have eyes everywhere." The leader said as he clasped a tooth with the pliers. "And you're going to tell me what you told Edward Koenig sooner or later." With that, he adjusted his center of gravity and yanked his elbow downward, as if working the levers of an old locomotive.

Jenny cried out in writhing agony. Koenig turned his head in disgust once more, unable to face the abhorrent sight. He held onto the ledge and stared downwards, watching as the rain splashed against tiny tendrils of grass and then dissolved into the blanket of dirt below. Her howls continued as the man jerked her tooth from its root. Amidst the buzz of rain and the distant claps of thunder, Koenig heard the soft crunch of her molar giving in and releasing from its root.

By the time he mustered the courage to look once more the man was already working on another tooth. Koenig's blood stanched as he discerned Jenny's molar, a speck of white, gleaming on the table. The robed leader was now twisting in labored jerks at the second tooth, but just as he was about to pry it out, the flashlight began to wane again.

"Power it up once more, I need light," the leader said as he stood over Jenny, his foot propped against her chair for leverage. Koenig was through watching such macabre actions. His hatred for the sadistic men had reached a pinnacle, and he decided to use the intermittent darkness to his advantage. Just as one of the henchmen was moving to pick up the flickering crank-light, Koenig braced his foot against the wall and pulled with all his might until his center of gravity had shifted over the window pane, and then he lurched himself inside.

"You monsters!" he cried as he drove himself into the leader's body, knocking the unsuspecting man clear off his feet and into the refrigerator. Without a moment's hesitation, he threw his arms around Jenny and hoisted her to her feet. Astonished gasps sounded throughout the shack, and the flashlight began to falter entirely, leaving the room in a black that was nearly pitch.

Koenig spun on his feet and pulled Jenny towards the front door as shadows descended upon them from all sides. Before a single robed man made contact, Koenig burst through the door and was assaulted by a blanket of daylight. Disoriented and carrying the weight of two people, he knew he could not afford a single blunder. He pivoted to the right and thrust Jenny towards the back of the house, while heavy footfalls paraded against the soft earth behind them. A cascade of voices reverberated from inside and outside the shack.

Refusing to glance behind, Koenig felt the breath of one of the men graze his neck. Before the figure could grab them, a soft thud sounded behind; the assailant slipped on a pad of wet earth and fell aside. Several shadowy objects stepped over him and continued driving towards the fleeing couple.

When they reached the southern slope, Koenig pulled Jenny's body against his own and wrapped his arms around her waist. As they dove towards the ravine, he felt a hand grasp the collar of his jacket. The combined weight of his and Jenny's bodies was too great, however, and the man holding his collar was lurched forward by their momentum and jerked down the muddy slope in tow.

Koenig felt as though he was gliding on a melting pat of butter. Globs of mud that Jenny's body displaced volleyed upwards and splashed his face. He shoved the heel of his palm into his eye to remove a caking of sludge and craned his neck to see if they were being pursued. Several dark silhouettes hovered at the top of the slope. The figures stood there and watched for a moment and then one by one, they slowly turned and stalked out of sight.

The farther they fell down the slant, the harder the earth hit back. Trees whizzed by at an increasing rate, and Koenig was powerless to prevent himself or Jenny from being dismembered by a branch or split open on a boulder. The robed man behind Koenig screamed unintelligibly under his hood. He fell silent as his body was clipped by a passing tree, and then plummeted down the hill in an enervated slump.

Koenig made an effort to avoid hitting his head on the ground when he reached the bottom of the hill, which he feared would severely compress his spine at such a speed. He thrust his right shoulder forward and rolled over it, subjecting his body to a series of spins and tumultuous somersaults before finally coming to a full stop.

He laid still for a long moment and prayed that he hadn't broken anything. It didn't feel like he had, but the only sensation he entertained was a debilitating dizziness. White flashes darted across his eyes until his vision stabilized and his equilibrium returned. As he finally normalized, he slowly eased himself onto his feet.

Overtaken by a rush of nausea that swelled from his stomach to his head, he hunched over and released a multi-colored spew of bile.

"Juh-Juh-Jenny." Koenig turned and stumbled toward the hill. Two bodies laid immobile at the base of the decline. Jenny lay prone about ten yards from the slope, and the robed man was several paces beyond her. He was on his back, with his head propped against an elm tree. Koenig knelt over Jenny and touched her face.

"Jenny, can you hear me?" he glanced down at her arm. The burn wounds coruscated in the rain, turning a plastic-like sheen of blue. "Jenny, it's Edward. Oh Jenny, please wake up," he begged, tapping her face repeatedly. After an agonizing moment, she emitted a low grumble and began to stir.

"Mr. Kenning?" Her eyes fluttered and then opened. They were murky and distant, a horrifying contrast to the warm vibrancy that he saw in the Seaside Diner. That upbeat, vivacious girl was long gone, and only the remnants of one who had been forced to endure far more than anyone should remained. Ten paces away, the robed man grumbled and twitched.

"I'll be right back," Koenig told Jenny. He stood up and hobbled on languid legs to where the robed man lay, picking up a sizable rock as a precaution. He yanked off the hood and exposed the face of a man probably in his twenties, whose youth was nearly masked by an aging process that made him appear older than he was. He wore a soiled complexion that bespoke a man of corruption and greed. Something else lay within the fabric of premature wrinkles that tarnished the young man's face too, something more disarming. Pain.

Whatever motive dominated this hooded clan, it was something that had taken a great toll on him. He was suffering, and simply looking at him, Koenig could tell he was beyond reparation.

"Who are you people?" Koenig demanded. "What do you want from me? What did you want with Jenny?"

"I take it you are Edward Koenig?" the man asked, his face curling into a sneer. "You have no idea what you're in for." The man gargled a mixture of blood and saliva, and then spat a tooth onto the wet earth. He hadn't fared well on the journey down the hillside.

"What's going on here? Who was that old man I saw in the road?" Koenig was frantic. "Who is Kendric?"

"She looks more like Eveline than you," the man spat. "She's beautiful."

"What did you say?" Koenig grabbed the man by the throat and began to shake him. "What did you say? Where is my family, you miserable piece of shit?" The man let out a cackle and scooped up the rock Koenig had dropped. Koenig backed away instinctively, but it wasn't him the man was aiming for. A hollow crack sounded as the man battered his own forehead with the rock, leaving a jagged crevice, under which the stark white of his skull was visible.

Maintaining eye contact with Koenig, he lowered the rock back down with a steady hand and cackled once more before swinging it up again. His arm followed an identical arc to his head and with another sickening crunch, the rock met with his skull, penetrating the bone and into the tissue beneath. The man continued bashing his own skull in while Koenig stood by and watched, horrified.

After several blows, the man dropped the rock and his languorous body slumped against the tree. All that remained of the left side of his face was a soupy mash of bone fragments, blood soaked clumps of hair, and a gash that leaked bits of brain tissue down his robes. The rest of his face remained intact, and upon it lay the sinister grin of a man whose sanity had long since been relinquished.

"What sickness would drive a man to do something like that?" Koenig asked aloud, dumbfounded. Jenny moaned and attempted to turn onto her side. He rushed to her and grabbed her by the waist. "I'm gonna get you out of here, Jenny. We've got to get you to a doctor. If there is one in Pinemist Bay that we can trust…"

Koenig began to turn her over when she let out a stifled cry. Feeling the tingly caress of something warm and soggy on his hand, he pulled it away from her body and saw that it was coated in thick, black blood. There were minute strands of something stuck to the blood as well. He pulled his hand closer to his face and saw that there were tiny wooden splinters glued to his skin.

Koenig peered down Jenny's side and turned gray at the sight. The root of a tree jutted out of the earth, like a bone protruding out of a wound in a compound fracture, and was jammed into Jenny's side. *She must have landed on it on the way down. How deep is it embedded? I have got to get her out of here, and fast.*

He knelt beside her and stroked her head. "Jenny," he said, his voice laden with trepidation. "Jenny, we've got to get you on your back so I can get you out of here."

"I feel something in my stomach," she murmured. "It doesn't feel right."

"I know. You landed funny." He didn't have the courage to tell her the truth, and with the amount of blood she was losing, he wasn't sure if she would survive.

"On three," he said, fastening his arms around her waist. "Breathe, Jenny. One, two, three!" In one smooth motion, he pulled her onto her side. She let out a tortured cry and looked down at her own abdomen, which was now veiled with blood. Koenig ripped his jacket off and attempted to conceal the wound with it as best he could. Between the heavy rain and the torrents of blood, it was an onerous task, but he eventually managed a makeshift tourniquet over the wound.

"Oh god, I don't wanna die, I don't wanna die!" She descended into a panic, and began shaking violently. Koenig palmed her cheek and turned her face to his. She was pallid as a ghost.

"I'm going to get you back home, Jenny." He scooped her up by her legs and torso, cradling her close to his chest. She let out a whimper as he scrambled to his feet and began stumbling through Blackrock Peak's rain-coated forest.

"Mis-Mister Kenning," she whispered, her voice hoarse and soft. "You'll never make it with me weighin' you down."

"Don't say that," he choked.

"Put me down, I'm a goner…They have your family, and maybe you can still save them. But if you try to carry me, you're puttin' all of your lives at risk. Please…leave me here."

"I can't leave you." His voice hitched under an onslaught of tears.

"I did this to you." Jenny's stone-gray face relaxed, and her body began to loosen in his arms.

"Go to Ambrose Asylum." Jenny's lips continued moving, but she struggled to formulate the words. "My mother was put in there years ago…I think she knows someone in there who could help you…" Her eyes closed.

"No Jenny, stay with me!" Koenig spat.

"If you see her…don't tell her what happened to me." Jenny's eyes unfocused; a milky white glaze descended upon them. Her body slackened and her arms flapped as he walked. He stumbled to the ground and sat there for a long while, cradling her in his arms. Thunder rumbled all around and storm clouds swirled a hazy froth above. Koenig stared at the sky as his tears blended with the rainwater that tumbled down his face. Succumbing to weakness and disconsolation, his thoughts drifted to his family.

Chapter Eight
The Café

He burst through the double door and stalked the halls of the sheriff's office like a wolf sniffing out its prey. Streaks of rainwater trailed on the tile floor behind him, and several workers in the bullpen paused their duties to gaze at the sight of the man burning with intensity and purpose.

Darlene stood up to greet him, but he brushed past her and headed straight for Sheriff Grady's office.

"You can't go in there right now, Mr. Koenig," Darlene blurted. "You need an appointment!" Unconcerned with formalities, he threw the sheriff's door open. The entire room gave a low shudder as the door swung into the wall and then closed abruptly behind him. The sheriff was perched at his desk with his telephone in his hand.

"Uh listen Gerald, I've got to call you back. Somethin's just come up," Grady said into the receiver, and then slowly placed the phone down. "Well, Mr. Koenig, this is rather unexpected. Would you like some coffee? I'll have Darlene fetch us a pot."

"I don't want coffee," Koenig interrupted. "You need to listen closely to me, Grady. As sheriff of this town, you need to be aware of the things that are going on. What I have just witnessed, what I have just been through…I have scrambled all the way through the storm, sopping wet and exhausted because you need to know! As the authority of this town you need to gather your men and…"

Both of Grady's hands were placed attentively on his desk as he listened to Koenig speak, and what Koenig noticed was so peculiar that it caused him to freeze mid-sentence.

Covering the fingers of the sheriff's left hand was a thick layer of bandages, under which Koenig saw the faint spread of blood seeping through several layers. His mind whipped back to the abandoned shack with Jenny and the robed men.

"What happened to your hand, sheriff?" he inquired. Grady looked down and paused for a moment; gave an insouciant shrug.

"Darn near chopped it off splittin' some firewood last night," the sheriff grunted. "It's not too bad though, I think it'll heal just fine. Now, what did you need to tell me?" he said, gliding his good hand across his nearly bald head.

"Um, nothing," Koenig said in a listless tone. "I just remembered that I forgot to call my wife." He backed away as the sheriff eyed him in a dumb, open-mouthed gaze. "I'll make an appointment with Darlene and come back another time." He turned and passed through the sheriff's door so deep in consternation that he didn't hear it latch behind him.

"Are you alright, Mr. Koenig?" Darlene asked, breaking him from his trance. She was leaning across her desk with one eyebrow raised, watching his every move.

"Yes." He gathered himself. *Could Grady have been one of those insane hooded men? It might be a coincidence, and he really did just injure his hand like he said...* "I'm fine." She looked down the hall with an enigmatic glint in her eye, and then began writing something down on a green post-it note.

"The sheriff really is quite busy at the moment." There was a tremulous lilt in her voice. "But he can see you at this time." She handed him the post-it note while staring abstrusely at him, as if she were trying to tell him something with her gaze. He held her stare for a moment and then looked down at the note. It laconically read:

Blackrock Café – midnight.

Koenig glanced back up at Darlene, whose eyes were wide and alert. She cleared her throat, picked up a ream of papers and began stacking them in an implicit gesture that she couldn't talk further. He folded the note and slipped it into his shirt pocket.

"Thank you," he said, and walked away. Upon rounding the corner, everyone in the bullpen sheepishly avoided eye contact with him, but he could feel the burn of their gazes as he walked out of the building and into the rainy twilight.

****

Finding Blackrock Café was simple once Koenig received directions. He was in no mood for her blather after what he had been through, but he figured Sarah Schubert at the hotel's front desk was the most sensible choice for assistance. He approached Sarah, dripping wet and wielding a fire in his eyes that should have, but did not faze the young girl.

She stood behind the desk in a nearly identical outfit to the one she was wearing the night Koenig had arrived, twirling her hair and making sweeping and pointing gestures with her hand.

"You go southwest two blocks and follow the street down to the old gaslight district called, Moriarty's Foundries." Her directions were basic, but Koenig didn't expect the café was far from the hotel. Nothing in the small town was.

"Are you alright, Mr. Koenig?" she asked as he was turning to leave. He paused for a moment and did a half-turn.

"You guys have an interesting town," was his reply.

Koenig walked briskly down two blocks and continued south. The street, which had been following the sloped gradient of the terrain, leveled out and gave way to an old business district. Worn, chalky brick buildings lined the walkways on either side, and looming tall over the murk of the street were gas lamps that threw a foreboding flicker over the environment.

Blackrock Café was bookended by a large two story business to the north called Moriarty and Sons, and a huge bedding of rock to the south. Fir trees jutted out amidst chunks of granite and mica that, along with the sizable building next door, composed an effective veil around the café. The little building exuded a homey warmth against a backdrop of grays and whites, and Koenig noticed the house lights of the café ebbing out of a small side window. It looked like Darlene was already waiting for him.

He walked up the steps and onto the large oak deck. The original structure was immaculately upheld, and Koenig could tell that the windows were all that had been altered. An antiquated brand image printed on the left side of the wall suggested that it was once a metal factory or a welding shop. The brick was peeling and faded, however, reducing the luster of the print to that of a worn tapestry languishing in the sun.

The front façade of the café was made up of two floor-to-ceiling windows and, peering in, Koenig could see a man sitting at one of the tables with a binder and a few loose leaves of paper. Another man was working behind the counter. Darlene appeared from the back room after a moment and when she noticed Koenig, she smiled and gave a broad wave. His breathing deepened and his taut body eased upon seeing her.

"Mr. Koenig, I'm glad you made it! C'mon in," she said, ushering him in with her hand. She looked cautiously up and down the dimly lit street before closing the door and locking it up behind them.

"Please, call me Edward," he insisted, mustering up a smile and nodding.

"Edward it is," she said. "Come, I have some friends I'd like you to meet." The man sitting at the café table stood up promptly. He had a lanky build, short blonde hair, and a studious, almost geeky look, complete with a cardigan and a collared shirt underneath. The man adjusted his glasses and held out his hand.

"This is Adam Trevin. He's an architect here in Pinemist Bay, and a close friend of mine," Darlene said. Koenig shook Adam's hand. *Well, he's certainly not a contractor.* Adam's hand was soft, and his grip tentative.

"It's nice to meet you, Edward," he was British. "You're taller than I thought you'd be." *Did Darlene give him my description?*

"You get much work around here?" Koenig asked, shrugging off the odd comment. "Almost all I've seen in Pinemist Bay is ancient buildings with ancient architecture."

"Good question. My primary focus is restoring and preserving preexisting local structures, as well as working with contractors to reinforce buildings against quakes and the like. Around here, that's quite important." Conforming to the same mannerisms of most of the Brits Koenig had met, Adam Trevin had a quick and rigorous way of spewing syllables.

"And this," Darlene said, leading Koenig to the bar, "is Zachary Roussel. We went to school together in Portland." Zachary was hard at work at an old espresso machine. The contraption was made of copper and brass, with wooden levers and handles, and an ergonomic design. "He owns

Blackrock Café."

"What's up, man?" Zachary said, smiling from behind the antiquated machine. He had a slightly dark skin tone and wavy black hair that was pulled behind his ears where it trailed down to his lower jawline. The stubble on his face showed a nice, clean growth pattern, and meshed with his features to complete an unkempt style that bespoke a young bohemian. He wore a loose-fitting gray sweater and had an orange sling bag on his back. *He definitely fits the archetype of a young man wrenched out of Portland.*

"Oh, and call me Zach. Want something to drink, boss? Midnight is, in fact, the best time for caffeination."

"Nice to meet you, Zach," Koenig said and turned to Darlene. "With all due respect, can we cut to the chase? What I've experienced today has been really overwhelming, and my family may be in grave danger even as we speak." The glimmer in Darlene's eyes, the one that he was becoming increasingly fond of, faltered.

"Of course," she said. "I'm sure you have many questions. I promise we're your friends and we're here to help. You can trust us."

"You guys are just about the only normal-seeming people here," Koenig sighed.

With an expressive click of his tongue, Zach said, "I know just what you need, my friend. A double espresso, neat."

"If you've got a double whiskey, neat, I'll take that too," Koenig jibed.

"Come, sit down Edward." Darlene motioned to the table where Adam was situated, now hunched over his binder working on some sketches. Koenig sat down, took a breath, and looked around. The café had a mixture of rustic and modern style. Wood lined the walls and floor, but the tables and chairs, as well as the bar, were made of contemporary materials and finishes. On the far end was a raised set of booths that had gaudy, plush red seats, beneath which were rusty mechanical joints that connected the booths together.

"Pretty cool, huh?" Zach said, nodding to the booths. "I nabbed that from an old train car that's been out of commission for a long time. The whole line of booths, including the attachments, were lifted directly from the carriage. I think the train was built in 1908 or something, right around when the national rail system was being completed here. Man, what a process that must have been. I heard that the mountainous terrain was so unforgiving that it took months to lay down short strips of track. Lots of people died during construction of the tracks, too; from hunger, exhaustion, hypothermia..."

Koenig nodded politely through Zach Roussel's prattle and then glanced at Darlene in an insinuative manner.

"Well, Edward," Darlene began. "I suppose it makes sense to start with the three of us and our story. We have been researching the history of Pinemist Bay and its residents for some time now. Particularly, we've been following the Vucari and their role in yearwalking."

"The Vucari," Koenig interjected. "I've heard that term a few times now, what is it?"

"We don't know too much about them. It's a group of men, a cult, if you will, that conceal themselves in robes and terrorize people in Pinemist Bay. It's hard to explain to an outsider like you, but there's another world on top of our own; a spiritual world. And legend says there are various ways to enter this world, one of which is through the ritual known as yearwalking," Darlene said. "The Vucari have some sort of attraction to this world, but what it is we don't know."

"I'm familiar with Drugoy Mir by now, or at least, the basic definition of it," Koenig added.

"Good. So, the Vucari prey mainly on visitors to Pinemist Bay, less on residents as far as we know. Their primary hotspot is the Pinemist Hotel, which is where you're staying right, Edward?" Adam Trevin looked up from his work, inquisitively waiting for Koenig's response. Zach placed a tiny cup of espresso in front of Koenig and joined them at the table, sipping on his own frothy cappuccino.

"Yes," he said, which procured an odd expression from the two men, who leaned towards each other and engaged in indistinct, burbling clatter.

"Has anybody taken you out of your hotel room, Edward?" Adam Trevin asked. "Have you ever been transported to a different world?" His voice trailed off and he shuddered violently.

"Adam went to Drugoy Mir himself," Darlene said. "Back when he first moved to Pinemist Bay, he stayed at the hotel while the current owners vacated his new house. One of the locals informed him of the ritual, yearwalking, told him it was a longstanding tradition in Pinemist Bay, and so he tried it out of curiosity. Whatever happened to him during the divination, only he knows, and it has haunted him since." She put her hand on Adam's shoulder.

"You would know," Adam continued, "If you had been to Drugoy Mir. Someone or something must be blocking them from getting to you in your room."

"So, you guys are trying to tell me that this group of hooded figures is trying to sneak into my hotel room while I sleep and abduct me?" Koenig scoffed.

"It's not a laughing matter," Darlene snapped. "And they've had quite some time to perfect their methods. Based on the research we've done it seems like the Vucari have been around for a while now, passing down their knowledge generation to generation. The process for joining their ranks is still unknown to us, though."

"I'm sorry, I didn't mean to offend you," Koenig said to Adam. "I've seen the Vucari myself, just today."

"Where?" Zach inquired.

"At Blackrock Peak. They were in this old angler's house, and they had kidnapped a girl from town named Jenny. They were torturing her because I had been asking her questions about Pinemist Bay and about yearwalking. I rescued her from them, but when we were in the midst of escaping, she landed on an upturned root of a tree and... she didn't make it."

He sat in oppressive silence, reflecting on the terrible event. Tears began to mist over his vision, turning the illuminated objects of the café into a patchwork of spotty hues.

"I'm so sorry, Edward. I had no idea," Darlene's voice stirred with compassion. Zach and Adam looked at each other with furrowed brows, and then at Koenig.

"They've been more active lately. Something is about to happen," Adam said.

"One more thing," Koenig told Darlene. "I can't be certain, but I think the sheriff is one of them." She took in a sharp breath.

"It's true. He is one of the Vucari," she whispered. Koenig shook his head, nearly slamming his fist against the table in frustration. "I found out after I began working as his secretary, and since then I've been using my position in the office to learn more about them."

"So, why do they abduct people from the Pinemist Hotel? What do they do with them?"

"We're not sure yet. Information is so hard to come by, and it's basically just the three of us working on this in a covert manner," she said. "The Scandinavian tradition of yearwalking is a voluntary act one does in order to try to gain insight into future events, or gain some sort of wisdom or skill. Using their Slavic origins, which introduces a bevy of new mythological creatures and superstitions, the Vucari have been trying to find other ways to access Drugoy Mir; to what end I have no clue. There seems to be some catalyst driving all of this. Someone from inside Drugoy Mir perhaps...like an unknown leader, lurking in the shadows."

"According to Scandinavian folklore, there are a great number of supernatural entities one can encounter during a yearwalk. Some of them are downright unsettling, and with the Vucari snooping about, god only knows what they might unleash on accident."

"I'm partial to The Draugen, myself," Zach interjected. "It's this mythical sea beast, kind of like the Kraken, only it lingers near coastlines, where it spreads a mist that covers the lighthouses in darkness. Legend has it that if you see a shipwreck on a dark and foggy night, the Draugen is near."

"Spooky," said Adam.

Zach and Koenig nodded in agreement.

"Pretty far-fetched is what I would have told you just days ago, but based on what I've encountered here it seems almost plausible," Koenig said.

"Some of these creatures are apparently real," Darlene shrugged. "I heard Robert talking on the phone in his office once, and he was describing various monsters that supposedly lurk in Drugoy Mir. He also mentioned other terms that I didn't grasp like Pesta, Kikimora and Fossegrim.

"There are forces at work here, and not just a bunch of demented robed men preying on townsfolk. We need to be careful going forward, Edward, especially you. You stirred up the hornet's nest coming here, and the Vucari seem particularly interested in you."

"In a sense, we're all endangering our lives simply interacting with you," Adam said. "But if you had been through what I have, you too would crave answers."

"So, we are working together to learn more about the Vucari, and also to figure out whatever is going on in Drugoy Mir," Darlene said. "I've lived here several years and I can say that I have witnessed people engaging in yearwalks. Through history people have chosen several prominent days of the year to perform the rite, including Christmas Eve, New Year's Eve..."

"The first night of summer solstice..." Adam added.

"The first night of winter solstice..." Zach said between two interminable sips of his cappuccino.

"Easter night is also one of the commonly chosen dates," Darlene finished. "So, anyway, a few years ago on the first day of winter, I saw someone on a yearwalk. I had been at a party on Pinemist Drive. I'd had a little to drink but what I saw sobered me right up. I was walking home around 1 o'clock in the morning when I saw this woman. She looked like a ghost at first, dressed in this pale nightgown and looking as if she was floating slowly across the street.

"We crossed paths and I remember asking her if she was alright, but she either couldn't hear me, or she just flat out ignored me. She was catatonic. I remember watching her stalk across the street, silent as a thought, but twitching and shaking violently. Then she just disappeared into the woods. As you can imagine, I didn't really sleep that night."

"She was twitching and shaking violently..." Koenig thought aloud. "Just like the old man in the road."

"Who?" Zach asked.

"It was very bizarre." Koenig picked up his espresso cup and took a sip of the potently rich drink. "On my way up to Pinemist Bay, I ran into this naked old man right in the middle of the road. He had the same muscular spasms as the woman you mentioned. He knew who I was, and warned me to 'not let the Vucari find me,' and of 'a darkness inside Drugoy Mir.'"

Adam shifted uncomfortably in his seat, and continuously ran his middle finger and thumb across his forehead as if to soothe an intangible ache in his mind.

"Interesting," Darlene broke the silence. "You see, there are other forces at work here. So, Edward, are you in? I know it's a huge proposition, but it seems like you have a lot invested in this situation already. Do they have your family?"

"I think they do, yes." His voice was cold and despondent. "I'm in." Darlene studied him for a moment and then looked down at Adam's sketches.

"Now, as you know, Pinemist Bay is an old town. It's been around since the mid-1800s. Back when it was known as Alistair's Brigand, the town was divided into larger sections than what it is made up of now. There was the harbor section of the town, which is pretty much what Pinemist Bay is today.

"There was also a secondary portion of Pinemist Bay, known largely as Old Town today, that served largely as the main residential neighborhood. They built this section out of necessity when the town grew from a small trade port to a bustling community. Old Town was east of here, higher up in the Cascades.

"Now, between the port and Old Town is an abandoned coal mine.

As you may or may not know, the original settlers of Pinemist Bay were miners from the California Gold Rush. They already had much of the necessary mining equipment when they arrived. When they discovered coal nearby, they built an installation in the mountain, and used the newly established port to put their findings on the market.

"The mines were constructed in the 1880s and were active until a particularly hefty earthquake decimated a large portion of them, rendering the entire installation useless. They've been pretty much untouched ever since."

"How do you know where all of this is located, Old Town and the mines?" Koenig inquired. Darlene smirked.

"I lifted an old diagram off of Robert's desk one day. It was handwritten and smudged nearly beyond comprehension, but I figured it out with some help." She nodded to Adam. "Now, the main road that led to the neighborhood was morphed through the years by earthquakes and rockslides and is no longer accessible. We've been monitoring the Vucari's movements, and for the observable past they've been working tirelessly to get to the old eastern part of Alistair's Brigand. We're wondering if the coal mine may be the last accessible through-way to the old neighborhood."

"The terrain up in those eastern mountains gets increasingly vertical and impossible to maneuver." Adam gestured the angle of incline with his arm. "It's reminiscent of medieval castles where impenetrability was paramount; as if Alistair and his men crafted this community in the upper reaches of the mountains in anticipation of a great siege. A hundred armed men couldn't tackle the geography now that the main road is mangled with boulders and debris."

"We're assuming that once you get up amidst the mountain peaks, though, it's reasonably stable footing," Zach chimed in. "I mean, based on our research, there were quite a few people living up there in Old Town."

"Returning to the coal mine, Adam assumes that the air inside is still ripe with toxins from when it collapsed," said Darlene.

"Or maybe it just gets really twisty and confusing in there. Probably pretty dark, too," said Zach. "Like one giant, pitch-black hedge maze."

"Don't forget the potential of a black damp in there. Carbon dioxide, nitrogen, hydrogen sulfide…there might be several airborne compounds trapped in there," Adam said.

"So, we're looking at a giant, pitch black, poison-filled hedge maze of floating death. My bad."

"You must pardon our friend Zach," Adam chuckled. "He has a penchant for the extreme and the terrifying."

"So, what are we getting at here?" asked Koenig. "Are we going to go to the lost town of Alistair's Brigand?"

"We're going to try," Darlene said. "And we'd like you to help us. Some of the citizens of Pinemist Bay are aware of what's going on, most aren't, and things won't change without someone taking the initiative."

"It's imperative to remember, though, that we are meddling with an evil that we don't understand, and we shouldn't expect help from anyone else around the town," said Adam.

"Well, maybe you guys shouldn't have led with the whole 'poisoned death trap in the abandoned mines' bit but, count me in. I don't have too many leads to work with here, and I might be running out of time. I just feel like there must be another way up there…"

Darlene clasped her hands together and kissed Koenig on the cheek, proceeding to look away in haste as a pocket of crimson swelled on her cheeks. After seven years, Koenig's marriage with Eveline had become a blur of increasingly perfunctory moments of affection. The subtle, sweet caress of a woman's lips on his skin, however, made him yearn for nothing more than another chance to lose himself in the reverie of his wife's embrace; to become intertwined with her on a metaphysical level like he did when their love was fresh and exciting and new. It seemed his wife had to be eradicated from his life in order for him to realize he needed her.

"What is that in front of you, Adam?" Koenig motioned to his sketches.

"This is what we know thus far of the layout of the mines." He raised a piece of paper that had crude pencil markings akin to an architect's initial sketch of a new project.

"So, you've actually gone in there?"

"I did," Zach said. "With this." He undid the clasp of his sling bag and unearthed a fusty old gas mask, which he promptly handed to Koenig.

"Is that from World War I?" Koenig turned the device over in his hands. The mask was crafted out of dyed-black leather, and the eye lenses were composed of several geometric shapes that emitted a dim yellow glow under the café lights. The filter canister was fitted directly onto the muzzle of the mask, completing a respiration system that had to be an impressive feat of engineering for its time.

"Good call," Zach said. "It was my great grandfather's in the French Fifth Army. He nabbed it off a dead German soldier during a raid. And good thing he did, because otherwise I wouldn't be here. This mask saved his ass when the Germans flung shell gas into his trench." It was eerie holding the equipment of a long-deceased French soldier. The glaring lenses emulated the wide-eyed semblance of a horror-stricken man.

"Cool," Koenig remarked. "What do you do about the filter? Surely you're not using the original one that was issued with the mask?"

"No sir. My father was employed as a miner while we lived near Portland. So, I've learned a few tricks of the trade growing up. I take a couple of ordinary coffee filters, anymore and it gets tough to breathe through, and coat them with activated charcoal. The stuff works miracles. It absorbs harmful particles and toxins, while allowing enough air to flow through.

"If it's a blackdamp in that mine, though, the oxygen will be sucked out of the air and you simply suffocate. So, I bought a miner's lamp." He proceeded to pull a foot-long cylinder out of his bag and propped it on the table. The contraption looked similar to a normal gas lamp, and had solid copper and iron components on the shell, a small glass cylinder in the middle, and a torch mechanism inside.

"Essentially it works as a warning tool," Zach said, proudly eyeing his device. "The mechanism inside the glass ignites a little flame that dies off when the ambient oxygen becomes too low, as fire needs oxygen. If that happens, you just need to run back to where you came from, screaming and flailing your arms for dramatic effect."

"How much equipment do you have in there?" Koenig asked, stupefied by the man's collection of antiquated gadgets.

"That's his little bag of goodies." Adam shook his head. "But it's been useful up to now, as we've managed to make it this far into the mines without cocking up." He held up his sketch. "I've mapped a rough layout of the mine's initial workings based on what Zach described to me on the other end of a two-way transmitter—"

"Walkie-talkie," Zach corrected, jostling Adam with his elbow in a playful manner. "Or at least that's what we call them here in America."

"That whole situation sounds risky," Koenig advised. "You could have been killed in there with your makeshift tools, no offense."

"What's life without a little risk?" Zach shrugged. "Especially when it's for a noble cause."

"So, what made you stop exploring the coal mine?" Koenig inquired.

"I heard something," Zach whispered.

"He just chickened out," Adam argued. "Which is totally understandable, to be honest."

"No, I'm serious," Zach persisted. "Someone was shuffling around in there, making some kind of noise. So, naturally, I assumed it could have been one of the Vucari and I booked it."

"Well I must say, you guys really are crafty. I mean, for a three-man operation, I'm impressed." Koenig earnestly appreciated their hard work, especially since his family might be in trouble.

"Well, I too have a personal stake in this." In a dramatic shift of expression, Zach gave Koenig a somber, tenebrous look. "My sister was abducted by them a while ago. At least I'm pretty certain that's what happened. She was visiting me from Portland, and one night during her stay she just disappeared without a trace."

"Oh my god. I'm so sorry," Koenig said. Adam's and Zach's motivations were apparent to him now. Adam had been through a hellish experience during a yearwalk and needed answers, and Zach's sister had been abducted by the Vucari, just like Dalla and Eveline. "Do you think she is with my wife and daughter?"

"I don't know," Zach sighed. "Possibly. What we do know is that the Vucari are getting more desperate, as if they're running out of time or something. It seems like a ballsy move even for them to yank a 20-year-old girl from her brother's house in the middle of the night."

"We will find her, Zach," Darlene consoled him. "We will."

"It's going on 2 AM, guys," Adam said.

"Let's call it a night, then," Darlene nodded. "Edward is up to speed, and probably very tired."

"When should we meet again?" asked Adam.

"I'll give you guys a call," she responded. "The sooner, the better."

Zach rose from his seat and began closing down the shop. Adam busied himself with his papers.

"One more thing," Koenig ran a hand through his hair. "It's about that girl, Jenny. Before she died, she mentioned Ambrose Asylum; said her mom was in there, and that she might know someone who can help me."

Darlene considered Koenig's proposal for a minute. "How well did you know Jenny?"

"Not well at all, but those were essentially her dying words. She seemed pretty trustworthy, too, like she wanted to help."

"We'll visit the asylum in the morning," Darlene decided, nodding her head. "And for the foreseeable future, you'll be staying at my place." Her proposal hit Koenig like an errant train against a building. His track record of restraint in the presence of an unfamiliar woman was after all, abysmal.

This is different though, Edward. That is the last thing on your mind right now, especially under these circumstances—regardless of how alluring she is.

****

Darlene had a small bungalow on top of a hill overlooking the southern stretch of Main Street. With his mounting fatigue, and the scant lighting that the side streets offered, Koenig felt disoriented.

Darlene led the way into a cozy living room with high ceilings and an eclectic offering of furniture. Her living space was, without a doubt, favorable to the gaudy green and yellow walls, and the old-world upholstery of his hotel room. Sizing up Darlene's living room with his eyes, he breathed a sigh of relief in knowing that the Vucari would not be stealing him away as he slept this night.

Darlene showed him to the couch and provided him with a set of blankets and pillows. As she retired to her room, he stripped to his underwear and, reveling in the warmth of the sheets, sank with ease into a ponderous slumber.

Chapter Nine
The Asylum

    The road adjacent to Wanderer's Way branched off in a southeastern direction and up into the steep base of the Cascade Mountains. Darlene took this road in her weathered 1980s Toyota with Koenig riding in the passenger seat. He took note of the increasingly rocky terrain as they broke off of Pinemist Bay and began a sloped ascent toward the mountains.

    "Where is the asylum?" he inquired. He had found himself becoming aware of her little charms the more time he spent with Darlene. The way she carried herself without relying on the little affectations Koenig knew people employed in the presence of the opposite sex; the way she looked at him, with an expression of constant warmth and wide-set eyes that bespoke a woman who had managed to retain her youthful disposition in a dark life.

    Perhaps that was what drew him to her the most. Koenig felt like his own soul was all but spent. From the years of alcohol addiction to the occurrences of infidelity, he believed that he was beyond requiting the love of his wife. He could never pay her back for all she had done for him; could never make up for the damage he had done to her.

    Here beside him was this shining beacon of light in the form of a woman; one who was unbound by insecurity and petty habits of self-destruction; one who breathed exaltation. Being around Darlene made him feel as though her qualities were bleeding over to him, as if he could capture them like fireflies in a mason jar.

    "It's right around the first corner at the base of that mountain," she pointed ahead, her expression softening. "I just want to let you know that I think you're really brave, Edward. What you must be going through…" He flashed a tepid smile at the undeserved condolence and looked out the window. The sky was a milky gray that blended with the dull hues of the mountain, and caused the fir trees that dotted the landscape to pop with a sprightly green.

    "Thanks." His voice was soft. "It's more about what I've put them through." Darlene glanced at him in confusion, but didn't pry. "Honestly, I'm just trying to process this all. To say it seems surreal is a gross understatement."

    "Pinemist Bay has been my home for a long time," Darlene said. "And it took a while to realize what was going on. Believe it or not, there is a thread of regular life here." Her eyes were watching the road, but they were hazy as she seemed to reminisce about her past; a past Koenig found himself growing curious about. "Here we are," she exclaimed. "Creepy."

They went around a hairpin turn and came upon a black gate that could have spanned a football field. It was a tall, oppressive object looming in the haze; ornate in decoration and wrought with rust. They stopped at the entryway, where the gate elegantly peaked in an arc. In gothic lettering, the wrought iron placard declared the residence beyond the gate, Ambrose Asylum, established in 1881.

Beyond the entrance was a lengthy courtyard muddled with an overgrowth of grasses, vines, and shrubs; all manner of foliage that manages to creep, tangle and spread when it grows unchecked. The focal point of the courtyard was a circular fountain upon which was hewn the likeness of four cherubs. Under a blanket of electrically charged clouds, the frames of the cherubs appeared to dance and shimmer, beckoning Koenig and Darlene into the compound. The grounds were serene and quiet, yet underneath the peaceful image, pulsed an intangible malign energy. Koenig didn't relish the thought of entering the asylum.

The building itself would have appeared monolithic in comparison to the grounds, but it laid against a mountainous backdrop that towered above and cast an eerie gloom over it. The asylum looked old, but sturdy, and had a pale, ghostly hue emanating from its marble surface. Two massive pillars bookended the front doors, completing an appearance that was more befitting of a federal courthouse than a mental hospital.

They exited the Toyota and Darlene gazed up at the building. "I haven't been here in a long, long time," she said.

"Oh, did you know someone that was admitted here?" inquired Koenig. Darlene's eyes quivered, but she didn't respond. Instead, she ended the discourse by walking into the building.

Silvers and grays suffused the uniformly simple, yet elegant facility. The foyer was massive and square and made entirely out of polished stone, and it echoed like a cavern as they stepped into it. To the immediate left and right were matching doors, upon both of which were inscribed the words: Faculty Only. Directly ahead was the service counter, which looked like an island in the middle of an ocean of space. Behind the service desk on either side, a pair of staircases led up to a second story catwalk.

"Hello, and welcome to Ambrose Asylum," said a middle-aged woman whose stern complexion was glaring at them from behind the counter. Her nametag read Charity, a name Koenig thought was incongruous with her appearance. Darlene and Koenig approached the service desk. Two other women in nurse's uniforms were going about their business beside her, seeming not to notice the two visitors.

"Hi," Koenig responded. "I'm here to visit a Mrs. Wilbur."

"Alright, are you friends or family?" Charity asked, pulling out a Manila folder.

"Uh, friends of friends, more like." Koenig shrugged.

"No problem." Charity's rigid face upturned into a cracked and wavering smile, looking as if the simple nicety taxed her. She had a network of wrinkles along her cheeks and neck, and wore a thick layer of ruddy lipstick that contrasted with her pallid face to give her a gaudy, Barbie doll look. "I'll just have you sign this visitor's form before you enter the wards." Koenig handed the papers to Darlene.

"Here you go, babe." He hoped they could elude suspicion if they appeared to be a married couple. "I let the wife do all the paperwork," he said to Charity, who smiled with all the charisma of a dead fish. She turned to one of the nurses beside her.

"Mr. and Mrs., uh…"

"Donaldson," he said, glancing at Darlene, who looked perplexed. "William and Ruth Donaldson."

"Mr. and Mrs. Donaldson are here to visit Beatrice Wilbur. Will you take them to her room, please?" The young nurse smiled and nodded.

"Of course," she said. "Nice to meet you, I'm Nurse Holbrooke." They followed the nurse around the service counter and up the polished steps to the second tier.

"So, we're married now?" Darlene whispered, chuckling. Koenig simply smiled and looked onward.

The nurse led them by several doors, until they came upon an entryway labeled, North Wing, and entered.

This section of the mental asylum was dissonant in appearance from the foyer. Koenig thought it looked like a typical hospital wing, complete with tile floors and scintillating overhead light, which splashed the long hall in a stark glow. Each room had a bolted plaque beside it, displaying the name of the resident.

Channeled through speakers in the hall was the floating, meandering style of one of Erik Satie's compositions. The melody was spacey and resonant, but occasionally a discordant note was struck with precision and fervor, catching Koenig off guard. The lonely, yearning composition was wrought with irony in the context of the asylum.

"You guys always have classical music playing?" Koenig asked.

"Through the day, yes," Nurse Holbrooke responded. "We feel it has a relaxing effect on the residents."

A feeling of dread pervaded Koenig as they walked down the hall, their footsteps clacking and bouncing off the walls as they went. A muffled yell resounded from one of the rooms. Darlene flinched.

"What was the nature of your visit today?" Nurse Holbrooke asked, apparently unaffected by the suppressed outburst.

"Our families were friendly awhile back," Koenig lied. "Just coming to say hi again."

"How nice of you. Now, Pinemist Bay isn't the largest community and most of us here know each other pretty well. I'm not sure I've ever heard of a William or Ruth Donaldson, are you just visiting?" Nurse Holbrooke asked.

"Uh yeah, we live near Portland." Koenig attempted to be as vague as possible. As far as he was concerned, no stranger in Pinemist Bay was to be trusted.

"Well it's very nice of you to come all this way," the nurse exclaimed. "Are you enjoying your time in Pinemist Bay so far?"

Clenching his jaw, he responded, "It's a very scenic town."

"It certainly is," the nurse agreed. "And this venerable establishment you're in is quite the landmark. We're very proud of it. Erected in 1881 by one Sheldon Voight Ambrose. Now, he moved here from England and brought some...questionable medical practices with him. Rumor has it the original medical wing of the hospital, the one that Ambrose himself built, is still intact. It would be a few levels down, in the underground portion of the asylum, but you probably wouldn't want to see whatever is in there. From what I hear, he kept a secret ward in his original medical wing reserved for *experimental procedures*."

Sheldon Voight Ambrose. The man in the obituary at Safe Haven, Koenig reminded himself.

Nurse Holbrooke turned back and smiled with raised eyebrows. "Either way, local legislation doesn't want us digging around underneath the hospital. They say it could jeopardize the integrity of the whole structure and bring it down. So, we don't exactly go looking for the missing wing on the daily."

They came to the end of the hall and took a left. A lone restraining bed obstructed the path about halfway down the corridor, awash in the pallid brilliance of the hall light. Something about the image awoke a primal fear in Koenig. His curious mind ran wild as he imagined what the patient tied to that bed might have been like; what afflictions might have tormented them.

"What's that doing here?" Nurse Holbrooke asked aloud. "My apologies, Mr. and Mrs. Donaldson, our staff is a little sparse today." Koenig let out a gasp as they came upon the bed. Upon the arm restraints were smears of encrusted blood. Darlene's usually radiant face became devoid of color as she, too, noticed the dreadful and incriminating sight. The nurse deftly nabbed the top sheet and pulled it over the restraints, and then wheeled the bed out of the way.

Looks like they're still operating an experimental facility, Koenig thought, exchanging a knowing glance with Darlene. He reached out and clasped Darlene's hand in his. Her eyes were darting around nervously, and his reassuring touch appeared to calm her. The nurse came upon a room towards the left end of the hall and stopped.

"Now, Beatrice is a lovely lady, but she may be a little different from when you last saw her. She is suffering from dementia, the poor dear. She tends not to remember some things, particularly people, very well." Koenig and Darlene both nodded and Nurse Holbrooke opened the door.

It was a small cell. The walls were alabaster white and the bed was quaint and narrow. Much to Koenig's relief, it did not have any restraining belts on it. On the bed was the figure of a woman, perhaps at one time resolute and vibrant, but now shrunken by atrophy and broken by destitution.

Mrs. Wilbur was sitting up on the bed, gazing at Nurse Holbrooke with magnanimous eyes. She had frizzy black hair that resembled Jenny's, only it was speckled with grey and white. Her languid, bedridden frame sank into her gown in a petite lump on the bed. Time had eroded any muscle on her structure, adding to Koenig's assumption that she had been lying there for years.

"Hello, Beatrice," the nurse said with an expressive lilt in her voice, as if she were talking to a dog. "You have some visitors."

"Visitors?" Beatrice's voice was hoarse and tired. "I love visitors!" The nurse turned to Koenig and smiled.

"If there is anything you need, I'll be down the hall at the nurse's station." Koenig nodded and Nurse Holbrooke walked out and closed the door behind her.

"Hello Mrs. Wilbur. My name is Edward and this is my friend Darlene. We're friends of your daughter's."

"Friends of my daughter, eh?" Beatrice asked. "Well it is nice to meet you two. I haven't seen my Jenny in some time. How is the dear?" Koenig gave a saturnine glance to Darlene.

"She's uh, she's doing really well, Beatrice." Tears pooled in his eyes as he told the lie. His mind was playing the terrible event of Jenny's death over and over again. "She just barely moved actually." He cleared his throat. "To California."

"California, eh? Good for her, my daughter has been here darn near her entire life. Slavin' away at that diner for a while, too. I always knew she wanted to pack up and get out, but I couldn't help her there." She held up her bony arms and looked around the room. "I've been in Ambrose Asylum for most of her life. For the first while she would visit me real regular, but, over the years…well, that came to an end when we had an argument over her father. Man could scam his way into a six-figure deal, but couldn't for the life of him figure out how to care for a family."

"I'm so sorry to hear that, Beatrice," Darlene said, approaching the bedside.

"Oh I've come to peace with it, dear. That was all so long ago it feels like another life," Beatrice said, and took Darlene's hand in her own.

"But, why are you in here?" Darlene inquired.

"Oh, honey, it's a long story." She patted Darlene on the hand. "I'm so happy for my daughter," she said, lost in her thoughts.

"Mr. Koenig and I just wanted to pass the news to you of your daughter's departure," said Darlene. "She would have done it herself, but she knew she might not have been able to leave if she came and said goodbye to you in person." Darlene was taking liberties with the situation to console the woman, but Koenig didn't mind. She was a gentle soul, and spoke with ardency.

"I understand, honey," Beatrice said, and then looked past Darlene to Koenig. "What did you say your name was again, young man?"

"Edward Koenig, ma'am."

"Huh," Beatrice said after a moment. "I knew a Koenig once. It's not exactly a common name 'round here, that one." Koenig shot a glance at Darlene.

"You knew a Koenig?" he asked, the inflection in his voice wavering.

"He was more an acquaintance," she said. "Fine young man, though. That must have been at least twenty years ago, maybe more."

"Was his name George?" he choked.

"Aw, honey, that was so long ago, I can't remember all the details. My memory is like a sifter that's too wide to hold anything in. Especially with how sedated they like to keep us in here." She paused, raising her eyebrows. "Although…I think he had a friend who is in this hospital."

"Really?" Darlene gasped. "Do you know who, Beatrice?"

"Sure I do. Heavens, I'm not that senile. Not yet," she chuckled. "I'm not sure what you're both on about, but I'll help you with what you want to know. Her name is Ella Nylund. She's in this wing, or she was. They like to move us around in here, as if they want to keep us from gettin' tired of our surroundings." Beatrice let out a ratcheting laugh. "I've known Ella for many years; since we were girls actually…haven't been able to talk with her much since I've been here, despite bein' within arm's reach. The nurses keep a pretty close watch on us residents. Don't want us talkin' too much amongst each other."

"You've been most accommodating, Beatrice," Koenig said, delicately. "Thanks for allowing this impromptu visit, and for everything you've shared." He approached the bedside, stifling a swell of tears and an onslaught of emotion. After a pause, he softly picked up her hand and said, "You should be proud of your daughter, Jenny. She's a brave and honorable young woman." Beatrice's lower lip began to quiver.

"I know. I couldn't be more proud of my beautiful little girl. I'm glad she's movin' up in the world." Koenig cast his eyes to the floor in shame. He couldn't muster the courage to look at Beatrice under the ponderous weight of his deception. Even if lying to her was Jenny's last wish, there was no escaping the fact that Koenig unintentionally set the terrible events that led to Jenny's death in motion.

"Take care of yourself, Beatrice," he said. Darlene had moved to the doorway, and was glancing up and down the hall.

"You too, young man," replied Mrs. Wilbur. "Stay out of trouble now. Wouldn't want you to end up in here, with a frontal lobotomy like Mr. Scott across the hall." The vulgarity of her comment caused a chill to course down his spine and twist in his gut. A warm hand grazed his shoulder.

"We should look for that Nylund person's room now. The hallway is clear," Darlene whispered. He released Beatrice's hand and closed the door softly. Before they continued down the hall, Koenig glanced across the way. The plaque by the door opposite Mrs. Wilbur's room read, Alvareth Scott.

At the end of the corridor and to the right was the nurse's station. With Darlene hugging tightly to him, Koenig made the peremptory move to go left and avoid a possible confrontation with the staff. There was no sign of life down the left corridor save for a janitor, who was sweeping the floor with rancorous motions and cussing under her breath.

On a golden plaque to the left, the name Williams reflected in the harsh light. To the right: Perkins. They kept moving, occasionally darting nervous glances behind, even though the hallway echoed enough to alert their ears just as promptly as their eyes.

"You read the names on the right, Darlene, and I'll read off the ones on the left. We can get through the hallway quicker that way," he said in a low, gravelly tone.

"Okay, I've got a Brunswick," she responded.

"Wong," he said.

"Wharton," she whispered. A terrible sob came from within Wharton's room that gave both of them pause. A woman was crying. Not the typical cry that might implicate casual distress, but the kind of slow, tired whimper of a woman knowing she was at the end of her road.

For a moment, they both stood in the corridor and listened to the lonely moans and quivering sighs that fought to escape the cell door. With a lump in his throat, Koenig continued down the hall.

"Mendel," he said.

"I hope we're in the right wing," she replied. "Gonzalez."

"Hendrikson. Me too," he grunted. They had reached the end of the hall. A sharp right turn met them with a plain black door which concluded the north wing of the asylum. A golden plaque upon the door read, Patient Overflow.

A soft cascade of noises brought Koenig's attention to their flank. He stepped back a few paces and peeked down the corridor. Nurse Holbrooke was walking down the hall in their direction at a brisk pace. He ducked behind the wall, listening to the clacking of her steps, and prayed that she didn't see him. Her footfalls resounded ever louder until they stopped abruptly. He leaned with excessive diligence from the ridge of the wall and looked once more.

The nurse had stopped at a room about halfway down the hall and was fiddling with a large set of keys.

"What is it?" Darlene hissed. "Do you see someone?"

"It's Nurse Holbrooke," grunted Koenig. "She's stopping in one of the rooms. It's hard to tell but it might be Mrs. Wilbur's. We need to keep moving." He waited during the intermittent jingles while the nurse tried various keys for fitment. Then, there was silence followed by the closing of a door. "Let's go," he said.

He turned the knob and eased the door all the way until it made contact with the rubber stopper. Darlene slipped through and Koenig followed, pulling lightly back on the door to abate the force of its close. Darlene touched his cheek upon his shutting the door, and pointed forward. They were standing in a large, well-lit ward with at least a dozen beds, each one afforded a meager privacy by sets of curtain tracks. A few of these were ajar, allowing Koenig glimpses of some of the patients within.

They moved among the beds, employing great care to stifle the sound of their footfalls. Some of the residents slept, while others simply watched the two strangers shuffle through the room. Koenig smiled and nodded at an older man, who didn't acknowledge his gesture, but followed him with his eyes.

They have these people living on top of each other like animals in a slaughterhouse. This is despicable.

The concentration of beds thinned as they made their way through the room towards a door on the far side. Just before reaching the exit, Koenig heard the wisp of a voice emanating from a bed by the window.

"You look just like him," the voice said. "I mean, the spitting image." The speaker was obscured by a brilliant light shaft that shone through the window. With his heart thumping in his chest, Koenig slowly approached the bed.

Her blonde hair was thinning, and was peppered with grey. She had an elegant facial structure. Well defined curves made up her jawline, and above it, high cheekbones like little mountain peaks, jutted out. Between these peaks lay radiant blue eyes and a sharp nose. Even in her advanced age, this woman was quite beautiful. In her prime, Koenig thought, she must have enraptured men.

"Ella?" Koenig asked tentatively. "Ella Nylund?"

"Oh kiddo, you have no idea how long I've waited for this moment." A swell of tears pooled from her eyes and danced down her cheeks.

"I'm confused," Koenig stated, and looked back at Darlene. She simply shrugged.

"He said that you'd come; told me it may take a very long time, but that he knew it would happen. And here you are. A grown man, and a mighty handsome one at that."

"Did I know you?" asked Koenig. "You must be my dad's old friend, Ella Nylund." The woman considered his question.

"Friend? Yes, you could say that. Go on, kiddo, pull the curtain. And you may want to sit down. You can come in too, dear." She ushered Darlene inside while Koenig drew the curtain taut against its track. "You must be Mrs. Koenig?"

Darlene blushed. "Oh, no, I'm just a friend. My name is Darlene." Koenig knelt beside the woman's bed, not letting his gaze leave her.

"Yes, I am Ella. It is so nice to finally meet you, Edward," Ella said, beaming.

"So, you know who I am, too?" he replied. "And how did you know my father? He made one trip up here what must have been twenty-five years ago. How did you guys become friends in such a short time?"

"Oh, kiddo, you've got a lot of catching up to do," Ella said. "Brace yourself." She patted him on the hand. "Your father didn't come to Pinemist Bay just once. He was here many times."

"No," Koenig contested. "He was always off on business trips, but he only came through Pinemist Bay once on his way to Vancouver. He told me that many times."

"Well, maybe Vancouver was his destination the first time he came here," Ella said. "But he never made it there."

Koenig turned to Darlene. "He lied to me? What for?"

"Well, honey. Before I continue, I want to say that your father was a beautiful, conflicted, flawed human being. Much like yourself, I assume." She raised an eyebrow at him implicitly. "And he loved your mother very much. But, on his first visit here we met at the Seaside Diner, and, as if by the powers above, we were struck. Struck with raw, dumb, young love. And…we made a child, Edward." She began to choke up. "And that child was you."

A surge of emotion swept over Koenig like an errant tidal wave capping a pier. He withdrew his hand from the bed. "No!" He shook his head. "No, my mother was Irene Grace Koenig. She was my world. She read me stories when I was a child. She took me to the park…" He glanced again at Darlene, this time with a desperate countenance. "And she always looked after me. Even through everything with my father…I don't believe you."

"Yes, she was your mother. And she raised you beautifully, Edward, but she was not the one who birthed you. I was. Edward…" She reached out with a trembling arm. "I know this is so much to take in, but it doesn't have to change anything. Your mother and father were very real, and as honest with you as the situation allowed."

"What situation?" he asked, while an inexorable tempest of emotion spun around his head.

"Oh dear," Ella sighed. "Well, I suppose it's not a good sign that you're here, kiddo. Your father had a vision that you would show up at some point. He also stated that if you did, it meant you were in grave trouble."

"A vision? Was it something he saw on a yearwalk?" Darlene asked.

"Yes, dear. His first visit here, George stayed at the Pinemist Hotel, as do all of Pinemist Bay's visitors, and, mingling with the locals, he became acquainted with their customs."

"Of course!" Koenig said. "My father went on a yearwalk, too, and when he completed it, he was given visions of this moment."

"Visions of other things, too," Ella nodded, and Koenig thought he saw her shrink in her bed. "There is a lot to discuss, kiddo. What's your situation, why are you here?"

"My wife and daughter were abducted from my home in Chicago. We assume it was the Vucari. I'm trying to find them, but I don't have much to go off of. I have so many questions. Primarily, who are the Vucari and what is the purpose of this yearwalking that I hear so much about?"

"The Vucari are an ancient cult." Her voice became quiet. "This all might be hard to grasp, especially for a rational man such as yourself. But please believe me, I speak the truth." Edward showed his compliance with a slight nod.

"In old Russian folklore, Vucari, meaning 'Wolf-Men,' were a type of creature whose legend endured and became what people today call 'Werewolves.' These creatures were intrinsic to old Slavic culture, but where I think the Vucari of Pinemist Bay got their moniker was in a folktale not of actual wolf-men, but the young men in villages who would engage in a peculiar custom to protect their homes. At times when demons invaded, which was usually during the winter solstice, they would wield frightening masks and great staffs. Equipped like this, they would roam the village, supposedly warding off the evil spirits and protecting their families.

"The Vucari that we know are a violent dichotomy from those in the Slavic tradition. They are blindly devoted to this man…well, he's not exactly a man, not anymore. They say he once was. But Drugoy Mir has changed him somehow, morphed him into a hideous and tormented being."

"We've heard a decent amount about that man," Koenig said,

turning to Darlene.

"Yes," said Darlene. "That is as much as we know of him, we don't even have a name to use...seems out of this world. So, the Vucari are loyally following this deranged evil spirit, who is inside the world of Drugoy Mir?"

"Yes. Think of Drugoy Mir as a world between worlds. It's sprinkled throughout generations of Slavic folklore, in a similar vein to their parallel worlds-theory. You see, in Slavic folklore, there are other worlds existing alongside our own; whole landscapes that we cannot see or touch, but are believed to be there nonetheless. The Slavs had names for at least three of these worlds: Prav is the spiritual world above our own. It's said that when we die, our spirits go to Prav, where they become the stars that shine above us. Yav is our world, but adjacent to it are many other dimensions that are invisible to us except in rare circumstances. Nav is the world below, the underworld, where it is said certain spirits go after death.

"Reincarnation is very important to Eastern European culture, and intrinsic to their belief system, so perhaps some of these alternate world theories pertain to that as well. There is the belief that you are given certain tasks to accomplish in the world of Yav, and if you complete them before you die, you will be sent to another world, perhaps Prav. But if you don't complete your tasks, you are reincarnated in the world of Yav until you do. It is believed that Drugoy Mir is one of these alternate worlds that is connected to our own, and one can access it only in very specific ways.

"It is said that these 'spirit worlds,' as the ancient Slavs viewed them, contain the Unclean Force, which is essentially a mixture of various spirits, demons, and creatures; most of them evil by nature. Among the Unclean Force are supposedly the souls of all those who have committed suicide in our world. There are many stories about Drugoy Mir and its spirits; pick your favorite one, kiddo."

"Did my father tell you all of this?"

"Just some of it. I've lived here long enough to hear plenty of ideas from plenty of intrepid people. He did, however, encounter the man to whom the Vucari claim allegiance, among some other hellish creatures, while he was in Drugoy Mir."

"My father was there more than once?" Koenig inquired.

"Well, his first time up to Pinemist Bay he stayed about three days if I remember correctly, and it was then that he first went to Drugoy Mir. He didn't understand what was happening, but he managed to escape the Vucari leader's clutches, even if just barely. But some of his visions upon completing the trial were truly terrible, and there were things he saw that he refused to tell me about."

"Escaped his clutches? What did he want with my dad?"

"Your guess is as good as mine, kiddo," Ella shrugged. "Anyways, George returned once every so often, and we shared a secret, intermittent romance for a few years. I'm really sorry to have to tell you this. I imagine it rather desecrates your image of George. We were young and I think we both hungered for something exciting and dangerous; the passion was too much.

"So, on one of his trips, I informed him of my pregnancy, at which point he resolutely isolated himself for a day and initiated another yearwalk."

"So, why are the Vucari interested in this other world?" Koenig asked, incredulous.

"I'm not really sure, since I've never seen them myself, but I know they speak an ancient language; a Slavic dialect of some type. One with ties to paganism, and teeming with ritualistic passages and demonic mumbo-jumbo.

"It would help if you understood that the practices of paganism date back quite far, and lots of their rituals and beliefs are rooted in the craft of changing one's own consciousness on command. Yearwalking is an extreme, but quintessential example of this. People have been practicing the divination across Scandinavia since the Middle Ages, and maybe this folk tradition has been a way for the Scandinavians to communicate with their own gods.

"The Vucari have taken an interest in this world because they think it will aid their cause. What that is, I'm not sure, but I digress. What George saw on his yearwalk scared the hell out of him. He blabbed on and on to me about how the Vucari will hunt for our baby, that the monster will send his minions to find my child, and that they will stop at nothing to get to him.

"He mentioned something about you having the *essence*, and how Muka Vechny needed it."

"Muka Vechny?" asked Koenig, who was growing increasingly perplexed.

"To this day I don't know what he was talking about, but he took you from me shortly after you were born. Took you home and Irene, however heartbroken she must have been, raised you as her own.

"Your family prospered far away from the evils of this place. I never once met her, but Irene was a hell of a woman for putting up with all of your father's shortcomings." She chuckled and patted Koenig on the hand.

Like father like son. I can't believe this, Koenig couldn't reconcile that both he and his dad had betrayed their families.

"So, why are you here rotting away in this...this prison?" Koenig spat. His contempt for Ambrose Asylum was a welcome feeling; having something tangible to despise somehow eased his pains. His fledgling compassion for his estranged mother, however, caught him off guard. Ella sighed.

"Well honey, your father was right. The Vucari did come for me. Two of them came to my house in these long, gothic-looking robes and inquired about my baby. I told them the truth—that your father took you away. But I'm not daft, I was vague about the details. I told them he lived somewhere on the east coast and that he was never coming back.

"I was certain that they'd torture me to be sure, or perhaps just kill me. Alas, they spared my life, in a manner of speaking; took me from my home in the dead of night and brought me here, to Ambrose Asylum. Only this place is hardly a mental asylum." She eyed the walls. "You were right to call this a prison, kiddo."

Darlene's big hazel eyes widened in an agitated and fearful response to Ella's statement. "A prison for anyone who learns of their dealings and then tries to escape Pinemist Bay to tell outsiders what's going on. In my case, they locked me up for being a liability; I knew too much."

"You mean to tell us that everyone in here has discovered valuable information about the Vucari and this Muka Vechny guy, and are suffering life sentences for it?" Koenig looked down at his hand, which had balled into a fist.

"I'd say that almost everyone in here was found to be too risky for the Vucari not to keep locked up. You see, kiddos, they're more or less the clandestine police force in Pinemist Bay. And as long as we're in here, they're able to keep us contained and organized like animals. It's easier to watch over us this way. They keep many of us on some kind of medication, too."

"What kind of medication?" Koenig inquired, thinking his pharmaceutical background could be of use.

"It varies, kiddo. Sometimes it's intravenous, sometimes it's a capsule. Whatever substance it is, it's been in my system continuously for years. I think they dope us up in order to keep us calm and to make our minds fuzzy."

"You poor dear." Darlene swooped in and stroked Ella's cheek with her hand. "You've got to be one of the strongest women I've met." In a fit of frustration and brewing mania, Koenig clenched his jaw and ground his teeth together until his head churned.

"I've got to get you out of here," he said softly, but with resolve. "I've gotta get you out."

"Aw honey, I've been in here so long I'm at peace with my existence. And besides, you've got a lot on your plate with the disappearance your family and everything you're going through. I'd simply be endangering your lives." Koenig found himself becoming aware of the little foibles of his long-lost mother, and discovered himself inadvertently comparing the subtle similarities, as well as the glaring differences, to himself.

Even after suffering years of solitude and neglect, Ella was a woman of grace and compassion. Her little mannerisms seemed premeditated and commanded respect, and every little movement she made, even the way her eyes fell upon Koenig as she talked to him, seemed elegant and dignified; two qualities that Koenig began to wish had been passed onto himself. Instead, he had become his father's shadow.

"Mom, I can't leave you here. Not after all you've been through."

"There was someone else I wanted to tell you about, kiddo, someone who can help us."

Suddenly, a shrill sound swept through the overflow hall. Darlene jumped, and the gasps and grunts of consternated residents burbled through the room. A red light blared above the doorway that Koenig and Darlene had come through.

"That's not good." Ella exclaimed. "That signal is reserved for critical situations, like escaped patients. You have to go!" She warned Koenig. "Now!" He hesitated for a moment, clutching onto her bed frame.

"I didn't know you even existed until now. I can't just leave you in here. I won't, you're my mother!"

"You have to, kiddo. You can come see me another time and we can work something out. But, right now you have to go. That might be the sheriff. When that signal goes off, it usually is. Now listen, go through that door, down the hall, and take a right. When you get to the stairwell, go to the basement floor and take a left. That should lead you safely out and away from the compound." Koenig looked at Darlene, his eyes coursing with furious determination.

"I'm not abandoning you! I will come back for you Ella." He bit his lower lip and threw the curtain aside.

"Good luck, my dear." She smiled at him with a remarkable placidity. He rallied an unsteady smile in return and flew with Darlene to the end of the room. Warm pulses of red light flashed on the walls as he burst through the door and ushered Darlene through. Just before the door snapped shut, he caught a glimpse of the sheriff busting through the opposing door in full uniform, accompanied by a few other officers and Nurse Holbrooke.

"It's the sheriff!" Koenig yelled. "He's right on our heels. Go, go!" They blazed through a long service hallway and made a sharp right turn. Koenig could feel his shoes slipping and sliding about on the polished tile, as if he were dancing on marbles. There was a door at the end of the hall and Koenig slammed his body against it, disregarding the chance to look behind at their pursuers.

"Did they see us?" Darlene heaved.

"I couldn't tell, but they were moving fast!" Koenig grunted.

Darlene began down a series of stairs. Following her lead, Koenig was astounded by the facile way in which she moved. Her footfalls didn't reverberate like thunder as his did, but were brilliantly soft. He crashed after her as they volleyed down four flights to the lowest level, where a marker indicated they had reached the basement floor. Pushing through the door, Koenig thought he heard the clatter of footsteps on the stairs above. The door closed behind them, ushering in an icy silence.

They were in what looked like an old service pantry, unlit and musty. Koenig considered the possibility of hiding behind the heaps of clutter in the darkness, but a firm tug from Darlene on his collar persuaded him to keep moving. In the left corner of the room was a narrow doorway, under which Koenig could discern the faint trickle of light.

Darlene burst through first and Koenig felt his heart lurch in his chest when he saw what lay ahead. He came to a screeching halt to avoid smashing into the wall not six feet from the door. They had flung themselves into what looked like a janitor's closet.

"Fuck!" Darlene exclaimed. "I swear we followed her directions exactly! It's a dead end!"

Roughly the size of an office cubicle, the closet was covered in rotting and dingy alabaster tile. A greasy looking center drain sucked strands of water down its gape. Koenig took note of the fixtures, which were curiously older than those in the rest of the asylum. The overhead light was a senescent brass fixture with a cord bolstered to the ceiling. It looked like a primitive ceiling light in an old home.

"We're definitely in an older part of the asylum," he stated. "We're not near an exit, we're getting deeper!" A small flash of light on the lower left corner of the wall caught his attention. Behind a heap of janitorial equipment lay the reflective sheen of something metal.

"What are we going to do?" Darlene pleaded. "They'll find us at any minute!"

He reached down and pulled aside a mop bucket and two containers of solvent, unearthing an aluminum utility panel in the lower left corner of the wall that was roughly the size of a manhole. The panel was slightly ajar, as if the last person to use it hadn't managed to seal it shut upon exiting.

Without hesitation, he wrenched the panel from the wall and became inhumed in the stench of damp earth mixed with festering moldy wood. Shoving his head through the hole, he darted glances both ways. The closet light cast a pale glow over the first few feet of the crevice.

"Come on!" he motioned to Darlene. "You first."

"Is it safe in there? Where does that lead?" she asked.

"We'll find out once were inside, but we've gotta go now!" he barked. Darlene crouched down and shuffled into the service tunnel. Koenig followed briskly after and grabbed the utility panel by its handles once he was inside. He lined it up against the edges of the wall and pulled until all of the light was sealed out, and the panel clicked shut.

Chapter Ten
The Clandestra

For a moment, Koenig was embraced by total darkness. He felt an oppressive thickness to the air, which had become heavy and stagnant in the moldy space. Wooden floorboards cracked and moaned beneath as he redistributed his weight in the tiny crawl space. Up ahead, Darlene was coughing.

"Can you see anything?" he asked her.

"A little," she said. He could make out her form shimmying forward, and felt the floorboards shift as she moved.

"Who puts the access to a crawl space in the janitor's closet?" Darlene asked.

"Someone who built their asylum for some shady business," Koenig replied.

They crawled forward, listening to the dim sound of footfalls on the other side of the wall. Grady and his men were searching. Koenig hoped they wouldn't think to look in the janitors closet or else he and Darlene were sitting ducks waiting to be killed, or potentially worse. Thin slices of light poked out ahead.

"There are holes in the wall!" Darlene whispered. "I can barely see in but there's a room. We must be inside the walls between rooms or something. I wonder how long it's been since anyone used this passage."

Koenig's eyes had fully adjusted to the darkness, and he found he could decipher trifles of information about his surroundings. Water pipes that were warm to the touch ran beside him, and steel braces ran vertically along the wall every several paces. It appeared he and Darlene were crawling in the very foundations of the building.

He came upon the gashes in the wall and peered in. The room on the other side was slightly more luminous than the crawl space, and he could discern a couple of tables, upon which brass instruments with pressure gauges lay. The room's composition reminded him of an old laboratory in a science fiction movie.

"Maybe this is the old section of the asylum that the nurse mentioned. The original secret facility," he said.

"Creepy," Darlene replied during a fatigued, drawn out exhale. He began to feel a pervading feeling of sympathy and concern for her. Over the past few days he had been subject to a number of situations that tested in parity his spirit and his body, and he hoped that Darlene's involvement in his mess would not tarnish her innocence and magnanimity.

"How are you holding up?" he asked.

"Well, I'll admit that I didn't think I'd ever be crawling through the ancient foundations of an insane asylum while trying to duck the sheriff, but what's life without a little adventure? I am worried about you, though."

"I'll be fine once I get to my family," he grunted.

The old service tunnel widened and they found enough headroom to stand. Koenig dusted himself off in the darkness and began sidling along the wall. He groped for Darlene's hand and when he found it, she squeezed back and held on hard.

"I wonder who tipped the sheriff off?" Koenig pondered aloud.

"Your guess is as good as mine," she said. "They have eyes everywhere here. That's why what we're doing is so risky. But you and Zach need to find your loved ones. That's all that really matters." They bumped into a crumbling wooden wall that ended the passage. Koenig ran his fingers along the wall and his spirits lifted upon feeling the smooth surface of another access panel.

He gripped the handles and pressed, but it didn't budge. Squeezing firmly, he shook the panel with all his might, but it remained fastened to the wall.

"Shit! It's either locked from the outside, or completely stuck," he exclaimed.

Darlene gasped. "Are you sure? Maybe it's just rusted on or something." He shook the panel vehemently one more time, feeling claustrophobia start to set in.

"It's really on there," he sighed. "Well we can't go back the way we came, that's for sure. Hang on." He shuffled back down the passage. Darlene nodded, hugging the wall and watching him move about. When he reached the small cluster of holes in the wall, he put his back against an opposing steel support column and kicked hard at one of the openings.

The old wood splintered instantaneously, leaving a sizeable slit in the wall. He kicked several more times in quick succession, feeling shards of wood graze his face and clack against the column behind him, until there was an opening large enough to fit their bodies.

"Let's hope nobody heard that," he said, and shimmied through the opening. He drew a lengthy breath to push out the damp air clinging to his lungs, and began stumbling through the dark room. The silence on this side of the tunnel was unnerving, and the air was suffused with the ripe, tangy scent of mildew and rot.

"We need to find a circuit breaker. There's got to be something that powers this old facility." With no source of light to aid his steps, Koenig felt his way out of the room containing scientific bobbles and instruments, and into a hallway. Tile floor clacked beneath his feet as he pawed the walls for a breaker box.

His finger grazed an old push button light switch, and he pressed it without hesitation. When the only outcome was a simple clunk of the button's mechanism inside the wall, Koenig made a dissatisfied grunting noise and then continued fumbling through the hallway.

"Do you hear that?" Darlene asked abruptly.

"Hear what?"

"That buzzing noise," she said. Koenig stood in the acute stillness of the facility for a moment. She was right. He thought he could hear a faint trickle of sound emanating directly ahead of where they were standing. He tip-toed forward as the low hum grew louder, until his hand met a doorknob. The mysterious sound originated from behind the door.

"It's in here," he whispered. With a gentle pull Koenig opened the door, gritting his teeth and hoping he wasn't stumbling in on the Vucari, the mysterious Muka Vechny, or any other sinister entity that Pinemist Bay could deftly conjure. A pit developed in his stomach when his eyes fell on an idle flashlight on a countertop in the middle of the room. It was still lit.

"Somebody has been here recently," he warned Darlene. The dying device gave off a dull and flickering stream of light, illuminating what appeared to be an old electrical room.

He retrieved the flashlight and scanned along the wall until he came upon the source of the buzzing. An old circuit breaker lay on the wall near the where they were standing, with the main lever in the ON position.

"Somebody has definitely been using this facility recently," he said in a grave voice. "Stay close to me."

In the dim wash of light, he could see her beautiful, soot covered face squinting at him. She nodded in compliance and darted a cautious glance behind. He held the light to the breaker box and began scanning a crumpled power distribution chart that lay on the wall next to it. In old cursive handwriting, he saw the words, Lights – main, and flicked the switch.

There was nothing but silence at first. Then a swooshing, grating noise burbled around them, as if several large turbines were set in motion after a lengthy period of inactivity. Koenig squinted as feeble, ancient ceiling lights flickered on throughout the electrical room and down the hallway. They gave off barely enough light for Koenig and Darlene to see down the length of the corridor, but he could discern enough to tell that the section of the asylum they were in was old. Old and eerie.

"This must be Ambrose's secret laboratory," Koenig whispered, still uncertain if they were alone.

He walked into the hallway, each step laced with trepidation. The tile floor was cracked and brittle in many areas, and caked with soot and dirt, but its moon-white quality managed to poke through and glow under the lights. Koenig walked back to where they had broken through and investigated the wall.

The tile, and most of the inner wall behind it, was rotted and falling apart in that particular spot. Fragments of tile and large hunks of wood were strewn across the tile from his vigorous kicks. Koenig sighed in relief upon realizing that they wouldn't have been able to kick through the wall had its integrity not been compromised with creeping rot.

Flickering flashlight in hand, he turned around and continued past the electrical room. Boxes and equipment were scattered across the narrow corridor, with a tarpaulin of cobwebs enveloping them. Stepping into this facility was like uncovering a time vault, or unearthing a collection of archeological findings; everything seemed significant and mysterious.

They came upon a room. Written on the door amidst a network of encrusted dirt and filth, was the phrase, Test Room Alpha. He grabbed the knob, startled by the cold that resonated from it, and entered.

The room's aesthetic was similar to an old-fashioned operating room; stark white and sterile throughout. Antique instruments lined a countertop to the left, and on a pedestal in the middle of the room was a restraining chair that made Darlene gasp. A powerful overhead lamp illuminated the chair, highlighting its heavily worn condition.

"Well, I think it's safe to assume that we're in Sheldon Ambrose's secret wing." Koenig's voice was shaking slightly. "What the hell were they doing in here?"

"I don't know," Darlene said as she gently picked up an unusually large brass scalpel from the collection of medical instruments. "But I'm not sure if I want to know."

"Look at this." Koenig waved her over, peering closer at the operating chair. "Whoever was strapped to this struggled a lot." The leather arm and leg restraints were frayed and tattered. "Some of these look like teeth marks."

"Ick." Darlene shivered. She crept over to the shadowy corner of the room where the counter ended and some objects loomed in the dark. "There are old wooden cabinets over here!" With a grating screech, she pried open one of the cabinets. The brittle hinges stretched to their limits and snapped, causing the old door to clatter to the floor. Darlene squatted there with only the knob left in her hand, and peered inside.

Koenig aimed the dying flashlight at the contents of the drawers and exhumed a ream of yellowed papers from one of the shelves. He pocketed the flashlight and walked back to the well-lit counter. Rubbing his hands together, he watched a cloud of dust snake through the air and disperse into the shadows.

"I wonder if Ella knows about all of this; if she wanted us to find this place."

"Could be," Darlene replied. "She did lead us here, intentionally or unintentionally." Koenig nodded and studied the documents.

"These are some old handwritten notes." The penmanship was extravagant and embellished, reminding Koenig of old documents written with a quill pen and inkwell, like the Declaration of Independence or the Gettysburg Address. Decoding the aged cursive scrawls was a chore, but he was able to salvage most of the words.

"The penmanship is excellent," he squinted. "It's dated February 17th, 1883. And I quote,

"'Patient 17C—Operation 4. Electroshock treatment persists to accredit my belief that alternating the flow of brain waves in a controlled and invasive manner may perhaps inhibit the function of certain lobes of the brain. Patient has become less resilient through the course of the procedures; dare I say, he displays an equable demeanor and a murky intellect of late.

"'It is a welcome observation, this gradating dissolve of conscience in the patient. It is incongruent with my dignified history of medical practice to employ the alternative, more barbaric methods of operation; methods which I have been utilizing for some time in this, the Clandestra. To keep this patient at hand during the proceeding events would be wise. I think I will relocate him to the holding cells down the hall. For posterity's sake, I will continue to employ this method as well as the others, in hopes that patient 17C's cerebral cortex responds exponentially to the stimuli.'"

"Jesus," Koenig said. "There's a sort of diagram at the bottom of the page. It looks like he was cutting into this person's skull and placing electrodes directly onto their brain tissue." Darlene leaned in and studied the notes. "I mean I'm no doctor, but that's what it looks like. He was torturing these people, probably patients from the asylum, to some twisted scientific end."

"My god. What have we stumbled upon?" she uttered. "What a sicko."

"Let's keep moving. This place is giving me the creeps," Koenig said, receiving nothing but a fervent nod from Darlene. They left the experiment room and continued down the desolate corridor, passing rooms containing more forgotten devices and instruments from an era of burgeoning medical practices. Through a half-open door, Koenig saw a heavy wooden operating table with restraints dangling off the sides.

"Despite being malicious and horrifying, this place is like a treasure trove of historically relevant secrets. A lot of people would pay a lot of money to be in here," Koenig suggested. They passed by several patient cells, dissecting each one with their eyes as they went.

An overturned chair lay in the middle of one of the cells. Decrepit strips of bedding haunted the left corner of the room, painting an image in Koenig's mind of the prisoner that was confined there; left destitute and afraid, until it was time for more torturous experimentation at the hands of a psychotic doctor.

In the next cell was another grueling image. The white tile panels on a section of the wall had been ripped away and on the boards underneath, lay the impressions of what looked like fingernail scratches left by a prisoner. Shorter scratches dotted the wall, while longer tendrils of fingernail indentations ran down its length.

On the tile surrounding the damaged chunk of wall were faded smears of blood. Time had discolored the marks, which looked more like coffee stains than blood. On the floor near the scuffed wall, a strip of canvas with only the word 'INDEMNITY' written in blood on it.

Koenig forced himself to move on, trying not to get lost in the myriad of tangible memories that littered the forgotten catacomb. Once they reached the end of the hall, they came upon a single door that had two electrical lights designed like old candelabras on either end. It was Ambrose's private quarters.

"Jackpot," Koenig muttered. He grasped the brass door handle and turned. The door swung wide of its own accord and revealed a small box of a room. Resembling what Koenig always imagined Sigmund Freud's study looked like, Ambrose's office was cramped and full of various items archetypal of a scientist's quarters. Research objects on the desk, portraits of pertinent 19th century innovators on the wall, and a bookcase chock full of medical encyclopedias against the back made up the contents of the room. Centered behind the desk was an artist's rendering of Sheldon Ambrose himself. In the painting, he appeared aged and bald, with a long, sloping forehead, and mutton chops that met a substantial white beard below.

Reacting to the deepening chill that enveloped the old facility, Koenig crossed his arms and held them taut against his body. He rounded the massive oak desk and began sifting through its contents.

"Nikola Tesla," Darlene said, eyeing an old-fashioned portrait of a young man with a mustache and short black hair that had an ostentatious part down the middle.

"'I tell you, this man had some money. Nurse Holbrooke said that he came from England. Wonder who his family was?" Koenig shuffled through old handwritten medical documents on the desktop, and began digging in the drawers below. Dust plumed about him every time he withdrew an item from the ancient shelves. He found himself constantly waving it away with his hand as he rifled through various irrelevant papers and articles.

"Gregor Mendel." Darlene was staring at another face on the wall. Mendel was wearing glasses, and had an altruistic disposition. He was just about the only person from the era Koenig could remember having seen to intrepidly pose with a smile.

"Didn't he discover heredity or something that had to do with genetics?" Koenig inquired. His hand disappeared once more into the darkness of the top left drawer of Ambrose's desk and fondled the rim of a book. He unearthed what looked to be an antiquated journal, leather bound and coarse to the touch.

"Louis Pasteur," she listed the name of another figure. This one was a stern, calculated older man with a rough and wiry beard.

"I think I found Ambrose's personal diary!" Koenig exclaimed. The pages were brittle and cracked, and threatened to deteriorate with even the slightest pressure. "The Diary of Sheldon Voight Ambrose," he quoted. "The first entry is dated March 8th, 1879."

"The breadth of my profundity is nigh boundless," Koenig read. "However, it alone will not suffice in bringing my daughter, Alyssa, back to the vital and vigorous seven-year-old girl she was but a few months ago. It is a dreadful concept to grasp, and a situation I suppose many a father must endure, to have one's dreams for their offspring squandered at the cold hands of fate.

"Since her birth, I have deemed little Alyssa a candidate for a propitious future, one brimming with discovery, and subsequent praise from esteemed inventors and scientists the world across. Lord knows, it would not be a fortuitous circumstance, for both her parents came from good stock, and, before Cassandra's abrupt and untimely passing to a bout with acute pneumonia, we raised Alyssa with only the utmost devotion to the development of her cognizance and fledgling curiosity.

"Why, when I reminisce of antecedent years, an activity I confess I succumb to more and more of late, and what my pejorative father viewed as frivolous, I can recall times when little Alyssa would trot over to me with some marvelous thing in her hands and a flame surging in the forge of her young mind.

"On one such occasion, little Alyssa had cupped in her palm a katydid that she procured from the garden adjacent to our home. She instructed me to speculate as to what was in her hand, and suggested that the insect was from the cricket family, and had nocturnal eating habits. Not being proficient in the nature of insects, I shrugged in reply. When she uncurled her tender little palm to reveal the katydid, it lay crushed and very surely dead.

"Articulating thanatology in even such a trivial matter as an insect's death to a small child without causing them disturbance is a daunting endeavor, and I remember quite well the saturnine glaze in my little Alyssa's eyes following the explanation. How am I to educate my precious daughter of her current conundrum? Alas, they pronounce the greatest tragedy to be when a father outlives his own child, but tuberculosis is a tricky affliction, and despite the knowledge and experience I profess to command, I find myself at a loss.

"Dear, sweet Alyssa, I must apologize, and turn to my last bastion of hope," Koenig finished. The silence around Koenig and Darlene was palpable. Ambrose's words were heavy, and Koenig couldn't help but feel a connection with the man—his daughter was in danger, he didn't want to lose her.

"Well it looks like this Sheldon Ambrose guy had a heart, in at least some form," Koenig said.

"His wife died and his daughter was very sick, but he was tending to her health," Darlene added. "So, after she fell ill, he created this evil place?"

"Doesn't really add up, I know." Koenig turned the archaic page with the care of a surgeon.

March 19, 1879

I had foreseen the voyage to America to be an arduous one, alas, had I been afforded the luxury of foresight I may well have not undertaken such a rugged, albeit calculated risk. We suffered a tenuous demurrage on the frigate, during which the capacity of the ship's holding quarters was determined insufficient for the quantity of personal items carried by us emigrating souls. I must confess that our small family's cargo exceeded the standard travelers fare by roughly three-fold, nevertheless I held fastidiously against the suggestion of leaving any item behind. A man of science must have at hand the items pertinent to his craft anywhere his travels may take him.

The journey has proven a grueling challenge for my daughter, who was relegated to the bristly charms of a small cot on the vessel for days on end. The ambient air onboard was abysmal and dewy, and at one point, became caustic to her feeble lungs nigh to the extent of suffocation.

While our fortnight of travel took its toll on her, little Alyssa's metaphysical-self exuded a favorable and wholly welcome segue from the morose temperament her condition has hitherto afforded her. Much to my disbelief, whilst she wasn't afflicted with a spat of cough or fatigue, my little girl was vehemently engaging in dialogue with myself and any passenger she could find. At one moment, it was conjecture concerning what species of marine animals might have been speeding by underneath the vessel, the next moment it was a question regarding the reinforcement of the frigate in which we were traveling; her interest stemming from a story I read to her a year prior concerning the sinking of a whaling ship by a giant albino whale off the coast of South Africa.

I recall with a smile when Alyssa turned to a young man residing in an adjacent bunk and enlightened him of Herman Melville's enthralling tale. Attempting to maintain a reticent countenance, he received her story until a palpable fear brewed in his eyes, whereupon the poor boy briskly cradled his head in his shoulder to veil a whimper, and scuttled away to hide his emasculated demeanor from my indomitable little lady.

After suffering the cumbersome effect of sea legs, we found ourselves confined to the cabin of a steam train for a journey of a half-fortnight across the American heartland. Here at least, we had the relief of a shred of privacy.

Alyssa and I reached Alistair's Brigand in the glum shroud of night, where the very atmosphere threatened to absorb us into its being like an untiring, unrelenting machine of malicious thirst. Astute men such as I tend not to fritter away time nor energy with the supernatural; indeed, something foul rests in these mountains. It be not of a tangible nature, but a brooding darkness that hangs in the air like tendrils of death, tremulous in the anticipation of wrapping lost souls in its chilly bosom, never to hear or be heard from again.

I may seem a stark lunatic with such ramblings, alas, insufficient rest has clouded my perception like a potent rotgut. Be that as it may, my refined sense of judgment, as well as my keen fatherly instincts, is exhorting me to turn us round and flee for home.

But, what is home? Without Cassandra at my side, the affectations of Liverpool wane, sure as the muggy city air threatens little Alyssa's life. I, a rigid man of science and by virtue subscriber to no faith, take to my knees to pray that my peremptory tactic to relocate to a higher, arid climate proves invaluable in the recovery of my daughter. Cassandra would approve of our moving here. Time shall tell if Alyssa's condition improves amidst the crisp air and bounteous sprawl of nature.

I must keep my wits about me.

April 11, 1879

Improvement of my Alyssa's condition has yet to become evident. In the depth of night, she still awakens in fits of cough, whereupon she proceeds to choke and sputter until minute strains of bloody mucus lay at her feet. During such episodes, the only comfort I can provide is to rub her tender little back until the struggle subsides, and retire to the hearth to procure a concoction consisting of an herbal blend that I have deemed therapeutic.

The various pertinent and intensive studies of mine that are yet to be completed have been shelved, as I am allotting the entirety of my time and willpower to finding a cure for this most unnerving of complications. 'Tis a shame that a man long committed to his scrupulous methods of research should find himself baffled by a devilish infection such as this. Have I not treated hundreds of ailments in my day, from the common flu to the more abstract afflictions of the human psyche? My relevance as a health practitioner and scholar stands on my illustrious history of servitude to the commonwealth, and not just on my merits and accolades that line the halls of Cambridge.

My initial consternations upon reaching Alistair's Brigand are resolutely unchanged. Though the townsfolk are amiable, a sense of dread pervades me even now. A collectively uneducated and detrimentally isolated lot, these people fervently divulge in superstitious beliefs and practices of olden times. According to what Alistair himself has told me, a Swedish family emigrated here right as these northwestern states became settled some thirty years ago. They may have brought with them an archaic pagan rite to which the townsfolk have taken a shine.

May 13, 1879

A man without need for money has the liberty to occupy his time as he sees fit. My influence on the townsfolk of this rural and burgeoning settlement, Alistair's Brigand, has been arguably impactful thus far. I am employing my various methods as a doctor to inoculate and provide care for the citizens who recruit me. I have set up, in my brief time here, something of a meager laboratory and physician's office in my own home.

As an outsider and non-conformist to the traditional belief set of this community, I anticipated some opposition to my methods. A particular group of men have approached me on multiple occasions, inquiring about my history as a doctor, and the services I am adamant in providing for the people of Alistair's Brigand. Reminiscent of Roman-Catholic priests, they have adorned on each of their persons, long brown robes and hoods effective in the concealment of their faces. If such nuisances persist, I shall bring a grievance to the local legislation in regard to these mysterious cultists.

Meanwhile, the condition of my poor, sweet little girl has continued to regress. Dare I say, she seems to be experiencing a deterioration, the intensity of which has increased since our arrival. Dear Cassandra, what I have done by bringing her here, and what shall I do?

A method that appears to be aiding her health, or at least abating her torment, is to place a warm, damp cloth over her mouth and allow her to breathe in the moist and saturated air. Perhaps if the arid and chilly climate helps not, then the moisture from the cloth will mop up the bacteria from her

lungs as she exhales.
As I walk about the port town, I hear more chatter in regard to one ancient pagan rite that pervades the community. It involves a primitive and simple procedure characteristic of most archaic divinations, both religious and non-religious, in which one is afforded the ability to foresee the events of the following year, or perhaps even further into the future. It is most reminiscent of Seidr in Norse mythology; a most intriguing form of shamanism and prophecy thought to be given to man by the all-god Odin himself. They are calling this form of Seidr: Yearwalking. I ordain it, pagan crockery. Alas, I must admit that the temptation of participating in such an act grows stronger, as my little Alyssa grows weaker.

May 29, 1879

It is with immense effort and psychological fortitude, as well as a tenuous grasp on my quill, that I scribe these notes. Forever will I condemn my soul for my failings as a scientist, and further, for my failings as a husband and father. It confounds me that I might spend a glowing career mustering my efforts towards the betterment of society, only to have my accomplishments squandered and thrown asunder in the undoing of the lives of my loved ones. Might I have saved Cassandra? I know not.
Alyssa is bedridden and pallid. The frangibility of her sick body has proved too great for the tenacity of her spirit and mind. Having exhausted every legitimate method known to me, and many other more experimental and extemporaneous methods, I am at a loss. There is a local parish in the proximity of my house, as well as a cemetery next to the neighborhood of this parish. On morrow's inception, I, Sheldon Voight Ambrose, shall fruitlessly endeavor on a yearwalk, with only the aspiration of discovering the prognosis of my daughter's condition. I am left with no other option.

"There's just one other entry," Koenig stated, flipping the tattered book over to double check. "There's no date on it either, and the penmanship is...different. The lettering is no longer precise and embellished. It looks as if he was writing with a broken hand."

What an eccentric and yet electrifying experience! It be as if my eyes were open for the first time. The yearwalk transcended me to a level of wisdom and enlightenment my entire life of science hitherto could never touch. My daughter Alyssa passed into the next life last night, like a wisp of dust dispersing into a maelstrom and twirling about until every last particle is absorbed fully into the atmosphere. Indiscernible as a shadow in the night, her soul fled on silken wings from the security of my arms and into the blessed dark.
Alas, it is alright, for I follow Him now. Upon meeting Him in the murky fathoms of my trials, I was awoken. It all makes sense now, how could I, an antiquated and dithering dog of a man, have been so obtuse? It matters not; I heed His call now. For even as I write, I finish my greatest

achievement yet, the Ambrose Asylum. Clandestra, my private wing, is coming to fruition, as will all my future endeavors in the science of memory erasure – my newfound métier. In the end, what man aims to clutch tenaciously to all his faults and limitations, his squandered dreams and somber love, which burns scant and faint, like the dying embers of his life's hearth? That, indeed, would be a brave man.

After a long and thoughtful pause, Koenig turned to Darlene.
"The poor, tortured soul."
"Well, yes," Koenig responded. "It's very sad what happened to him, however, he did create this…torture chamber, and in the name of that Muka Vechny person, by the sound of it. What could have happened during the yearwalk that caused him to lose his moral compass and essentially become mentally enslaved by this creepy monster? Whoever, or whatever, Muka Vechny is, he is powerful and cunning."
Darlene nodded. "What a shame," she said with a stormy, saturnine glow on her face. "And Alyssa…"
"So, what I gather is this: he initiated the divination to discover the fate of his daughter, and in all likelihood encountered Muka Vechny while in Drugoy Mir. He became hypnotized, more or less, by this evil man, and built Ambrose Asylum at the man's bidding. Then, he created the Clandestra to experiment with the mental manipulation of his patients." Koenig shook his head in disbelief.
"Sounds about right," Darlene said. "Although I wonder how much of his spiral into madness was from an outside influence like Muka Vechny, and how much of it was caused by the slow deterioration and death of his daughter. That really broke his heart, Edward. The guy tried to cure her in every way possible. Imagine losing your daughter to something like…" She paused and wrapped a hand over her mouth.
"I'm sorry, Edward," she said, touching him on the shoulder in a conciliatory gesture. "I was so caught up with Ambrose's journal that I forgot about your situation with Dalla and Eveline."
"It's alright," Koenig grunted, patting her soft, alabaster-like hand. "Let's just try to find a way out of here." He stood up, pocketed Sheldon Ambrose's journal, and meandered into the hallway. "I wonder why he created the Clandestra after all? To erase the memories of the people who had experienced the divination and might spill the bea-"
An overwhelming surge of fear and surprise jolted through Koenig's nerves and simmered in his chest. Standing in a dim section of the corridor was the shadowy figure of a man. Muted, but visible by effect of a far-reaching ceiling light was a gaunt, disfigured face that seemed nearly to fester underneath the brim of a tall hat. The dark figure stood there for only a moment, leering at them, and then it dashed into one of the patient cells.
"What the fuck was that?" Darlene asked in a hollow, coarse whisper.
"I think…I think it was Kendric," Koenig stammered. "It had to be." Pushing Darlene behind himself, he gently tiptoed toward the room that the mysterious man had disappeared into, his heart hammering on his

sternum like a violent fist. He turned to look into the room, and a cooling rush of relief washed over him upon discovering that the room was empty.

"Where did he go?"

"I don't know. He's disappeared on me once before." Koenig shrugged.

"How do you know it was him?" she inquired. "I could barely see him."

"Kendric is instantly recognizable. He has these old burn wounds or scars of some type on his face. Where could he have gone?" Koenig entered the cell and dithered about. "The overturned chair is still here, just as it was when we first walked by. There's nothing else in this room except..."

He approached the left rear corner of the tiny room. He had noticed the emaciated ribbons of bedding when they passed by the cell before, but hadn't looked closely enough to discern what lay partially concealed beneath them. With a tremulous hand, he pulled the tattered cloth aside and revealed a man-sized hole.

"My god," Darlene's voice quivered behind him. Koenig brandished the flashlight from his pocket and clicked it on. Although the light weaned and flickered, it produced enough light to see well into the gape.

"It looks like a tunnel," he grunted. "Earthy and rough. Manmade perhaps."

"I don't want to go down there." Darlene shook her head fervently. "Especially if that weird Kendric guy just did."

"I don't like it any more than you do, Darlene, but I think this may be the only physical way out of the Clandestra; that is, besides relinquishing ourselves to the sheriff and his men back there. I vote we take the tunnel and see where it leads."

"Okay," she relented. "What if it collapses on us?" Koenig considered this for a moment, and then hopped inside. Already feeling the anxious prickle of claustrophobia on his neck, he delved deeper into the passage. There was enough space to stand in an awkward hunch and shuffle along on his feet, under which, the earth was moist and impressionable. Together Darlene and Koenig produced a symphony of clustered thumps as they continued down the dark tunnel for some time.

Every several minutes, they found it necessary to pause and rest their backs, which had built up a searing discomfort from the constant strain of bending over. The flashlight illuminated nothing but chunks of brown and green earth, intermittently sprinkled with sheets of rock, and Koenig found himself in the throes of a terrible headache brought on by the struggling effects of the failing device.

After what felt like the better part of an hour, and long after his flashlight had failed to operate, Koenig saw a warm shaft of light looming just yards ahead.

"I think we're coming to the end of it!" he exclaimed, and Darlene zealously moaned in anticipation of gulping in the fresh mountain air. They came upon what appeared to be a trellis made out of chunks of wood that served as a sort of door from the passage. Rivulets of light puckered through the latticework and shined brilliantly in Koenig's eyes. He pushed aside the makeshift door with one arduous stroke of his arm, and was instantly bathed in the bilious light of the sun.

    The initial sensation that overtook him was one of nausea and lightheadedness, but as he crept out of the cavernous dark and into the open world, his eyes adjusted, and he was overtaken by a feeling of splendor and gratitude. Darlene emerged ponderous as a turtle, but she too, was overcome with relief upon exiting the tunnel. She fell to the earth and dug her nails into the grass, succumbing to a fit of laughter.

    Koenig knelt beside her and allowed himself to appreciate her display of joy, basking in the radiant energy of her laugh. He followed the curves of her prostrate body with his eyes, and reprimanded himself upon developing the urge to embrace her in a frenetic celebration of victory, in this forgotten field tucked away in the manifolds of the mountain.

    He slowly rose to his feet and took a cumbersome, but intrepid step forward.

    "We made it out," he sighed. "I'm not gonna lie, for a minute back there with the sheriff and his henchmen, I thought we were goners." Darlene rolled onto her back, yielding to the warmth of the sun's rays.

    "Me too," she said. Koenig observed her high cheekbones as she lay there, and her bulbous eyes that matched the color of the grass beneath her. He shook his head to dismiss a bubbling fit of passion, and perused the scenery.

    They had emerged into a glen that was wedged between two vertical walls of mountain. Sequences of aspen and pine trees dotted the narrow landscape, and placid ribbons of mountain streams flowed about them. It was a striking scene. Koenig took a deep inhale and surveyed the land, wondering what kinds of secrets and long untouched memories rested in this furtive, secluded forest.

    "We must be higher up in elevation," he surmised. "We started out at Ambrose Asylum, which was at the base of the Cascade mountain range. We followed a tunnel through God knows how much earth and came out here. I guess we're in between two mountains above the sanitarium…I wonder if we're near old Alistair's Brigand?"

    Darlene gathered her thoughts and spoke with brevity. "Edward, it's getting late in the day. We don't even know where we are or who else might be around, except for that Kendric guy, who could be waiting in the bushes somewhere. We need to try to get back home. For now."

    "Right," he concurred, and helped her to her feet. "I wonder what his deal is. He's been haunting me since I got here." They meandered through the corridor of woods, and through dense, overgrown thickets, and droves of grassy knolls, but the surrounding mountains refused to yield a passage. As night began to fall, and an oppressive haunt of cold air fell upon them, Darlene spotted a gnarled path that split a recess in the mountainside.

    Steps laced with eagerness and exhaustion, they followed the unassuming path through the thickness of the mountain and out the other side. To the northwest, Darlene eyed the blotched glimmer of street lights.

****

Entering Darlene's house was, after the day he'd had, the most tranquil and comforting moment Koenig could remember. The simple and rustic décor was a pastoral embrace in a world gone mad, and the woman beside Koenig was, in his eyes, a spirited semblance of Aphrodite. Darlene and Koenig had been through turmoil together and come out unscathed, but somehow changed. He observed a closeness between them that had budded not from maundering conversation, as it normally would between acquaintances, but from the bond created by the life-threatening situation they had mutually endured. He embraced the newfound sensation of familiarity between them.

As she stepped into the living room, the mosaic of colors around her melted and faded away, until all that Koenig could see before him, was the glowing figure of Darlene.

"I'm gonna call Adam and Zach to make plans really quick. Make yourself at home, Edward." She disappeared into the kitchen and Koenig readily heeded her advice, sinking into a plush red couch.

After a few minutes of phone chatter that Koenig couldn't articulate, Darlene appeared and, in a terrifying instant that struck Koenig like a lightning bolt, he saw not Darlene, but the face of his wife staring at him over the kitchen counter. He saw Eveline's rosy cheeks juxtaposed with her elegant blonde locks, and the corners of her mouth were puckered in a smile. He felt his knees buckle at the illusion of his wife, and a wave of worry and anxious thought consumed him.

He slid forward on the couch and thrust his head into his hands. "Edward, are you alright?" Darlene gasped.

"Yes." He gathered himself and looked back at Darlene. The vision of Eveline had vanished. Rubbing his eyes, he assumed the brief visual blunder was a desperate exhort from his subconscious mind that he needed to stay focused. His family needed him, and he was determined to step off his father's beaten path and remain faithful to his wife henceforth.

"I'm just a little overwhelmed," he admitted, burying his head once more. "My wife and daughter are still missing, and I don't feel any closer to finding them. I just learned that the woman who raised me, the woman I have always known as my mother, was a lie, and that my birth mother is wasting away, wrongfully imprisoned, in an insane asylum here in Pinemist Bay.

"My father was a cheater and a liar, and he is the cause of her continuous suffering, while..." He took a long, shaky breath. "...I am the cause of my own family's suffering." He chuckled cynically. "Like father, like son, eh?"

"What do you mean?" Darlene asked. Koenig snorted in reply.

"Let's not talk about it right now. Do you have anything to drink? Anything that will take the edge off?" He looked up to the warm greeting of Darlene's eyes, which glowed with compassion. He wondered what his own countenance must have exhibited.

"I think I can help you there, Edward." She disappeared into the kitchen and returned with a bottle of whiskey and two shot glasses in her hands. "I figured you'd want it straight-up." She smirked. Koenig took the bottle from her and frenetically uncapped it, like a lost man in the desert stumbling upon a canteen. He took a deep swig and palmed the bottle, whereupon he began to laugh horridly.

"It's pretty good, huh? What's so funny?" Darlene asked, sitting down beside him. He ran a finger along the label that read, 'Mt. Hood Single Malt Whiskey.'

"Looks like you and Sheriff Grady have a similar taste in spirits," he said. "I spied this same brand in his desk the night I arrived." Darlene rolled her eyes and snatched the bottle from his hands, gulping down a significant portion of the drink.

"That insufferable fuck," she snorted. "He's regularly intoxicated on the job." Sneering, Koenig grabbed the bottle again and felt the warm liquid burn a path down his throat.

"But I guess the question is…" A dull buzz simmered in his head. "…Aren't there any other distilleries in the Pacific fuckin' Northwest?" To this, Darlene laughed unabashedly. Koenig knew his juvenile retort didn't merit such a fit of humor, but the alcohol was affecting them rapidly in their state of exhaustion.

He relinquished the half-empty bottle to Darlene. Being in a safe and trusting environment was a welcome change, and Koenig found himself utterly disarmed in the moment.

"Hey Darlene?" There was a tremble in the husk of his voice. "Do you think my family is still alive?" She nodded after a lengthy sip.

"Yes I do, Edward. I don't think they just abduct people at random and slaughter them. They take them for a purpose. We just have to figure out what that purpose is, and how we can get them back."

Koenig cocked his head back and took one more pull, watching the ceiling start to churn. As a blanket of numbness encompassed him, he felt, or thought he felt, Darlene's soft hand caress his. Then, his mind detached from conscious thought in the unrelenting grasp of intoxication that he knew too well.

Chapter Eleven
Discovery

Sometime after dawn, Koenig awoke to a suffocating pressure on his throat. Somebody was on top of him. He opened his eyes to a blurry haze of inscrutable commotion. Unable to determine whether the jarring ache in his head was an after effect of the liquor the night before, or from a lack of oxygen to his brain, he gulped in as much air as was permitted by the hands coiled around his throat. As his mind rapidly reached a state of lucidity, he began to panic.

Thrusting his arms forward, he groped with shaking hands until he found a firm, strong pair of arms, and pushed with every fiber of his being.

"Looks like somebody's ready to wake up," a familiar voice rang. The clenched hands released Koenig's throat and, like a kinked water hose unraveling, an uncontrollable flood of air cascaded into his lungs. He fell to his knees and began sputtering and coughing.

He fervently darted his eyes from side to side in a fruitless attempt to see. At first he was overcome by a dizzying array of stars that popped in and out of sight, and gradually, lights and colors, and then objects eked into view. He was kneeling in Darlene's living room, right beside the plush red couch he must have passed out on. As his vision normalized, he discovered in horror that Darlene was on her knees in front of him, with her hands bound behind her head.

Two robed men stood motionless behind her, and in between Koenig and Darlene was Sheriff Grady, who had adorned the robes of the Vucari. He was staring at Koenig with his hood drawn back, and upon his countenance was a malicious sneer. Koenig attempted to rise to his feet in an effort to thrust himself at the evil man, but his body was ponderous and inept, and his chest was still heaving after the strangulation.

"Don't even try to get on your feet," Grady barked. "You're outnumbered and probably so out of it that you couldn't tell your asshole from your own mouth." After this, he chuckled officiously. "Oh boy, you two have caused me a lot of grief. You're just lucky that He is heavily invested in you, Edward, or else I'd have had you strung up and slowly cut you to pieces, alive and screamin.'"

How did...how did he find us? Koenig looked at Darlene, who's mouth was covered with a strip of duct tape. Her eyes were wide with fear, and her body was in a tremulous fit of shakes and spasms. *How did he connect Darlene to this? How did he...the car. We left Darlene's car at the asylum.*

"And you." Grady turned to Darlene. "You've been working against me right under my own nose, you conniving bitch!" In a swift motion, Grady's hand danced across Darlene's face with such force that she stumbled forward.

"Leave her...leave her alone," Koenig panted, helpless as a fish out of water.

"Come, brother. Let us get on with it," said the cloaked man on the right.

"Yeah, I just wanted to savor the moment a little," Grady said in gruff satisfaction. "Hold him down." He pointed to Koenig. The robed man on the right bowed and stalked over to Koenig, placing cold, firm hands on his shoulders. Grady pulled his hood over his head, rummaged through his robes, and brandished a long dagger. Darlene began to moan and shake in her tethers at the sight of the glimmering weapon.

"Crying, into the world I came," Grady chanted in a fierce and almost unrecognizable tone. He stepped towards Darlene.

"No!" Languid and terrified, Koenig struggled against the robed man's grasp in vain.

"No grave shall there be, to bear my name." The timbre of Grady's voice strengthened as he raised the terrible dagger in front of his face with two steady hands.

"The earth, the wind, the rain, the fire. My life's design, to build a pyre." Koenig's heart lurched in his chest, and his jugular was pounding hard and fast in his throat.

"The embers of my soul shall kiss the sky." Grady was nearly shouting now. "Return to earth, let me to die!" Darlene made a desperate, muffled shriek as Grady placed the dagger against her throat. Just before he sliced into her windpipe, the cloaked man behind her reached out and grabbed him by the wrist. With a flurry of his robes, the man brandished his own weapon, which scintillated under the light and shone a strange ornamentation upon the blade. A deafening shriek filled the living room as the tip of what looked like a giant spearhead sank through Sheriff Grady's robes and into his skin.

The mysterious robed figure drove his body forward and plunged the lengthy steel deeper into Grady's stomach, until the handle was nearly flush against his garments. Koenig's captor stumbled forward in a baffled motion, but Grady's assailant was ready. In a quick, sopping slush of a noise, he exhumed the blade from Grady's body, which toppled to the floor inanimately, and the mysterious figure launched itself upon the remaining Vucari.

The two bodies landed beside Koenig and became a whirl of flailing garments. Grady's killer overpowered the other man and drove the scarlet-speckled blade through his hood and into his skull with a brilliant crunch. The man moaned and twitched, as blood burbled out of his hood and pooled on the wooden floor. Then, the room fell deathly silent.

Neither Koenig nor Darlene dared even to fidget, fearful of the mysterious assailant and his unknown motives. With a queer elegance, the man stood and approached Sheriff Grady's body. He placed a finger on the dead man's throat for a moment, and then ripped the tape from Darlene's mouth and approached Koenig, who stumbled backwards in fright.

"I've been watching you for some time now, Edward," the man said in a voice Koenig thought he recognized. "And it appears that we are out of time." The man reached up and slowly drew his hood back to reveal a decrepit and mutilated face. It was Kendric.

Awestruck, Koenig gasped and shook his head in declaration of his stupor. "Kendric? It's you? How did you know…but why didn't you just tell me in the diner…I've thought you were out to get me this whole time?"

"There is much you need to know, Edward, but now is not the time. Suffice it to say that Pinemist Bay is a dangerous town, increasingly so with your arrival. The Vucari are out in full strength hunting for you," Kendric said, his leathery jowl stretching. "This place is not safe. We would be wise to flee now."

Kendric aided Koenig to his feet, and then tended to Darlene's restraints. "I have something to show you, Edward," he said, whereupon the front door swung open, and two voices cried out in alarm. Zach Roussell and Adam Trevin stood in the doorway, mouths agape. Upon seeing the intruders, Kendric instinctively reached for his weapon.

"No, they're our friends! They're here to help, Kendric, I called them last night and told them to meet us here this morning." Darlene scrambled to her feet. "You can trust them."

"What the hell is all this?" Zach stammered.

"Are they…dead?" inquired Adam, who was pointing to the bodies with a shaking hand.

"Yes," said Darlene. "That's Sheriff Grady, and that's another member of the Vucari—"

"And who are you?" Zach interrupted. "And what's with your face?" he sputtered at Kendric.

"There isn't any time for discussion, guys, but he just saved our lives," Koenig said.

"And I'm afraid I shan't be able to deal with the larger unit of Vucari that are surely on their way here, right now. We must go!" Kendric ushered them through the doorway and into a street lit with the warm hues of morning.

"I know this town better than I know myself," Kendric stated. "Keep a low profile, stay silent, and follow me." He led them through the waking neighborhood; behind houses, across gardens and to the southeastern corner of the town without incident.

As they passed a network of apartments, Koenig noticed a little girl staring out of one of the lower windows. Her hands were pressed against the pane as she observed the odd group stalking across the lawn.

"Where are we going?" Zach questioned.

"To the mountains, my dear boy. The only place I can keep you out of harm's way." They arduously ascended the long slope, toward the crevice in the mountainside, which Koenig and Darlene had traversed the previous night. He began to notice a perplexing energy emulating from Darlene, and an indistinct expression on her countenance. Every so often she leaned towards him as if to say something, and then turned away in silence.

When the group reached the path that cut through the mountain, they slowed their pace, and Zach ventured a question.

"Does this path lead to old Pinemist Bay?"

"It is in that direction, yes," Kendric responded.

"How did we not find this Adam? I mean, I realize that it's out of the way, but we were trying to get straight through the mines in order to reach Old Pinemist Bay. And the Vucari don't know about this route either?" Kendric glanced over his shoulder at Zach before he spoke, who shriveled backwards at the mysterious man's unsightly face.

"They are aware of this route," he said gravely. "We must be ever diligent even this far out of town. There is a way deeper into the mountains that the Vucari are none the wiser of yet. You are crafty though, young man, considering the old coal mines as an option. What is your stake in all of this?"

The shadows cast across Zach's face under the midday sun exaggerated his sudden sepulchral demeanor. He cleared his throat. "My uh, my sister was taken by those monsters a couple months ago. I've been desperately trying to learn their whereabouts since then." Kendric remained silent.

"Alright Kendric, it's about time you told me your part in all of this. Why have you been following me, and why are you helping us now?" Koenig blurted. The pathway opened and they entered the secluded forest, retracing the steps he and Darlene had taken the day before.

After a long pause, Kendric slowed his pace just enough to fall in line with Koenig, while the others trailed behind a few steps. "You three back there, keep your eyes peeled for anything suspicious," Kendric barked at the others, and then glanced at Koenig in a sagacious manner, as if he was absorbing information from Koenig's face and judging how to proceed based on what he saw.

"My name is Alistair Kendric."

"Oh, are you related to the founder of Alistair's Brigand? A great grandson, or something?" Koenig inquired.

"No, young Edward, I am the Alistair who created Alistair's Brigand."

"What?" Koenig was utterly confounded by the statement. "Surely you're joking? Alistair's Brigand was founded in the 1850s."

"How else do you think I found you in Ambrose's Clandestra, where the sheriff and his men got lost? I built those linking passages years ago, and have many more peppered throughout Pinemist Bay. I developed, essentially, an entire subsection of Pinemist Bay upon the arrival of Muka Vechny, a name you have likely come to know during your visit. By the time Sheldon Ambrose came to America and built Ambrose Asylum, I had already been forced into exile for years."

"Muka Vechny?" Koenig repeated, a bitter look of contempt pervading his complexion. "So that *is* the name of the man who's behind all of this. The man who got my mother locked up in the asylum, and has my daughter and wife, as well as Zach's sister, in captivity."

"Yes, although I don't know if I would call him a man, we will get to all of that. Perhaps tomorrow we can rescue Ella, but for now, you need to follow me and listen carefully." He brandished the peculiar weapon he had used on Sheriff Grady. "You asked how I could possibly be one and a half centuries old. In short, it is thanks to this device."

Resembling an ancient metal spear with a massive spearhead and a curiously short shaft, the weapon gleamed in the midday light. Along the hilt, Koenig could discern various ancient symbols and five brilliantly carved settings which suggested the absence of jewels or adornments of some type. One of the five settings along the hilt contained an onyx colored gem.

"This is called the 'Runkavle' in Swedish. In English, the 'Rune Relay,'" he said. "It is an item of mystical power that one may acquire during a yearwalk. You see, when one sets out on this quest, he or she has the opportunity to encounter an armored man riding a horse, who contains this item in his possession.

"His name is Brynjar Eindride, and it is believed that he was a great Norse warrior during the Viking Age. He now endlessly wanders the land of Drugoy Mir, relinquishing the Runkavle to whomever proves worthy of possessing it. The legend states that if one possesses the necessary physical and mental faculties to obtain the Runkavle from Brynjar Eindride, and then is able to complete their yearwalk, they are endowed with one wish.

"It is an incredibly rare opportunity to encounter Brynjar while in Drugoy Mir, and a dear friend of mine was fortuitous enough to do so. Upon seeing the mounted man, my inordinately brave and headstrong friend was able to pry the Runkavle from his grasp. He then attempted to use this powerful item to kill Muka Vechny.

"Alas, Muka Vechny proved far mightier than anticipated, and he slew my friend. In the event of his death, I was left with this most powerful item in my possession. I then set out on my own vision quest with the Runkavle in hand, and a feverish vengeance on my mind.

"Upon completing my journey, I was visited by Brynjar Eindride, who offered to grant me one wish. I requested to be endowed with the gift of life until the evil of Muka Vechny was put to rest once and for all; a wish that will soon be fulfilled, I can feel it in my bones," Alistair said, nodding to Koenig.

"Who was this friend of yours, Alistair?" Koenig asked.

"I think you'll be acquainted with him soon enough," was his reply.

The group traversed the hidden valley until they came upon the surreptitious entrance to Sheldon Ambrose's Clandestra, where Alistair segued the group towards the eastern mountain. Enshrouded in shadow along the monolithic slab of earth was an orifice large enough for a man to fit through.

Alistair Kendric paused when he approached the hole. "Beyond this cave lies an old subterranean tomb. Now we need to be particularly cautious when we enter that place, because the Vucari use it as a dumping ground for many of their victims, and as a burial site for their own fallen brothers and sisters."

"We have to go in there?" Adam lamented, pointing at the cave. "I can't handle dark, cramped quarters very well."

"It is a brief passage since we're near the tip of the mountain," Alistair stated and disappeared into darkness. The others hesitantly followed him into the dank, echoing chamber one at a time.

As soon as he entered the cavern, Koenig was guided by soft ribbons of light that teased him from the other opening across the way. "Just watch your heads and keep your limbs close to your bodies. There are some sneaky stalagmites that will pop your eyes out in these mountainous caverns." He heard Alistair's voice divide into tiny echoes as it tumbled through the cavern.

"It's dark as fuck in here," Zach exclaimed. "Ow!"

"Be careful Zach! He just told you to watch yourself," Darlene's voice resounded throughout the cavern.

"I'm sorry. I can't see shit in here," Zach retorted.

"They say that this was a frequent hiding place for victuals and spirits during the prohibition era," said Alistair. "I remember when federal agents would raid the town, the visiting aristocrats and politicians would grab as much booze as they could carry, and disperse into the woods. I'm not sure if the tale is true that they hid in this cave, but I did find bottles of liquor in here now and again."

"I'll never forget the time," Alistair continued, "when one of King George the Fifth's nephews came to Pinemist Bay for a getaway of surreptitious frivolities, and federal agents raided all of the pubs. He had a naked girl on his lap, and a bottle of liquor in his hand; but I tell you, he was the first one up and out the back door when the Feds barged in," Alistair grunted a laugh.

"Those were some interesting times in Pinemist Bay. During the prohibition era, many a celebrity and politician flocked to these shores to partake in underhanded, and often times despicable, acts of reverie. The near complete isolation of this port town made it easy for the government to overlook the goings on, and just as effortless for any aristocrat or nobleman to indulge their darker sides in relative security."

"So, how is it that we are supposed to believe you are…at least 150 years old?" Zach inquired.

"Do you know anyone from this era who uses the term, 'victuals'?" Adam jibed.

"All in good time, my boy," was Alistair's response. The group came upon the cavern's exit, and Koenig was assaulted by a fiery blanket of sunlight. "Alright, the Tomb of the Irremediable, as it has come to be known by those few who know it, is just ahead."

Once the oppressive light in his eyes had subdued into muted strands of sunshine, Koenig observed that they were in another valley between looming mountains. This one was wider than the last, but yielded a denser vegetation. Wooded areas were plentiful, and, in the direction of what Koenig could only assume was north, a knoll rose over the foliage, overwrought with weeds and creeping grass.

They trotted towards what looked like a large cellar doorway that stood at a 45-degree angle off the earth. The entrance was hewn from oak and had a rustic, gnarled appearance. The structure upholding the doors consisted of stone, and in between its grooves, tendrils of grass and leafy vines prodded outward, as if attempting to escape their stony prison.

Alistair and Adam tugged the ponderous doors open, but before they entered, Alistair cautioned the group once more. "We must remain ever vigilant here. This tomb is dark as pitch and full of secrets; creeping, malevolent secrets that, if you dally in the rotting bosom of their home, will haunt you. Much evil has transpired here, and some things are best left untouched."

Alistair's comment seemed to pierce the three of them like a stark winter wind. Stripped of sanguinity, they entered the chilly crypt and walked down a stone stairway that led into a squat and lengthy corridor. Alistair pointed to sets of torches that lined the passage. "The embers burn nigh to their end. It appears no one has been here for days. This slice of fortuity may serve in our favor."

Darlene grabbed Koenig's hand and held on with a fervid strength that showed her dread. They continued down the length of the stony corridor until it gave way to a wider chamber; whereupon the stench of rancid meat crept into their nostrils.

"Ugh. What is that?" Adam coughed. Along the oval shaped walls lay dozens of compartments that were lined with caskets. Most of the chamber was wrought in darkness, but Koenig could see openings that led down dark subterranean corridors.

"Many a dead soul lay here," stated Alistair, with a spoil of disdain in his voice. "Come, let us not wander, and by all means, do not touch anything."

"No," uttered Zach. "No it can't be!" He dashed to the center of the room, where a sort of alter or shrine lay in shadow. "Hand me one of those lights!" he spat to Adam, who hurriedly dismantled a torch from the wall.

"What is it, Zach?" His voice was quivering.

"Just bring it here! Oh god, please," he pleaded. Adam thrust the torch forward, saturating the middle of the room in a brooding luminescence.

"No! Please, god, no!" Zach ululated.

When Darlene's gaze fell upon what Zach had found, she shrieked. He was standing before a mutilated body propped up on a stake. It was a woman who had been stripped bare and sliced horrifically across her torso. The wounds had puckered and bloated, and tiny insects were crawling along the gashes. Her head was bowed and veiled in darkness.

Zach touched her chin and gently lifted her head to his own. When her face shone under the light, he burst into tears. "No! Gen! Oh god!" He collapsed to the blood-smeared floor in front of the body and dissolved into a fit of tortured, haunting sobs that reverberated through the chamber.

Darlene rushed to Zach's side to comfort him, while Adam continued to hold the torch over the desecrated body with an unsteady hand. His face glowed like an alabaster moon.

"That's Genevieve," Adam whispered. "Zach's sister, the one that went missing."

"Oh my god," Koenig said. A twinge of guilt drove into his stomach when he realized how relieved he was that it wasn't his wife or daughter on the stake.

"The Vucari are under Muka Vechny's command," Alistair said softly. "They use archaic pagan rituals to carry out his will. Sometimes they sacrifice a living human to the tune of a powerful old incantation. This ritualistic offering temporarily breaks his tethers to Drugoy Mir and summons him in physical form. He uses this method to directly influence our world a bit at a time."

"This is what Robert Grady was attempting to do with Darlene back at the house. We cannot linger here," he said to Koenig. His disfigured face played horrors under the dim flicker of the torchlight in a fashion similar to the body of Zach's sister. "They could find us, especially in a group as large as this. We must keep moving until we are out of their reach."

"What happened to your face, Alistair?" Koenig inquired, nodding to Genevieve's demented corpse in comparison. Alistair stared at him in silent remembrance until a somber, brooding look washed over his face.

"The Vucari have touched many of our lives and bodies with a fierce, unrelenting hand," he said and turned to the others to imply a disinterest in elaborating. Zach was moaning and writhing on the cold stone floor while Darlene and Adam tried their best to assuage him.

"How do you comfort a man in the throes of losing someone so dear?" Koenig asked Alistair. "And in such a way..."

After a few minutes, they were able to reduce Zach's raw, unbridled frenzy of shouts to a low moan. He raised a shaking hand and placed it on his sister's foot. "We will avenge you, Gen. These monsters will pay for what they have done."

He glanced up at Koenig and wiped his sopping brow. "I will return and give my sister a proper burial, you have my word on that. I won't leave her body to fester down here with the rats. It's just not right. Oh god, how could I have let them take her from right under my nose?"

"You couldn't have done anything to help her, Zach. You did absolutely nothing wrong," Darlene consoled him.

"I could have gone in her stead," he declared. "I could have stopped this somehow."

"Please," Alistair interjected in an alarmingly sympathetic tone. "We cannot stay here. I understand that this is very difficult for you, and I am sorry for your loss, but we must move on Zachary."

"Just...just give me a minute alone with her, please?" Zach's somber voice resonated through the chamber. With a trembling hand, Darlene stroked his cheek, which, even under the dim glow of the torches were puffy and red. Tears were coursing down his cheeks, and his face was in a tortured grimace.

"Of course," she said.

"Come," Alistair said, dodging nervous glances around the chamber for something that might have been lurking in the shadows. "I'll show you a passage that I've used for over a century now."

Their feet clacked on the hard floor as they walked single file past the chamber and into a foreboding passage. Light emanating from the torches in the chamber splashed along the cavernous walls, providing only enough light with which to follow Alistair.

They hobbled down the earthy tunnel and came upon the entrance to another room. It was large and narrow, and the end of it was far enough back to be enshrouded in shadow. A smattering of additional torches threw a feeble light over this chamber as well.

"God, what kind of an installation is this?" Koenig inquired.

"This is all property of the Vucari now," Alistair said. "Which is why it is ill advised for so many of us to be here, but if we move fast and soft, we shouldn't be compromised. The dead cannot warn them of our presence. At least, not these ragged old souls." He pointed to one of the many coffins that lay about.

"This is one of their many crypts. A network of rooms like this constitute the majority of the catacombs." Alistair led them into the crypt, and Koenig had to plug his nose to gain respite from the layers of stench that permeated the air.

"Shouldn't we wait for Zach?" As the request escaped Darlene's lips, the aftershocks of a yell tumbled through the corridor.

"Oh god," Adam uttered. Distant footfalls padded toward them at an alarming rate. Then, more sets joined them; it was impossible for Koenig to discern how many. Moments later, Zach stampeded in from the corridor, his face flushed and hot, and still varnished with tears.

"They're here!" he gasped. "The Vucari!" Darlene shrieked, and Alistair coolly turned and stalked to the rear end of the crypt, where he brandished the Runkavle.

"We must fly!" he exclaimed. "Come." He kneeled to the floor and pulled a crumbling, soot-ridden box from underneath a casket. Behind it, a small brass trinket attached to the wall glimmered in the torchlight. He deftly placed the edge of the Runkavle into a slit in the object and a small chunk of the wall heaved into motion, giving way to a small passage behind.

"Edward, you first!" He motioned toward Koenig.

"No, Darlene goes first!" Koenig protested and pushed her towards the hole. The cascade of footsteps in the corridor resounded ever closer, and Adam and Zach bunched together behind Koenig. "You next Zach!" Koenig yelled. Zach squatted on his hands and knees and followed Darlene into the narrow gape in the wall.

Koenig and Alistair lined up to leap into the passage, while Adam seemed to linger behind them. "Come on, Adam!" Koenig shouted as he began to shuffle into the passage. Time for a clean escape had run out as two cloaked figures appeared ominously in the doorway.

Without a moment of hesitation, they darted forward, robes arcing in the darkness behind them. With the Runkavle still in hand, Alistair grunted and charged toward the men. "Onward, Koenig!" he commanded. He slammed into one of the Vucari and Koenig watched as their two bodies began to flail about the crypt, kicking up a whirl of dust in a desperate clash.

"Adam!" Koenig shouted hoarsely, watching as the second cloaked man sprinted toward them. "Come on!" In a gesture that was nearly subtle enough to be missed amid a sea of tumult, Adam made a somber smile with the corner of his mouth, and turned to face the charging figure.

Crammed halfway into the small opening, Koenig twisted and writhed to contort himself out of the passage, but it was too late. After a brief tussle, Adam collapsed to the floor with the hilt of a knife jutting out of his stomach. His killer was standing over him, and Koenig thought he could see the apparition of a crooked face leering at him in the murky depths of the hood.

Having dispatched the other attacker, Alistair rushed over while Koenig scrambled out of the opening. Finding himself outnumbered, Adam's killer gracefully turned on his heel and ducked before Alistair could drive his blade into him. The end of his robe whipped Koenig across the face and seconds later, the man had fled from the crypt and disappeared into the darkness.

"Adam!" Koenig fell to his knees and propped the injured man up on his leg. Alistair lingered in the clutches of a dark corner and kept watch for more intruders, while Darlene and Zach shuffled out of the crevice and looked upon the sight with horror.

"Ed-Edward." Adam coughed chunks of bloody mucus onto his chin as he struggled to produce the simple phonemes.

"Why did you do that, man?" Koenig chuckled nervously as he eyed the wound. Zach knelt beside him.

"Should we take it out?" His eyes were glassy. "Does anybody have something that we can use as a tourniquet?" Zach went to grab the handle of the knife when Adam pawed at him with a tremulous hand.

"Edward. You need to keep moving…" He gasped for breath. "What I saw on my yearwalk…I knew this was coming." Adam was smiling now. Not a joyous smile, but one rife with pain and something else that Koenig couldn't identify. It was the look of a man who had long since come to terms with his fate.

"You're the missing puzzle piece," he continued. "Go to her." With a final exhale, his body went limp and slid prostrate onto the floor.

Aside from the occasional sniffle and whimper, neither Koenig, Darlene, or Zach made a noise during the journey through the dusty tunnel. They followed Alistair's lead until the cramped quarters gave way to a dilapidated little shack. It was a barren, wooden room with a lopsided door, through which shown brilliant ribbons of light.

Alistair pushed the door open and they entered what appeared to be another mountain forest. Koenig had no idea where they were now, he only knew they had to be somewhere deep in the cluster of mountains.

Through a mess of tangled ferns and pine trees, lay a senescent stone cottage. It was snuggled right in with a landscape unhindered by man or machine, and the surrounding air pulsed with clandestine vigor. It was as if Koenig was stepping into a world of forgotten treasures.

Sunlight kissed their foreheads as they tackled the steepening terrain. Darlene was the first to brave a word. "We weren't able to give him a proper burial." Her head was down as she navigated a virgin path through the tall grass. Against the lush green background, her red locks were a flowing cynosure of color.

"Those monsters need to pay," she continued, with a bite of scorn.

"It was most unfortunate," Alistair said. "As is our predicament." Koenig glanced inquisitively at him. "I've managed to keep that passage a secret from the Vucari for over a century now, and the one that escaped is sure to inform the others. They could be on our heels at any time now."

"Where are we?" Koenig asked, as they passed a small collection of cottages that were gathered beneath a heaping outcrop of rock.

"Old Town," Alistair replied. Meanwhile, Zach was looking dreamily about the clustered landscape. Suffering the horrendous deaths of not one, but two loved ones had left him numb.

As Koenig traipsed through foliage representative of a jungle more than a northwestern forest, he felt a familiar buzz in his temples, the buzz that magnified into a ruckus of frenzied nerves and fired off in his skull. Then her voice split through the lithosphere of his mind like a seismic wave.

"Daddy," Dalla said. "I can see you."

"Edward, are you alright?" Darlene's voice pierced through the din. He turned to face her, and in the depths of her emerald eyes, his gaze fell upon his own reflection. The man in the reflection grimaced, and his eyes were bloodshot and glassy.

"I'm okay," he replied. Dalla, and the bluster in his head, were both gone.

"We're nigh upon the house," Alistair said.

"What house?" Koenig asked, but received no answer.

****

When the sun was high over the trees, and a glaze derived from its late afternoon shine waxed over the leaflets and branches, they reached a lone cottage. It sat on the crest of a small hill just behind a circular stone well that jutted through a plume of weeds. Peeled out before the house was a crumbling cobblestone path that made an eerily abrupt stop at their feet.

"I remember this," Koenig stated, hearing the clack of his shoe on the first stone step. "In my dream. Dalla told me about this place." They followed the path up to the old water well, where Koenig stopped and fell to his knees, overtaken by a swell of emotions that inexplicably didn't feel like his own.

"What's wrong Edward?" Darlene stooped beside him with the look of a concerned mother on her face.

"I...I don't know," he said. "I feel like I've seen this well before. Everything feels so familiar." He looked up at the worn, but solid roof of the old cottage. "Like when you return to the house you grew up in for the first time in years."

"Where are we?" he asked Alistair.

"First, I believe you should enter the house." Alistair pointed a bony finger to the oak door. Koenig stumbled to his feet and subconsciously grabbed Darlene's hand as he approached the building.

The stone structure of the old house shed a scent that tingled in the back of Koenig's nasal cavity, and when he looked at the oak door, it was as if he was gazing at it through the filter of a dream. He pushed hard and the hinges creaked into action.

The cottage was cramped and covered in layers of dust. Old papers, cracked at the edges, lined a wooden table, and archaic crimson drapes bled along the grey stone walls. Much of the house was draped in shadow, with fingers of light poking through two oblong and ornate windows on either side. Unlit candles oozed wax onto the tables and sills.

Koenig heard a commotion from below the floorboards. Someone was moving about beneath them. Alistair moved with deftness to the center of the room and threw open a heavy cellar door.

"Come on out, dear," he called. "I've brought someone for you." Koenig's eyes widened and his jaw fell as a little person climbed out of the cellar; a tiny ashen-haired girl in a dirt-smeared nightgown.

He would have cried her name had he been able to speak at all. Falling to both knees, he embraced his daughter with such alacrity that they almost tumbled over. This moment gave merit to everything that had happened the past few days, and Koenig reveled in it.

"Dalla!" he finally gasped. "Dalla, baby, oh my god, I've been worried sick about you!"

"Daddy, daddy, daddy!" she cried, holding onto rumples of his shirt with plump, coiled little fingers. "I knew you'd make it! I just knew it!"

"Oh Dalla, I'm so happy you're alright," he exclaimed. "Daddy was worried sick, honey. I'm so sorry I ever left you guys. Never, ever, ever again." He knelt back to look into her eyes, but with a face blanketed in tears, all he could discern was the little human shape in front of him. That was enough.

"Where's mommy?" he asked, with a smile still plastered on his face. Alistair, who was standing over him, simply shook his head.

"Mommy's not here, daddy," she said, flicking a curl of hair out of her face. "The bad men have her."

"This little one managed to escape from the pack," said Alistair.

"We were in a car with lots of the bad men, the-the Vuc-Vuc..."

"Vucari," Alistair finished with a nod of his head.

"Vucari. And mommy pushed me out." Dalla made a shoving gesture with her hands.

"I had been tracking their movements, as I often do, and picked her up in the forest," said Alistair. "Then I proceeded to bring her here. It's the only place that's relatively safe from the Vucari. They still have your wife as far as I know. I think they're going to hold onto her as collateral for you, Edward."

"Thank you." Koenig put a hand on Alistair's shoulder. "Thank you for rescuing my daughter and looking after her." Alistair nodded and, with his hands behind his back, he began to pace around the room in deep thought.

"I just need to find my wife," Koenig stated squarely. "So, is this your house?" he asked. Darlene bent down to greet Dalla.

"You have the most beautiful eyes, dear," she said, which lit up

Dalla's face like a lantern.

"It is one of my primary dwellings, yes," Alistair responded. "Edward, we have much to discuss, and indubitably not much time. Let us take a walk."

Koenig wiped his eyes once more and knelt down before Dalla. Now that he had found her, he was desperate to keep her in his sight. "Hey baby girl. Daddy's gonna go outside with Alistair for a minute, but Darlene and Zach will be right here."

He peered over at Zach, who was staring out the window with a vapid expression.

"He's rallying himself," Darlene whispered. Koenig nodded sympathetically. Dalla was sitting between them and gazing upward with a fleck of vehemence in her own eyes, as if she somehow knew the events that had transpired.

"We'll take care of her, Edward," Darlene said resolutely. "I won't let her leave my sight." Koenig kissed his daughter one more time and stood up to leave, halting in the doorway to gaze upon her visage in a larger frame. His little girl had changed. Upon the fusty and gnarled wooden floor, she exuded a hallowed dignity from her person bespoke of an old wise woman or perhaps a revered professor, but certainly not a four-year-old girl. He smiled once more at her, and left into the forest with Alistair.

****

They took the cobbled steps that led away from the old house and took to a rough, but somewhat stamped trail through the bounding vegetation.

"Mine are the only boots to have traipsed through this beguiling forest in many, many moons," Alistair stated with a placid look on his face; his arms still crossed behind his back. His horribly disfigured face had become somewhat endearing to Koenig in the small matter of hours since the daring rescue maneuver at Darlene's house.

Koenig understood that he may never know exactly what the man endured to suffer such a prominent and unsettling accolade of wounds, but he assumed they were derived from a struggle against the Vucari; and he was conscious of a tacit compassion between himself and his enigmatic savior.

"Poor Adam Trevin," Koenig sighed. "What was he thinking, throwing himself in front of that madman like that?" To this remark, Alistair dissented.

"No, no, Edward," he shook his head. "That act was no whim. Adam Trevin had been granted visions of at least some of these events in his yearwalk. What happened in the crypt was a premeditated action to spare your life, so that you might continue your quest.

"What he did or didn't know, drove him to an unabashed devotion to your cause. I'm not sure if Adam had foreseen the exact events that transpired, but I'm certain he would have repeated his actions during that confrontation, had he been given the chance. I hope you have come to the realization that you and your daughter are rather unique."

They had shuffled and kicked their way through acres of woods when Alistair held up his hand, signaling Koenig to halt. Just ahead of their position, a bleak haze crept across the forest. Surreptitious in its occurrence, the thicket of damp air had seemingly conjured in a matter of seconds.

The effervescence skirted towards them at an alarming rate, its smoggy arms stretching out like the fingers of a ghostly figure groping its way through the woods.

"Oh good, he has arrived," Alistair sighed. For an icy moment Koenig was caught in the haze, stymied by fear and the suspicion that he had been duped by his mysterious friend. Somewhere in the center of the cloud was a frightening splash of light and a tumultuous displacement of fog.

"Come." Alistair beckoned him forward with a motion from his fore and middle fingers.

"Where?" Koenig blurted. "What is this?"

"Just come hither." Alistair was pertinacious. The two men stumbled through the fog, one of them with a confidant gate, and the other, a shrunken figure lurking behind. They came upon the rocky side of a mountain, whereupon Alistair led Koenig into a dark and moody crevice.

Despite being blanketed in shadows, the eerie fog provided just enough light for Koenig to see the cavern's interior, which starkly reminded him of the cave in which Dalla was hiding when he found her in his dream the other night.

After a moment of wretched stillness, an ethereal figure materialized before them in the haze. The pallid, slick bald head came into view first. After, the entirety of the squalid figure became visible. It was the old man he had met on his way to Pinemist Bay.

"Oh my god." Koenig's jaw slacked and his eyes bulged incredulously.

"Edward, I'd like to introduce you to an old friend of mine. I know the two of you crossed paths recently." Alistair nodded.

"Edward Koenig," the old man said. The distrait manner of his bodily spasms was present same as before, and he seemed to find it difficult in maintaining eye contact with Koenig. "I have much to tell you, and very little time. The Vucari are regrouping and plotting their course of actions even as we speak.

"What I am about to impart will surely seem implausible, but take heed of its message. I would also like to apologize to you antecedently for what I have done. Please know that in the desperate state in which I found myself, I became inexorable in my quest to conquer evil."

Chapter Twelve
Runkavle

It was during the year 1847 of the Gregorian calendar that my people became aware of the sinister forces they were harboring. Like a seed of evil inhumed deep within the soil, this furtive demon abandoned its dormancy, and made itself known.

In the southern portion of Sweden, nearest on the map to the town Jönköping, there laid a sleepy village by the name of Dödkärr. It was a sordid, rural patch of land, and drearily isolated. Dödkärr was home to a quaint community of no more than a couple hundred countrymen. We were a sinewy people, whose hands were calloused from the tiller, and whose backs strained and grew rigid from toiling in the fields day and night.

Everything we had, we created out of necessity to survive. I cast myself upon the growing fields under the contemptuous summer sun, and thrust my axe upon countless spruce and pine, until I found myself owning a plot of land commensurate to the village leader's own.

Presently, I married a lofty and vivacious young lady by the name of Mary Eklund, whose blond locks seemed to shimmer even in the dead of winter. Together, we raised a prosperous, budding family consisting of an elder daughter Eva, and a younger son Edvard.

Reigning over the commoners' hearts and minds was Dödkärr's local parish, where our Lutheran minister gave many a sermon, and our community upheld their faith, as had been commonplace for generations. However, a clandestine undercurrent pervaded our community, as it swept its way through Norway and Sweden.

Centuries prior to the creation of our fledgling village of Dödkärr, in what was a cyclopean exodus unprecedented to rural folk in the forests of Sweden, thousands of outsiders emigrated across Europe to escape Christian persecution. Slavs from across Russia and along the Balkan slopes ventured far and wide in an attempt to make a life according to their ancestors' beliefs. New forms of Paganism became intertwined with the folk traditions of my own ancestors.

Among other forms of Seidr and Norse augury, the unholy ritual of yearwalking had become widespread throughout the land by the time the Slavs arrived. When I was born in Dödkärr, a portion of our own was already furtively partaking in the divination. Villagers went on their vision quests in secrecy and solitude, as any unholy rite was deemed heresy in the traditional viewpoints of our elders.

Yearwalking remained largely secret, but it was a staple practice in our village. The various visions granted to the townsfolk were put to use in pertinent ways, for life was unforgiving in the desolate hills of rural Sweden; the seasons rancorous and vile.

Stories and personal accounts told by yearwalkers spread like a cancer among us. Many of us, myself included, experienced immense trepidation at the thought of encountering the supernatural entities we were told we'd find lurking about on our own spirit journeys. The monsters that wove a foundational thread into our culture, the same ones we were raised to fear from youth, were allegedly waiting for us in the mysterious land of Drugoy Mir.

Alas, when our fortune took a turn for the worst, and our harvest saw itself diminish year after year, many of the townsfolk became helplessly desperate. My wife fell ill with a violent fever and passed during this callous time, exacerbating my own tenuous grip on reality. A resoluteness spread amongst the younger and more indomitable of us, and soon, most of the youths in the village were engaging in the dangerous divination of which you have come to learn.

You must understand, such a fantastical activity allows little forbearance for a struggling farming community. We thirsted for a deeper knowledge of our dismal circumstance, and prayed to be granted with visions of a favorable outcome.

I believed that the benefits of such wisdom endowed upon me far exceeded any undesirable outcome that might result. Little did I know, I was about to reawaken an old and malevolent demon with my first foray into the pagan ritual.

I secluded myself in my cellar for a full day, without speaking to anyone or satiating my hunger. Towards the end of the meditation, it became an arduous challenge to restrain myself from clambering into the den and devouring the leftover meats and bread.

I'm ashamed to admit that a certain greed pervaded my soul after my first yearwalk. After I circled the church and blew into the keyhole, I was granted a glimpse not of my village's fate, but into the future life of my daughter. I saw her bearing a child.

How could I not indulge myself in the possibility of discovering the qualities of my daughter's future husband? How might I forego an opportunity to learn of my young son's future endeavors, and whether he would travel across Europe? You see, I yearned for him to escape the dreary clutches of our squalid little world, and blossom in the more propitious environment of Western Europe. I hastily dove into a yearwalk the following day.

During this event, I encountered a man of mighty presence on an enormous steed. He was wielding a magical scepter of some sort, and was moving with great celerity; far faster than any mortal man or beast could move. As I watched him approach, like a ghost flying on the wing of the night, my focus turned to the device in his hand. Unsure of its purpose or nature, I became instantly spellbound by the object. I craved it. Leaping forward with great vigor, I grasped the scepter and pulled with every fiber of my being. After a moment of immense concentration, I broke free the object from his gauntlet.

Upon reaching the end of my yearwalk, my path once again was crossed by this mysterious horse rider. He introduced himself as Brynjar Eindride and informed me that I had become an Odinian, a term I was unfamiliar with at the time. He stated that, having obtained the Runkavle, I had passed his test, and that he would grant me one wish.

Before I was able to utter a word, however, a cloud as pitch as black swept over me and consumed me inside its effervescent tendrils. Something, or someone, was malcontent with my possession of the Runkavle. After the dark shroud dissipated, I found myself in the murky depths of the forest. Brynjar Eindride had vanished. The yearwalk had ended.

The inexplicable events that took place that night left me desiring more. I had met a mystical being who would grant me a wish of my choosing, and how was I to let that opportunity slip? Perhaps I could wish for great fortune to fall upon Eva and Edvard. Perchance I might enable them to be whisked away to a more fruitful life than that which I could provide them in Dödkärr.

When the clock struck midnight, I journeyed from my cottage and out into the bleak embrace of the night. There was a particularly bitter and foreboding atmosphere that hung on the air that night, I still shudder upon the thought of it. The singular thing that kept my feet swift and my heart unyielding was the tantalizing possibility that I might gaze into my son Edvard's future, and take home with me something, some inkling of knowledge or hope which might keep my spirits aloft during such a wretched time.

The utter stillness of the forest that night, the hauntingly placid kiss of the breeze, awakened a dire fear in my heart. I sensed that something was amiss, but would not shirk from my mission and retreat home. Whereupon I reached the looming white of the parish, I was not met by Brynjar Eindride, rather I was assaulted by frightful visions of the man shrouded in clouds who had thwarted my encounter with the mysterious mounted man.

In a mere glimpse that felt like an eternity, I discovered his history and his motives; what he had lost, and what he desired in his cold flittering heart to gain. My meandering in the ancient world of Drugoy Mir had awoken him from his slumber, like a spider biding its time until an unsuspecting insect stumbles into its snare.

Muka Vechny was his name. For centuries he had been lurking in the shadows of Drugoy Mir, patiently awaiting the arrival of one strong enough in what is called 'the essence.' The essence is in all of us, every living thing. Its main constituent is the triumvirate of one's mind, body, and soul; the solidarity of these three elements. Most humans contain only shreds of the essence, minute amounts compared to a rare few. Only those born with inordinate amounts of the essence can hope to be quick enough and strong enough to snatch the Runkavle from Brynjar's grasp. Once they accomplish this, these people are called Odinians, as Brynjar Eindride had informed me during our encounter.

If you have ever heard of the term 'collective conscience,' or heard of an instance where two people very close to each other, perhaps siblings, were able to guess what the other was thinking, then you are aware of some everyday occurrences of this most peculiar force of nature. Many mediums and psychics are endowed with a keener essence than the average human as well, and they use this ability to earn a living through predictions and visions.

As far as I am aware, the quantity of essence one is endowed with is determined by genetics. Some family lines simply harbor more of this powerful force than others, and even within a single ancestral line, the gift seems to ebb and flow.

In what is an incredibly rare occasion, a baby might be born with a seemingly unlimited supply of the essence, and once they harness this innate power, they find they can achieve miraculous things using only their minds. Telepathic communication is one method of utilization. A much rarer and more powerful Odinian might be able to manipulate worldly objects without moving a muscle.

As for how this all relates to Muka Vechny, he has his own motives for exploiting the powers of one who is rich in the essence. What I discovered during my yearwalk was that my son was endowed with a near boundless supply of the gift, and as I stood in the desolate woods on that malevolent and brooding night, I witnessed horrific visions of this man's evil. I saw him tormenting my son and exploiting his powers in an effort to escape his confinement in the world of Drugoy Mir. I determined that I must never allow my child to fall into the clutches of such a desperately mad man.

With one child under each arm, I fled the bastion of our home, that which I built out of nothing but my own sweat and sacrifice. I set out to gain as much distance between us and that caustic swamp as I could manage. Our grueling journey saw us emigrating to the promising nation of America; particularly, to the developing territories of the Pacific Northwest.

We arrived here in the year of 1857. It was a tumultuous time, not merely for our fatigued and destitute family, but for the nomadic dwellers of these western territories as well, who were vibrant and zealous in the development of their new land. Upon reaching the isolated and rural trading port of Alistair's Brigand, my feelings of dread were allayed. Alistair himself saw us to our lodgings, the same place in which you are currently taking refuge.

He built upon the scraps of English we had gathered from our voyage until we were all somewhat literate. He entertained my children with outlandish tales of his adventures as a privateer on the Pacific Ocean, which were funded by the lucrative assets he procured during the California Gold Rush.

For a placid moment in our new world, my family thrived and flourished. My children, who had showcased a stout perseverance through our trials, developed a sanguine outlook on life. My daughter Eva found herself taken with the young and vibrant son of a carpenter, and devoted much of her time to being with him on his farm.

I was proud of my children, and felt for a brilliant moment that we were where we belonged. I dared not tell Alistair our reason for emigrating all the way from Sweden, and being a somewhat diffident man, he didn't ask.

Alas, the insidious demon who terrorized us in Dödkärr made his presence once again known. Inconceivably, he had followed us across the better part of the world; his bloodthirsty nature would not abate. The fool hearted man that I was, I found myself drawn once more into the guiles of yearwalking.

As a token of my appreciation for all that he had done for me, I introduced Alistair Kendric to the divination. He had invested much of his assets in the development of his port town, and was invigorated by the opportunity to attain knowledge of Brigand's success. Soon enough, much of the town was swept into the virulent tide of the ritual.

Thereafter, a thing of the most peculiar nature occurred. Some of the townsfolk began exhibiting strange behavior; mumbling to themselves on street corners, developing extreme antisocial tendencies. Over time people started disappearing from their homes entirely, and occasionally, we found townsfolk dead in the surrounding mountains.

And that was when they first emerged, this brilliantly pervasive clan. Brainwashed and loyal to Muka Vechny were the men and women who had fallen into his snare, and they metastasized like a cancer through the limb of our little society. Over time they became more prolific, and donned matching garments, like the robes you see today, towards a more unified and clandestine look. They were called the Vucari, and they acted as Muka Vechny's eyes and ears within a world that he could not penetrate.

I can imagine how outlandish this must be to you. However, what proceeds may truly discomfit you. Not long after their first appearance, the seemingly ubiquitous Vucari were at my doorstep making unwelcome inquiries. At first, the questions pertained to my family in general; where we were from, how long we had been in America, and so forth. Then, their unbridled curiosity turned to my son. I had to start keeping a diligent watch of my property day and night, and devised ways of hiding him from sight if anyone approached our property.

Alistair grew concerned for the well-being of his quaint town as it grappled with this devious cult. He also made more frequent visits to my cottage, as my mental health began to worry him. Recent events had put a tremendous strain on my tenuous faculties and with the developing threat of the Vucari, I was losing sleep. Reality started to slip away like sand through a clenching fist. The situation grew ever more dire from there until Alistair took matters into his own hands, for the safety of my children.

It was a cool April day when Alistair slipped into my home, quiet as an apparition, and swept my children away from me and into the security of his bastion. By this time, I was in the throes of such mental anguish that my mind decoupled from reality entirely. My daughter had been with child for some weeks, and of this I had no concept.

Even now I cannot surely say whether or not the proceeding event took place, or if it was a figment of my imagination. It was on a warm summer night sometime after Alistair had taken my children that two hooded figures swept into my bedroom, as soft and silent as clouds; robes flowing like diaphanous sheets of light. They lingered for a moment before the foot of my bed, peering down at me in a punishing silence.

I could distinguish no faces, no human qualities about them whatsoever, but from within my own mind their voices rose, and they informed me that they were agents of the Norn. They served as specters exhumed from the darkest reaches of night, to warn me of my son's imminent fate. Muka Vechny would not suffer a respite until Edvard was in his clutches. It was that night I learned that his evil, like a rolling winter haze, had been gathering its bitter strength for a millennium; biding its time for the sole opportunity of finding one strong enough in the essence to abet his escape.

These specters informed me thus, and vanished in the tenebrous embrace of night. I awoke the next morning very early and stumbled into the dewy woods with a singular focus. I made haste to Alistair's home and wrenched my son from the protection of my daughter's arms. Even now I remember the look upon her face; the fervid anguish on her countenance. It is a miserable thing, to have your own children fearful at the very sight of you.

However, I was possessed by my mission and could not afford to let such an evil enter our world, nor could I allow Muka Vechny to extract the essence from my son in the torturous ways I had witnessed in my visions. I dragged my boy, kicking and wailing, through the soft morning haze to my cottage, whereupon I thrust his face into the stone well and proceeded to drown him. A heinous moment which is forever burned in my memory. I can still feel the splash of cool water against my face, and the sobering sound of his struggling cries resound in my ears evermore.

I held him there until the thrashing subsided, watching the last bubble dance to the water's surface and pop. Can you imagine being in such a precarious mental state as to forego any feelings of mourning or guilt for killing your own helpless son? I sat by his lifeless body for a moment and my thoughts turned to my daughter's unborn child. The essence ran strong in our family, and if my son was endowed with a powerful degree of it, then my daughter's child may share the gift as well.

I was aware that the monster would stop at nothing to hunt down anyone with a strong essence. I could not allow my grandchild's fate to be that of Edvard's, nor could I allow her to serve as the catalyst to Muka Vechny's escape from Drugoy Mir. I returned to Alistair's house while he was away in town, took a knife, and attempted to kill my daughter and her unborn child, lest the little one should suffer the same fate from which I rescued my son. Eva's resolve was ferocious, however, and she held me at bay until Alistair returned and put an end to my attack.

Stricken with fear and remorse, Eva turned on her heel and retreated to her lover's house. They immediately fled Alistair's Brigand to elude my madness; for both Eva's sake, and that of her unborn child. The period after her departure is a hazy one in my memory, as I sunk further into my bitter tussle with depression and regret.

I had torn my family apart, and for what? In the moment, my actions had seemed the only way in which I could prevent the prolonged suffering of my kin as well as the unleashing of a terrible demon. But in the aftermath of the atrocities I committed, I was left with only my self-condemning thoughts to console me.

In my state of desperation, I thrust myself into another yearwalk. I yearned to find this demon of a man, and take from him whatever life pulsed inside his convulsing, vaporous entity. With my Runkavle in hand, the blade outstretched in the creeping night before me, I scoured the land of Drugoy Mir for Muka Vechny. After wandering through the dark ether for some time, I happened upon Brigand's local parish.

Upon reaching the parish, Brynjar Eindride galloped toward me on his fierce steed, proclaiming to fulfill his promise of a wish. Before I could react, however, I was enveloped in an icy broth of shadow. As I stood paralyzed with fear, something pierced my back and drove clean through my sternum.

Crippled by shock and searing agony, I gazed down upon that which had stabbed me and saw not a sword or a honed weapon, but the vacillating, contorting limb of a wholly inhuman being. Muka Vechny had found me. Stupefied and fading from life rapidly, I fell to my knees on the cold dirt. My final thoughts turned to my son, Edvard, and the life of which I had robbed him.

For a bittersweet moment that felt impossibly infinite, Edvard's visage gleamed before me. I could see his youthful face even after my vision faded to black and only a tenuous thread of life remained within me. Gripping the Runkavle taut against my chest, I stammered a few ponderous words:

I wish for my son to be endowed with the gift of life once more. To succeed where I have failed.

I then used the diminishing strength within me to wheel about and thrust the blade of the Runkavle into the vaporous body of my foe. As reality faded away, a gelid sheet of black wrapped around me and snuffed the life from my body.

Chapter Thirteen
Reconciliation

"That is where you come in, Edward Koenig," the old man said. "It has been a long time, my son. You have the same eyes."

"I'm confused," Koenig said. "You're my father...from a previous life?" Alistair nodded, looking between the old man and Koenig.

"Allow me to introduce Áki Koenig," he said. "You see, Edward, this is not your first time on this earth. It is your reawakening. And you, my young friend, are an Odinian; a very powerful one at that."

"Your daughter, Dalla," Áki added. "She is an Odinian as well. Perhaps the most powerful of any we have ever bared witness to, and she is but a child."

"That explains how she has been communicating to me in my mind," Koenig said. "So it was her who blocked the Vucari from getting in my room while I slept at the Pinemist Hotel...and maybe that's why I had a strange feeling about Sheriff Grady the night I arrived at Pinemist Bay. I got there to tell him about my encounter with you, Áki, and then I developed a mistrust of the sheriff while I was talking to him. Dalla was influencing my subconscious and I didn't even know it."

"Your daughter has been guiding your steps since the moment you stepped foot in Pinemist Bay," said Alistair. "Dalla is a keen little one, and her telepathic might is immensely appealing to Muka Vechny. His minions have been scouring the country for you and your family for quite some time.

"I believe that once they procured your location, they lay in wait until you and your family were separated. For you are an Odinian, and they were wary of your powers, and wanted not to directly confront you," he continued. "As soon as you and your wife had an altercation and you left home, the Vucari pounced on your wife and daughter.

"Dalla called to you for help from within her mind whilst they were being transported here. And you received her pleas because you too, are endowed with a strong essence, Edward. Although, she appears to be so powerful that she may even be able to probe a mind which possesses only a trace of the gift," Alistair suggested.

"So, what happened after Muka Vechny killed you?" Koenig inquired. "Are you dead?" Áki paused in contemplation for a long moment before responding.

"The phantom Muka Vechny has many wicked and powerful methods that he employs on his victims," he said scornfully. "He was born into the world of Drugoy Mir through a complicated pagan ritual; a process during which his killers vexed his soul with a potent combination of ancient Norse chants. In his current form, he is a dastardly powerful and corrupt being, and he uses his own essence as a conduit for his evil.

"You think the Vucari are but a simple group of men who have found loyalty to Muka Vechny, my son? Lord, no. They are the hollow, mindless, soulless shells of men and women that fell victim to him during life. Many of them encountered him during yearwalks and other situations that caused them to be pulled into the world of Drugoy Mir.

"With the Vucari, he is building an army of followers; insidiously spreading his reach across the world like a rampant disease. Alas, if he manages to ensnare you in his spectrum of evil, he will suck the essence out of you, siphoning it from your pores like a vapor. The essence satiates him as a hearty meal would a starving man, and magnifies his strength with each new victim.

"What remains of one whose essence is extracted depends on how much of it they possessed to begin with. Someone with a trivial amount may be too weak of mind, body and spirit to survive the aggress, and will simply perish. The entire Koenig family line evidently is made up of Odinians. Being a Koenig, I had enough essence not only to live through Muka Vechny's onslaught, but to retain my sentience and live on in the world of Drugoy Mir.

"When he finds an Odinian, Muka Vechny keeps them restrained in Drugoy Mir with him, whereupon he slowly feeds off their remaining essence through time. This has been my fate since the day Muka Vechny assaulted me on my final yearwalk. A well-deserved retribution for what I did to my family. To you, Edward, and your sister Eva. I cannot allow it to be your fate this time, my son. That is why I came to you on the desolate road that night."

"So, what happened after Muka Vechny caught you in Drugoy Mir? How did Alistair Kendric acquire the Runkavle?"

"When one obtains such a mystical and powerful item as a Runkavle, it remains tied to his being, in this world as well as in Drugoy Mir. When I awoke in Drugoy Mir after Muka Vechny ended my life, I was but a ghost of a man, a fragment of my former self. I found myself trapped inside the desolate and haunting world, but the Runkavle remained in my possession.

"As you may have divined by now, the local church, along with its adjacent cemetery, is the final destination of a yearwalk; the place where one might be endowed with some form of wisdom, or perhaps a mystical object. The keyhole to the church is considered a sacred portal, a junction between worlds if you will. It is believed by some that Drugoy Mir, and the magic that binds it to our world, was created during a Great War betwixt the gods of old. The name Drugoy Mir is of Slavic origin, and it is said that many tales from Slavic folklore are based upon this minatory and callous world. Ancient Slavic culture is rife with parallel world and multi-verse theories, and perhaps, at least this one is true.

"Now, if one blows into the keyhole, he temporarily relinquishes his connection to the traditional Catholic faith, allowing psychic visions of the future to invade his mind. I found that simply blowing into my parish's keyhole had no effect after Muka Vechny had slain me, however, if I slotted the tip of my mystical device into the keyhole, I opened a portal between Drugoy Mir and your world. I found that with this method, I could temporarily drop the shackles that bound me to Drugoy Mir and enter the world of the living.

"I first used this discovery to visit my dear friend, Alistair, the man who had taken in my family and I as if we were his own. A bitter realization awaited me, though. I discovered that the Vucari had reached him first, and were interrogating him as to the whereabouts of my daughter and her unborn child, as well as that of the peculiar scepter of Eindride.

"On a dreary night, I floated into the dank, convoluted cell in which the hooded demons kept him. What I found inside was a destitute, tremulous man lying in bitter anguish upon a heap of rubble. His frame was withered and slight, and upon his face lay a seething mess of boils and fresh wounds. So swollen and bloated was his visage that he was rendered temporarily blind.

"I swooped down and cupped his frail hand in my own. 'I am here, my friend,' I told him, and his shaking subsided. I reached out with the Runkavle and slashed the lock from the gate, and carried Alistair from that cruel prison. Deciding that I no longer had business in the world of the living, it was then that I relinquished my Runkavle to him. I told him to find the lone rider in the night, and make a single wish to him.

"Alas, Muka Vechny's minions are ever vigilant, always searching for something out of place..." Áki Koenig trailed off and stared vacuously, as if he was concentrating on a distant sound.

"I haven't much time now," he exclaimed. "Edward, listen to me; it all hinges on you now. I botched everything when I meddled with an evil I did not understand, all the while holding the key to Muka Vechny's demise in my very hands. You are the key, Edward, and I have faith you will succeed where I have failed."

"I have awaited this moment for a very long time, son." He reached out a pale, languid hand and cupped Koenig's cheek. An icy chill emanated from the old man's touch and spread through Koenig's body, curdling his blood and jarring his nerves. "It's peculiar that you can linger in anticipation for many a year in preparation for a singular moment, only to become stricken dumb in knowing that every word you can say, any idiom your mind can conjure, is vacuous and insufficient.

"I do not deserve an opportunity to apologize for what I have done to you, my son, but I have been afforded it. Please know that all of my actions were done with the best of intentions, for both your sake and that of any other Odinian to which Muka Vechny will give chase.

"My essence was robust in life, but, in the trinity of mind, body and soul, my mind proved the weak link. Had I protected you in your previous life, and allowed you to hone your abilities, perhaps you would have banished the monster from existence long ago and spared the suffering of many. Please Edward," Áki pleaded. "Cherish your daughter, and watch over her as she has watched over you."

In a wash of ethereal light, Áki Koenig materialized into the fog. Streams of diffused light crackled and sputtered as a wave of darkness engulfed the cavern. The old man was gone.

****

The walk back to the cottage was a contemplative one for Koenig. The concept of having been reborn in another life, to a different mother and father, was almost too much for his burdened mind to bear.

"So, I suppose my sister Eva fled from Alistair's Brigand and gave birth to her child. That child must have continued the Koenig family line when he or she grew up."

"Quite correct," said Alistair. "The father you grew up with, George, was your father in this life, but Áki Koenig was your father on your first iteration in life. Does it all make sense to you?" They passed by a gurgling morass that lay embedded between two lengthy fallen trees.

"Yes, I'm making heads and tails of it," was Koenig's reply. "I met a peculiar old woman at the Pinemist Bay Public Library, Doris. I think she was also a prisoner of Muka Vechny's. She had the same strange physical afflictions as Aki, like the muscular spasms, and she gave me a lead that helped put me on the correct path."

"Ah, Doris," Alistair sighed. "That's very perceptive of you, Edward. She was a dear friend of mine during the early days of Brigand. She knew your father Áki as well. Doris moved from Louisiana in 1856, if my memory serves me correctly. That old lady was instrumental in the development of our public services; schools, women's shelter, law enforcement…she filled in all of the holes that I had punctured while trying to build my settlement."

"So, Doris has a Runkavle as well?" asked Koenig. Alistair scoffed at his question.

"My dear boy, happening upon Brynjar Eindride during a yearwalk is immensely rare! And the requisite to having the combined strength, speed, and willpower to snatch the Runkavle from him, is for one to possess a quantity of essence greater than most men. Once one becomes an Odinian, their essence becomes truly immense.

"I had my wish of life extension granted to me because I completed a yearwalk with the Runkavle in my possession. If I were to attempt what Áki was readily able to do, I would fail, sure as you are his son," he said.

"So, someone has been conspiring with Doris and Aki, these long-dead spirits of Drugoy Mir, and allowing them to enter our world," Koenig declared, to which Alistair simply nodded.

"Then what is it about this mystical scepter that allows people to accomplish such things?"

"The mounted man, Brynjar Eindride is shrouded in mystery, even to your father and myself. Some believe he is a descendant of the Norse god of largess and prosperity, Njord. Some say the Runkavle is a piece of the divine spear that once belonged to the Norse all-god Odin. They say that Brynjar is the lone sentinel, the stolid warrior of old, who is waiting for the right time to return the fragmented spear to Odin, and herald the Ragnarök – the great and prophesied future war between the gods of old. What we do know about the man on the massive steed is that he appears to be a neutral force, fighting for neither side in our struggle.

"When your father's essence was extracted by Muka Vechny, morphing him into a phantom of Drugoy Mir, Brynjar must have snatched the Runkavle from your father's dying body and relinquished possession of it back to him in the afterlife," Alistair stated.

"The Runkavle itself, well..." He drew the device from his robes, and Koenig found himself staring in wonderment at it. "I like to believe it is in fact a fragment of the famed spear that belonged to the powerful Norse god Odin, and that Odin endowed it to the god of the sea, Njord, as a gesture of recompense. According to this theory, the Runkavle would have been handed down as a treasured family heirloom, eventually falling into the hands of Brynjar Eindride, who uses it to bestow fortune upon man. That is, should man prove worthy.

"Whether or not any of this is true, I have no knowledge. What we do know of the Runkavle is that it is a powerful totem with which Brynjar grants wishes. It also serves as a sort of portal between worlds, as Áki disclosed earlier. There is some connection between this device and Catholicism, for the sharp end must be thrust into a church keyhole in order to open the portal between worlds.

"Áki and I believe that whichever omnipotent being crafted the world of Drugoy Mir, and devised the mystical act of yearwalking, must have created Brynjar Eindride and the Runkavle as a method of salvation for man. Yearwalking would serve as the test of one's willpower and inner resolve. The psychic visions granted at the end of the divination, as well as Brynjar's scepter, should one be fortuitous enough to obtain it, would both serve as rewards for proving worthy in one's test."

"So, it's clear that Muka Vechny survived being stabbed by the Runkavle the night he killed Áki. What happened to him after that?" Koenig asked.

"He fell into a sort of slumber after that moment. Your father weakened him greatly, and since then he has been relying heavily on his minions, in both this world and Drugoy Mir. He has garnered much of his strength back, however, and we believe he is desperately seeking both you and your daughter, with the intent of consuming your essences and revitalizing his true power.

"You must now see, Edward." Alistair looked at him with a caustic intensity in his eyes. "You are the revenant, the reclaimer, and you must succeed where your father failed, and destroy this insidious evil once and for all."

They retraced their steps back through a wooded area into a clearing, which led to a cobblestone path and a ramshackle cottage. Koenig glanced at the brilliantly aged exterior of the stone house, knowing that at one time, many, many years ago, he trotted around the property as an unassuming child.

"Dalla!" he called, making a beeline straight for his daughter.

"Daddy's back. How was she?" Darlene shot a thumbs-up sign at him and smiled.

"Dalla and I have been getting to know each other a little. Isn't that right, cutie?" She tussled Dalla's hair, who was too preoccupied burying her face in her father's thigh to respond to Darlene.

"She's a sharp kid, Edward," Zach said, still perched near the window. Koenig could tell that the tepid smile on his face was forced. "She seems to have this sixth sense about things." Koenig crouched down to meet his daughter eye-to-eye.

"Yes, I'm very proud of her," he said, steeling himself in her storm-grey eyes. Looking at Dalla for the first time since discovering her true ability, and realizing what she had done to keep him safe through his journey, he entertained a peculiar sensation.

Somehow, Dalla was no longer his baby girl. As he focused his mind, he thought he could see the woman she would grow to become nestled deep in her visage. What he saw was a dignified woman. *Dalla, can you hear me?* The little girl did not reply, but Koenig intuited a confirmation from the way her face flinched and her eyes narrowed.

"Edward," said Alistair. "The Vucari are gathering their strength as we speak. They will come through my hidden passage at any time. We must make use of the time we have."

"What are you planning to do?" asked Darlene.

"Edward will enter Drugoy Mir, and confront Muka Vechny. He is our last hope," Alistair replied.

"Or I will be consumed by him, and allow him to grow all the stronger," Koenig husked. "But I need to find my wife, and bring her back safely. That is my main goal."

"Edward you'll be killed!" Darlene cried, throwing her arms around him. He motioned to Zach to take Dalla out of earshot. He was unaware of how cognizant his daughter was of the situation, but assumed that the conversation might upset her. Zach led Dalla out into the yard to look for flowers, telling her that he thought he could find one to match the color of her eyes.

"I have to try," Koenig said, folding his hands around Darlene's back and feeling the hot sting of tears in his eyes.

"Please be careful, Edward. We've all seen what he is capable of." Darlene followed them out the door and into the twilight. Over the treetops, the sun's strength waned and a stark chill set in the air. Zach brought Dalla over to them and she held out her tiny, pudgy hands toward Koenig.

I have to try to find mommy, but I'll be back darling. I promise. I hope you know that you are the light of my life, Dalla, and that will carry me through. Dalla beamed at him, causing a warm dizzying sensation to pervade his head until the hairs on his neck stood erect.

I love you, daddy. Koenig hugged his daughter one more time as Darlene and Zach stared quizzically at the silent embrace. He stood up, nodding to Zach and Darlene.

"Watch over my daughter, please. I'll be back soon." Their heads waved up and down, and Darlene wiped a stream of tears from her cheek.

She walked over to Dalla and pulled the little girl fast to her body. *Be careful,* she mouthed at him.

Koenig followed Alistair away from the house, not daring to glance back. They took a right at a thick patch of trees and began climbing a gentle slope. Subduing an onset of panic, Koenig paced his eyes from side to side across the scenery. The forest was vacuous and still, and elegiac rays of crimson light peeked between slits in the foliage overhead; a moody harbinger for what he felt was to come.

As he and Alistair walked in silence, a thin breeze stirred through the pines and enveloped Koenig. On the tail end of the air current whisked a delicate voice. *I'm with you, daddy. Always.*

Chapter Fourteen
Drugoy Mir

The tops of the pine trees quivered several yards above, and the water from a nearby brook sliced through the silence of the forest. Night had fallen over the Cascades like a raven-feathered tapestry, and the moon coughed a pale shroud over the rocks and ferns.

The wooded slope that Alistair and Koenig traversed evened out and bled into a wider region of densely overrun terrain. Koenig wondered how far he had gone from his daughter. He wondered if Darlene and Zach would watch over Dalla and protect her in his absence. He yearned to see his wife again; to hold her in his arms and tell her that everything would be alright.

"Are you coming with me to Drugoy Mir?" Koenig broke the silence.

"No," Alistair replied. "I will watch over your daughter. She is a priority target of the Vucari, and to allow her to fall into Muka Vechny's hands would mean the end of us. We will hide in the cellar and await your return. The Koenig residence is nestled deep in the mountains so you should be afforded adequate time while Muka Vechny's minions chew through the ruins of Old Town in search of us."

"I guess that is the best plan given the situation." Koenig shrugged. "Do you know where we're headed? I can barely see a stone's throw ahead of me."

"The moon looms large tonight and throws a meager glow over the forest," said Alistair. "Thankfully, I can traverse this land even on the darkest of nights." In a thicket to the right lay the remains of a small stone hovel; another melancholy remnant of a forgotten world.

"What happened to your people, Alistair?" Koenig asked. "To the people of Alistair's Brigand, once the Vucari came into being?"

"My humble little town was taken from me. Ignominiously I watched, as it slowly evolved from a legitimate coastal trading post to an isolated den of corruption and deceit. The Vucari preferred to stay elusive and discreet during their rise. Much of the town did not know of their existence until they spread their tendrils into each facet of society. Local legislation, law enforcement; they held positions of influence everywhere.

"Many of Muka Vechny's followers went so far as to live amongst the town's inhabitants, as unassuming as any other neighbor on the block. They quietly oversaw the development of my port town, which was eventually renamed 'Pinemist Bay.' They made the Pinemist Hotel; a station with which they can easily and quietly purloin their victims, relinquishing them to the world of Drugoy Mir, and into the voracious grasp of Muka Vechny.

"I was sick at the sight of it all, alas, what could I do? I was reduced to a hunted fugitive, carrying in his possession an item of great value to *Him*. So, I devised a collection of furtive passages with which to move about unseen, and waited for the time when my old friend's wish would come true."

"This morning you had the cloak of the Vucari on. Where did you get that from?" asked Koenig.

"Throughout the many cold and wearisome years which I waited, I was able to sabotage the Vucari from the inside," Alistair stated. "Over the years, I took to isolating, capturing, and interrogating members of the Vucari when I could. This provided necessary insight into the group, as well as gave me a disguise with which to infiltrate them. Just recently I abducted a younger, thus feebler and more impressionable, member of Muka Vechny's clan. William Hanley Wilson was his name.

"I can still very well see the raw terror in his eyes as I thrust him into my dwelling in Old Town. The sweat of his brow sopped to the floorboards beneath, and soon blood followed, as I began to work on him. I tortured the boy not for information, nor for anything valuable that he might give me, but to still the swell of anger, hatred, and bitterness for which my heart had betrayed me." Alistair spoke with a brooding self-contempt.

"I could not abate myself from destroying this man. Precisely how corrupt he had become from joining the Vucari, how much blood was on his hands, I did not know. However, his face gleamed with youth and a flaccid demure that haunts me today. Using the opportunity dispatching a member of the Vucari afforded me, I buried his body but retained his garments. The tactic has once again provided me with a great deal of information regarding the Vucari's whereabouts and plans."

"You've hidden amongst their ranks," Koenig reiterated. "If they had caught you..."

"It was a risk I was willing to take," he said. "It has opened doors for espionage that have proven fruitful. You think Jenny Wilbur and yourself were alone with the Vucari on Blackrock Peak that day?" Koenig's thoughts dashed back to the cold, grey day, and found that Jenny's screams resonated in his mind as vividly as they had then. He knew they would for the rest of his life. He remembered the frantic pursuit by a legion of cloaked figures, recalled nearly being nabbed by one of them just outside the abandoned shack.

"It was you," Koenig said. "You pulled that Vucari away from us and threw him to the ground, just before he caught us." He thought back to the occurrence at Safe Haven with the cloaked figures; how one had called the other Wilson. "And it was you up at Safe Haven that stormy day. You wore Wilson's robes and pretended to be him reporting to the other member of the cult. You've been with me every step of the way."

"We're nearly there now," Alistair segued the conversation. Koenig felt a bubbling sensation of warmth take hold in realizing the amount of people who had been surreptitiously guiding and protecting him in the dark and malicious town. He glanced ahead to see the moon illuminate a passage between two narrow chunks of mountain.

"You guys certainly built a life upon a rugged, mountainous terrain," he suggested, feeling a lash of soreness in his knees. As they stalked through the rocky pass, Koenig's eyes fell upon the ghostly white steeple of an old colonial-style parish. The building was partially buried in a forest of shrubs and tall grass. Its walls were overtaken with a cancerous spread of vines, looking as if the earth were attempting to swallow the ominous structure back into its ripe bosom.

A fervent chill shook Koenig's spine at the sight of the parish. "This is it," said Alistair. "The infamous sight of clairvoyance. Many people have stood where we tread now, and harbored visions of their futures...their family's futures." Alistair ceased his gait for a moment, his frame scintillating in the moonlight.

"I rarely return to this spot," he said. "Too many memories." They approached the building and climbed the gnarled steps to the tall front door. "This is where we part, Edward." He pulled the Runkavle from his robes and held it up. The embellished hilt threw fragments of moonlight in Koenig's eyes. "Remember, the world of Drugoy Mir is a hostile one. It is full of ancient energies and creatures, some of whom might be benevolent, some of whom will tear you asunder...or worse."

"This magical item resonates with Odinians. Keep it on your person at all times," he urged. "It will serve as a beacon for you, as it did your father." Just as Alistair handed the Runkavle to Koenig, a ferocious wind burbled up the pass and sliced through the trees overhead. "Take my robes, too. They will provide more protection than your button-up."

Koenig didn't relish the concept of wearing a dead man's uniform, no matter how long William Hanley Wilson had been dead. He took the heavy cloak and noticed that Alistair was wearing his pristine black suit underneath it.

"Why do you wear that?" he inquired. Alistair glanced down at his clothes curiously, as if he hadn't considered his adornments in some time.

"I suppose customs never die." He shrugged. "This is the same suit I used to wear to events during the heyday of my Brigand. The Vucari never ceased to hunt me, and showing myself in public remained dangerous. However, any event where it was customary to hide one's face, such as the many masquerade balls that were hosted during the early 1900s, I attended in secrecy, as is the procedure at such events.

"But we digress. Now, it's logical to assume that the Vucari will strike under the veil of night." He peered up at the darkening sky. "The clock ticks. Listen, you need to circle the parish in a counter clockwise fashion three times. Then you will thrust the tip of the Runkavle into the keyhole. The portal will remain open for only a matter of seconds, hurry through and do not let your guard down on the other side. Your experience in Drugoy Mir will be unique to you so I can only offer general wisdom. Stay quiet and keep moving.

"With the Runkavle, I believe that you will be able to finish what your father started when he impaled Muka Vechny years ago. If you defeat him, it may rid the curse upon his slaves and restore their essence."

Feeling his body tremble with anticipation, Koenig nodded. He stepped down into knee-high shrubs and began circling the old building. There was no moonlight covering the backside of the parish. His only visual marker was the husky, peeling frame of the building against the moonlit sky. He snaked through the foliage and came around the other side.

"Two more times, my boy," Alistair said as Koenig passed. He felt his heartbeat gyrate harder with each pass.

"Once more." Alistair nodded. "Alright, my boy, now come swiftly and place the Runkavle into the slot. Koenig extended the Runkavle towards the old door, with the blade pointed forward. After fumbling for a moment with the rusty old keyhole, he plunged the tip of the blade into it.

With a deafening crack the parish door melted from view, and an oval-shaped portal enveloped the blank space. Its greenish edges crackled and hissed in a foreboding tune, and a distorted image of the other side materialized before him. He turned to Alistair before entering. "Watch over Dalla, Alistair. Will you do that for me?"

"I will guard her with my life," Alistair hollered. "Now go Edward!" Koenig took a deep breath to steady his nerves, and plunged forward.

For a timeless moment, he tumbled through a vacuous space, as a thousand shards of icy fingers groped along his body. He found himself unable to inhale, or even force the smallest movement of his muscles. Then, as if being sucked from one end of a siphon out the other, he saw an opening just before himself. It began as tiny as a thread of light, which wriggled and contorted into a pulsating circle, and thrust itself upon him with such force that he lost consciousness.

Koenig awoke with the hood of Alistair's cloak blanketing his face. He felt a swathe of cold throughout his body, and a buzzing in his head. He was prostrate on the hard ground. Turning himself over, he gazed upon the diminishing pulses of green light, as the portal to the world closed on him.

"You are in a foreign and hostile world. Get up, and keep the Runkavle close!" Alistair's voice garbled through the air as if it were coming from a distant mountaintop. Koenig heeded his advice and stood erect. He found the Runkavle lying in the dirt beside himself and snatched it up. Turning to face the portal, he saw nothing but darkness in its place. He was now trapped in a disparate and mysterious world, with nothing to guide or protect him.

Feeling his heart slam against his chest, Koenig took in a few shallow breaths. Behind him lay the church, only it wasn't covered in vines and foliage. Around him was a deep and dark forest, but it didn't represent the forest that he had just traversed with Alistair. The trees appeared craggily and disproportionate, forming mutated shapes that stabbed into the shroud of night.

In the forest of Drugoy Mir, no wind stirred through the trees. Nor did an owl hoot, or a bush rustle. All was insidiously still and somber.

Thinking of his daughter awaiting his return, and of his wife languishing in the clutches of an evil spirit, he found the fortitude to tread forward.

He stalked through the desolate forest with only the rhythm of his heart and the rise and fall of his breathing body to carry him. He held the Runkavle firmly against his side, ready to swipe at anyone or anything that might approach him. Nothing did, however. No perceivable threats loomed in the darkness around him, or stalked his steps behind.

Koenig gazed up at the sky and found that there was no moon hovering above. The sky had been burning with the radiant glow of a full moon just minutes before, but transitioning to Drugoy Mir had stripped the world of it, and him, of any such comfort that its light might grant.

He stumbled onwards, feeling a slight downward grade in the terrain. He presumed he was traversing back down the mountainside, but couldn't see enough to determine where he was or if he was even on the same mountain as before.

A bleak, oppressive chill haunted the air and closed in around him. Behind a collection of scrawny, skeletal trees to the left, something stirred. Koenig began to feel the ethereal and devilish sensation that he was being watched. Daring not to look back in the direction of whatever lurked amidst those barren trees, he staunchly drove onward.

As he followed a rough dirt path through the woods, Koenig caught a small commotion once again to his left. Without slowing his gait, he peered over curiously. The forest lay in utter stillness and resolute silence until an erect figure stalked between two thin slices of trees and disappeared from sight once more.

Out of sheer terror, Koenig ceased to move. His blood stanched in his veins and his pulse blazed between his temples. Breaking through the placid demeanor of the forest, was a small sound. Breathing. A grunt that seemed to draw nearer. Before he could summon a thought, Koenig burst into flight. He dipped between limbs of trees and hurdled over any object that stood in his way, until he lost any sense of direction and dove off the small path and into a narrow ditch.

For an unquantifiable amount of time, he lay under the meager cover of the ravine and waited to hear the sound of an inhuman thing stalking the forest in search of him. He visualized the thing reaching down from the path and eviscerating him; his mind careening into a fit of distress.

He glanced left to right. The hood of William Hanley Wilson's cloak sliced his field of vision into sections of lesser and darker black. No footsteps thundered or crept on the path, and no hideous demon crawled along the ditch in either direction. He slowly clawed down a slope that led away from the dirt path, and found himself in a wooded gully.

The moon remained absent from the sky, but a muted light tingled around him. At first, it appeared as if it refracted off the tree trunks and grass with no definable origin, but Koenig found himself enshrouded by a thick mist, which soon betrayed the source of the light.

A small lantern bobbed in the air not two feet from the ground, throwing a ghostly white circle across the narrow gully. Even diffused through the stout mist that hung on the air, the light shone too brightly for

Koenig to peer directly at it. A mixture of fright and curiosity kept him from turning, however, and he slunk down between two sizable rocks as he watched the object bounce closer.

"A newcomer hath tread straight into my lair? Be not shy, young one, I have eyes everywhere," a squealing, ratcheting voice declared. Koenig's heart jerked with such force that he felt it might upheave from his chest and spill out onto the ground. "I saw you, ere you came to my plot. Encumbering your stride, your fear is not," the voice snarled in a rhythmic ramble.

Koenig stood to face the omniscient being. The lantern beamed directly in front of him now, and carrying it was a creature unlike any he had ever seen. A lanky, disproportionate monster stood before him. Its arms stretched well below its knees, and it carried a distended belly that protruded towards Koenig. Instead of skin, it had a hide comprised of a coarse green tissue. The creature wore checkered garments similar to that of a medieval court jester, and covering its face was a lopsided marble-white mask, which had an intoxicating gleam. It reminded Koenig of the tragedian masks that he had seen in theater, and the carved face was turned down in a sorrowful glare.

"Who are you?" he stammered. The masked thing cocked its head to the side, causing the already uneven mask to fall further out of place.

"My dear boy, thou art truly lost," the creature croaked. "Mine eyes cover this forest, the meadow, the moss. Thou mustn't take fright at what thou dost see. Heed what I say, and I shall let thou be." The creature stood with its arms dangling at its sides and its crude belly jutting forward, as it perfunctorily performed its rhyme.

"Thine fear and thine doubt, meager poisons without, a conscience of frailty, despondence and drought. Looketh past the stark image, of this pale and sad visage, and find what thou desires, yearns for, admires."

Koenig thrust himself to the left and gazed past the macabre, theatrical creature and saw two figures looming in the darkness behind. They appeared to be hovering over ten feet in the air, swaying ominously back and forth in a sky devoid of wind. He stepped past the monster, straining his eyes until he could decipher the image.

He saw two people dangling from a high branch of an enormous tree. One body was considerably smaller than the other. Thin ropes were notched around their necks, and the limp bodies reeked of death. Upon stepping closer, Koenig divined that one was an adult woman and the other was a child.

Warily, he took another step, and a fervent boil of anger churned in his head when he recognized their pallid faces. He snatched the lantern from the awkward creature and bathed the hanging bodies in light to confirm their identities. Eveline and Dalla.

Koenig cried out in fury and pain, causing a murmur of reverberations amongst the nearby trees. Overcome by a swell of contemptuous rage, he pivoted in his spot and threw his arms towards the creature. A torrent of air emitted from his hands and drove into the monster with such ferocious momentum that the unsuspecting thing was thrown several feet in the air, whereupon it came down hard and fast upon a bed of rocks.

Koenig stared in utter disbelief. A pool of light from the fallen lantern glittered over his tremulous hands. *What did I just do?*

"My name be Yggdrasil, and I have brooded so long, to find one like thee, an Odinian so strong," the voice continued, only now it emanated from the massive tree from which his family hung, and it had a baritone timbre that made the entire forest tremble.

"What is this?" Koenig cried. "This is not my family, it's just an illusion!" The lifeless bodies continued to sway above him. He couldn't bear to look at the grisly image of his wife and daughter, their usually ruddy faces covered in a sheen of bloodless white. A trail of blood oozed from Eveline's nose, black from oxidation.

"An illusion of mind, of heart and of soul, is what thou doth yet, with sorrow behold. Thou cometh to my lair with an item in tow, this item's unique, I need not see it to know. It hides 'neath thine robes, 'tis vain to conceal it. The power it holds, I sense it, I feel it."

Koenig instinctively groped for the Runkavle, which was resting in a pocket on the inside of his robes. The massive talking tree stood tall against the slope of the gully, its trunk must have been at least twelve feet in circumference.

"What do you want with me, Yggdrasil?" Koenig demanded, feeling a mix of haughty contempt and driving curiosity.

"There is one who doth search for this age-old relic, and an Odinian who wields it, whose power can tell it, to conjure up spells, to open up gates; the Odinian must face him, before it's too late." Koenig glared up at the bodies, assuming that the tree-spirit had conjured them up to illustrate the inference it was making.

"Turn 'round and relish thine eyes, no eschewing. At times our capricious acts be our own undoing." Koenig walked over to the creature with the glaring checkered costume and knelt beside it. The mouth on the mask was horrifically cranked upward into a smile now, as if sneering at him posthumously. In an apprehensive motion led by clumsy, nervous hands, Koenig pried the mask off of the creature.

Gazing up at him were puckered, dead eyes. The face, white as milk and inhumed under a curtain of blood, was not that of the green-skinned monster he saw just moments before, but himself. He averted his gaze, squeezed his eyelids shut, and then looked back feverishly at the sight.

A facsimile of Edward Koenig stared back at him, making him feel as if he was trapped in some abhorrent nightmare. Having seen his wife, daughter, and now himself in this horrid fashion was almost more than his soul could bare. He had never felt so isolated and so destitute in his life.

Daddy? Dalla's voice speared through the tranquil forest and drove Koenig to his feet.

Dalla? Can you hear me? he begged, staring into the dark sky.

Yes, daddy. I'm here with Alistair and Darlene. I can feel the Vucari daddy, I can feel them in my head. They are on their way to get us.

Don't worry, baby. Daddy just needs to do something and then he

will come back, and everything will be back to normal.
Watch out for the man of smoke daddy. He's wicked and he'll trick you, and take you away forever.
I'll be fine, honey. You watch over Darlene and Zach now, my wise little lady. I'll be back before you know it.

Buoyed by a newfound vigor, Koenig glanced once more at Yggdrasil before pushing on. The ghostly illusions of Eveline and Dalla had vanished from the branch, and the massive tree lay silent in the shadows. For the first time since arriving in Drugoy Mir, Koenig detected a minute current of air that streamed past his ears and flowed towards the slope of the gully. He scooped the lantern up and, like a hapless man lost in a cave would, clung to the rush of moving air.

He followed the ethereal breeze out of the gully and into a wood so dense, he was unable to see past the tops of the trees. He came upon a scrubby dirt path and the gentle current of air beckoned him to take it. Jutting out all around him were messes of tangled and sinister branches, and the skeletal trees that lined the path danced in the light of the lantern; their shadows shaking and writhing to and fro.

Not daring to let his hand wander too far from the Runkavle, Koenig continued down the path, which curved in arbitrary and lazy lines about the forest. The lantern was a welcome help, but he found that it afforded him a meager radius of illumination. Even with the added light he thrust his eyes exhaustively from side to side to watch for any threats.

He maneuvered through a tangle of trees and came upon a clearing when a noise broke the steely quiet of night. Like the clap of thunder, the mysterious sound reverberated in Koenig's head. Something shifted in the bushes just off of the path. Then, there was the subtle but ominous sound of breathing. Something lingered nearby.

Just then, Koenig discerned the soft beating of hooves. A large bull moose materialized in the tall grass of the clearing. As it drove toward the path, Koenig's gaze fell upon an aberration in its side. A gash the size of a child's blanket haunted the right side of the beast, from its shoulder to its haunch. Hunks of matted fur surrounded a naked rib cage, and a snake of intestine dangled below its malnourished belly.

The beast had vaporous red eyes that bled light through the darkness. Moving in long and languorous strides, it crossed the glen and came to a halt. Standing in close proximity, Koenig noticed that the creature had no lower jaw, only a gash from which flapped a long and dry tongue.

Koenig shivered spastically as the beast's eyes fell upon his own. It snorted a tuft of silvery breath into the cold mountain air as its head droned from side to side. Perched downwind in the stream of air Koenig was following, it appeared to be studying his scent or searching for that of another creature nearby.

He heard a rustle to the left, followed by a melodic, tortured moan. Not five feet from where he stood, something moved about in the dense grass. The moose's luminous eyes drifted from Koenig and fell upon a shady blob that slithered from the high grass and onto the path. Curious, but not daring to step closer, Koenig eased the lantern forward and found it to be a newborn calf floundering towards the decrepit beast. Letting out a low cry, the bull moose clopped towards it.

Koenig listened as the creatures began to fill the forest with an exchange of somber, dissonant tones that had a faintly musical rhythm. The father moose nudged its calf with a deformed snout, and the eager baby clambered onto its rickety legs in response. As the animals' cries softened, a distant and enigmatic sound tickled Koenig's ear.

Traversing the static temperament of the forest was a fragile, yearning sound. At first, Koenig had to concentrate to hear it, but the sound gyrated through the trees and grew resonant. It was a scratchy and fluctuating tone that matched the rhythm of the animals' cries distinctly. Upon hearing the sound, the bull moose urged the calf down the dirt path towards a cluster of trees.

Koenig trailed patiently behind the struggling calf and its chaperone as they lumbered toward the origin of the sound. The mystery sound grew into a wave of shrill musical notes followed by a collection of low, melancholy ones. It was a string instrument. He followed the peculiar animals into the wooded area beyond the clearing, whereupon he heard the silvery ramble of running water.

They came to a patch of land where a mossy bank was split in two by a gently flowing river. About thirty paces upstream was a frothy, virulent waterfall, roughly twelve feet in height. It spewed strings of glossy water into the air, which crashed down against a rocky outcropping and jettisoned downstream with bubbly fortitude.

Laden with fatigue, the baby moose collapsed a few feet short of the river. The bull moose leaned down, its long tongue unfurling from its deformed jaw, and gently pushed the calf on until the little creature's snout came in contact with the water's edge. It began lapping voraciously at the frothy liquid. Koenig peered left, his gaze fastening to the waterfall upon seeing a wavering figure inside it. The music emanated from whatever stood there.

He eased himself toward the ominous cascade and found the figure to be a man. He was of great stature, naked from head to toe, and kneeling underneath the waterfall on a great slat of rocks. Long strings of sopping hair clung to the man's face, and Koenig could divine nothing of his features, save for a long angular nose that jutted out from under his locks.

The powerful figure played vivaciously on an archaic violin, managing to drown out the thunderous water as it clapped on his back and on the rocks surrounding him. The flow and crash of the water seemed to emulate the temperament of his playing, as if the equivocal man controlled its very nature. When his strings resonated with a grandiose tune, the water would foam and curl and throw itself about. When he performed a sorrowful, slow lament, the flow of water would recede and hush.

Watching this enigmatic character perform, Koenig began to view the river as a giant, petulant baby; the musician, its assuaging father. Koenig found himself enamored with the lone figure's remarkable gift and aura. The weight of his cloak doubled as it soaked up rogue splashes of cold water, but he took no heed.

The fugue came to a close with a collection of solemn notes, at which point the stream attenuated and the musician raised his head. Koenig leaned forward. The man's face still obscured by pale clumps of hair, he appeared to be surveying the area.

In a slow, composed motion the man gazed upward, speckles of water accruing on his beard and neck. He wiped the glossy bow of the violin on his thigh and then poised it against the strings.

"Excellent," the man said in a tone of slate. With such a commanding presence, Koenig assumed he might be so aplomb in a burning room. "Water is the only salve for a beast who grazes in a hurricane." The man's head drooped toward the silvery rocks lining the cascade.

"What storm has swept this traveler from the verdant womb of life to a land whose only caretaker be the despotic maiden of neglect? He carries with him an easing burden; for each step he takes, his naivety drains like a decanter tipped by his trenchant spirit."

"You're playing...it attracted the animals," Koenig said. "And now they drink from a river you created."

"The father is very sick. His only tether to this existence is his calf, whose eyes are merely opening." The man appeared to brood over a thought for a moment, then resumed playing.

"Who are you?" Koenig inquired.

"I am one of the remaining shepherds of this land; a servant of the fjord and stream, and protector of souls. Fossegrim is what they used to call us." His arm moved back and forth weaving an elegant, swooning song into the air. "I call this piece Nocturne av Måne," he said before becoming encompassed once more in his craft.

Shafts of light crept over the trees, burning pale and strong on the river. A monolithic moon slid into the sky. Downstream, the calf continued to lap at the water while the bull moose craned its deformed head skyward. A single beam of light enveloped the beast, and what Koenig witnessed made his jaw drop.

Ethereal as a wisp of dust in a gale, the bull moose's body began to disintegrate and float skywards. Fragments of the animal danced about and glowed as they ascended the light shaft. Before it fully evaporated, the animal collapsed onto its legs and it gave the calf a final nudge, longer and more tender than the previous ones. The baby let out a wail as its guardian disappeared into the night.

Under the cascade, the sweeping melody strengthened into a climax and the Fossegrim became engulfed by the burbling wall of water. The moon wavered overhead, causing the light beam to shift and concentrate on the lone calf. Apparently stimulated by the moonlight, Koenig watched in awe as the creature struggled to its feet. Without hesitation, the calf pivoted on clumsy legs and wandered off into the forest.

As the musical piece drew to an end, the flow of water ebbed and revealed the Fossegrim once more. Koenig dropped the drenched lantern. The need for it diminished with the appearance of the moon.

"That bull moose had such tender compassion for its offspring. I thought everything I'd find in Drugoy Mir would be hostile and sinister." Koenig said.

"This place need not be so dichotomous from that whence you came," the Fossegrim bellowed. "You hold tenaciously to your desires, young one. And where there has been frailty in will, there is strength in spirit. There are those who would trump that strength, however, and exploit such a rare gift. Come forward, young one."

Koenig obliged the demand and cautiously stepped onto a rock just beneath the musician. "Give me your right hand," the Fossegrim said with clout. Furtively clutching the Runkavle with his left hand, he stretched out his right, and the man clamped his own giant, muscular fist around it. The Fossegrim jerked Koenig toward himself with such tremendous force that Koenig's feet temporarily lost contact with the ground.

He guided Koenig's hand further, placing it over the worn strings of his violin. Standing just a breath away from the instrument, Koenig discerned a tinge of dark red that ran down the strings, and cringed when he realized what had caused the discoloration.

The Fossegrim tightened his grip and thrust Koenig's fingers upon the bridge of the instrument. In a frenzied motion, the creature slid Koenig's fingers across the strings. A sound like fabric tearing into strips pierced Koenig's ears, followed by a searing pain in each of his fingers. Resisting the urge to scream, he found himself unable to retract his hand as the Fossegrim ran his fingers back over the body of the instrument.

A second wave of paralyzing agony shot through Koenig's hand. Though he pulled with all his might, he was unable to escape. The Fossegrim scraped his raw hand across strings coated in fresh, glistening blood, until Koenig's entire body started to flail back and forth from the momentum. At the height of the torment, the violin began to shake and vibrate, humming a discordant ballad that heightened Koenig's anguish.

He looked in horror at his blood-smeared hand as it raked back and forth across the instrument. Accumulating on the strings were scalloped bits of flesh, and Koenig feared the monster would soon begin to chisel away at the bone beneath. His head screamed with pain, and right as he felt he was losing consciousness, the deranged musician stopped. All fell silent, save for the din of running water.

The enormous man released him. He collapsed to his knees and then rolled onto his back as tremulous spasms overtook his body. A fuzzy tingle ran up and down his spine and through his limbs, while a concentration of explosions went off in his hand. After some time and with immense fortitude, he managed to steady his breathing. He clasped his left hand around his wrist and pulled the damaged fingers into view.

The shaking, shimmering pockets of flesh before him looked more like a descaled fish than a human hand. Koenig tried to cry out, to demand a reason for the creature's capricious turn to violence. A lump in his throat prevented any noise from escaping, however, and he was forced to gaze up at the Fossegrim with bitter, tortured eyes.

The musician raised his own prodigious and muscled hand through the raging torrent of water, pointing toward the river's edge.

"Dip your hand into my river, young one." His mighty timbre displaced the falling water around him, shooting jets of the frothy liquid upon the rocks. Curious but still wary, Koenig stumbled to his feet.

"Wh…why?" he stammered, clutching his arm.

"If one's will be strong enough, he might procure something from the silvery waters of my cascade." Koenig trudged to the side of the river and peered into the rhythmic flow of the water. "Pierce the surface with your right hand, young one. And only into the frenzied waters of the current, not the pockets of still water on the river's edge."

Watching the wavering sheen of the moon on the surface of the water, Koenig wondered what he might find in a body of liquid that is constantly dispersed and supplanted in an endless cycle. He timidly poked his raw hand into the river, lavishing the fresh, gelid sensation that overtook his arm.

Blood was purged from the wounds and began spreading in gooey tendrils through the water. Koenig's jaw dropped in amazement as the murky fluid coagulated, turning the volatile river into a static surface. He felt the voracious pain that had eaten his hand dissipate, and an image began to materialize on the still surface. At first it appeared abstract and dull but, like puckered stars in a darkening sky, it slowly intensified.

He gazed upon the wavering image of tall, bare trees standing in a hollow. Gleaming amongst the trees was a passageway of some sort, with a huge wooden door that looked as if it was sinking into the ground. It reminded Koenig of the Tomb of the Irremediable.

"Remember that upon which you gaze, for it is the place your heart seeks with an indomitable fire," the Fossegrim said. Then, like a dam breaking a levy, the cascade began to crash and churn until it flowed over the mysterious blood-soaked image. Koenig shot a glance at the waterfall in time to see the musician sink behind it and out of sight.

"Wait! I have more que—" He withdrew his hand from the river and was astonished to find the wound not only completely healed, but devoid of any signs of tissue damage.

"What the fuck?" He was flabbergasted. "Are you there, musician?" he yelled into the barbarous wall of water. No response, just patches of moonlight hovering over the waterfall.

Daddy, Dalla's voice pierced his mind.

Dalla! he gasped. *Are you okay, baby?*

Yes daddy, but the bad men are coming! They're in the dark and scary place, and they're breaking through to come get us. Somebody is leading them through the dark place. He saw you coming up here and knows how to get through Alistair's hiding spot.

"Dark and scary place—Alistair's hiding spot, they've made it to the Tomb of the Irremediable," he cursed. "I'm running out of time!" He closed his eyes, focusing on his daughter.

Alright, Dalla. Listen to daddy. Stay put. Do not leave Alistair's side; he will protect you. Daddy will be back soon, okay?

Please hurry, daddy. I'm scared, she said, her soft voice squeaking.

I will darling, he promised.

He drove his heels into the ground and climbed a low knoll next to the waterfall, his drenched garments trailing loosely behind. The continuation of the forest loomed ahead, oppressive and terrifying. He was uncertain which route to take in the foreboding labyrinth of trees that enveloped him, but he knew that if he wanted to save his daughter and the others, he needed to move fast.

He pushed on, the pale glow of the moon lacing through the treetops and fortifying his steps. He submerged into a dense thicket in which the pine trees appeared mutated and swollen, like gnarled, tumorous giants. Unkempt strands of grass nabbed at his knees, and he had to fight to find purchase through the foliage.

As he stumbled into the center of the thicket, he heard a low murmur. He stepped forward. A chuckle. He ducked under a tangle of branches and emerged in a bald pocket of the copse. Sprawled out before him was the body of some sort of creature, its upper back propped against a mangled trunk.

It looked old, like a decaying mummy long forgotten on the shelf of a cold, dry tomb. Wiry shreds of hair drooped over an angular, argentine head. A lanky, spindly body lay beneath. The thing was lacking a face, save for small gashes where eyes used to be, and a small puckered orifice for a mouth. It was fascinating, grotesque, unnerving, and pitiful all at once.

"You'll never make it out of here." The thing slowly tilted its head toward Koenig, who jumped, half expecting it to be long dead.

"What?" It let out a few hoarse chuckles before replying.

"It's your first time in Drugoy Mir. I know, I can tell."

"Everyone seems to have some sort of insight here." Koenig shrugged. "I can't make heads or tails of it; but I'm in a hurry, and lives are at stake. What are you? And why are you here?"

"I am a Leshy," it coughed.

"A Leshy?" The creature nodded.

"A spirit and guardian of the forest. I once was this, but that was before He entered our domain and cast his treacherous pall over it."

"He?" Koenig asked. "Meaning Muka Vechny?"

"The one you seek, yes. The man of smoke and mirrors who laid a ponderous seed of evil within this land many centuries ago."

"Every step I've taken in this place has echoed with a sense of evil. It's like one big rotting nightmare. Is this all his doing?"

"Drugoy Mir was once a place of great wonder and enchantment, brimming with spirits benevolent in nature. Legend tells that long ago, the powerful Norse deities known as the Aesir and the Vanir joined together to create this land," the Leshy continued with visible ardor.

"They were spirits of godlike status to you mortals; divine givers of wisdom, magic, fertility, and future sight. The Vanir created this world as a link between your world and their own worlds, chiefly: Vanaheim and Asgard. They called the world that surrounds you now, Andravärld."

"I thought it was called Drugoy Mir?" Koenig asked.

"It was given that moniker after a group of foreign deities from the Slavic pantheon invaded, but before then, it was called Andravärld. This was once a place where man might abscond to and divine knowledge of his future, of his actions and their consequences, of the nature of his plight, and perchance, to enlighten him with ways in which to ameliorate his woes and aid his brethren. It was a place where man might come seeking the counsel of the gods, beseeching them to provide him with the tools and the knowledge he needed to thrive in his own world.

"The Norse deity largely associated with fertility, nature and the land, Freya, created much of this world, including the aspects that would welcome and comfort man. Freya had a propensity towards selflessness and the betterment of others. She was also one of the gods primarily associated with Seidr, which is a type of shamanism and prophecy man likens to sorcery. Seidr comes in many forms, but it is often achieved with a type of meditation where one travels in their mind through the cosmos, picking up a degree of clairvoyance or some piercing insight on their journey.

"It is understood that Seidr was given to the gods by the Norn: three ancient and omnipotent witches who first discovered the runes, the same symbols prevalent in Norse history, and unlocked the magic residing within these symbols. It is not known why the gods practiced Seidr, but it's known that Freya helped create this land to impart upon man a way to search for the answers to his questions; to provide answers to life's mysteries. Årsgång, or yearwalking, is one method of divination Freya bestowed upon humankind.

"Njord was master of the sea and of crop fertility. Early Norsemen depended on this deity to bring them bountiful yields every spring. He and his wife, Nerthus, cared for and satiated man in harmony, and within Andravärld, they bore a child: Brynjar Eindride."

"Brynjar Eindride," Koenig interjected. "The man on the mount...I've heard of him."

"But the relationship between the Vanir and man could only last in harmony for so long. Legend has it that a group of deities worshipped by the people of Eastern Europe invaded this sacred land, jealous of the Vanir and their symbiotic relationship with man. Like the Norse gods, these Slavic gods have their own worlds surrounding yours, but in order to influence man directly, they must first have control over the Tree of Life, known in Northern Europe as Yggdrasil.

"The gods in the Slavic pantheon have long warred with the Norse gods over the Tree of Life, and at times when they had a strong foothold, they created their own unique and intriguing ways to interact with man. Theomancy was one way the Slavic gods communicated with humans, choosing a particular man or woman as a vessel through whom their messages could be sent.

"When the Slavic gods invaded Andravärld in an attempt to drive the Norse gods away from the world of man, and away from the Tree of Life, a titanic battle ensued. Fighting against the Vanir was Morena, the Slavic god of witchcraft, death, and winter; Svarog, the god of fire and forgery, who outfitted his brethren with the tools needed to battle the Vanir; Czernobog, the god of darkness and death; and Svetovid, the god of war and fertility, who heralded the first battle charge.

"It is prophesied that a great war between the gods shall come once more in the future, one in which the Norse gods will clash with the Slavic gods to regain what they lost all those years ago. This prophesied war is known as Ragnarök, and it is perceived to be the war to end all life as you know it. But some believe that Ragnarök was actually this previous conflict between the gods, and that the gods are forever done fighting over man. Evidence to the latter speaks to the device you carry on your person, the one that I have already referenced. You see, leading the fight against the Vanir was Perun, the Slavic all-god, who wielded the power of lightning and thunder.

"On the day of battle, Perun conjured up a mighty storm with his axe and led the charge. He alone was powerful enough to challenge the Norse all-god Odin, and it is said that during the duel he shattered Odin's spear with a bolt of lightning, severing the tip from its stock. Nobody knows what happened then, but it is speculated that the great and powerful Odin fled the battlefield that day, surrendering control of Andravärld and of the Tree of Life to the Slavic gods.

"Having witnessed their supreme ruler defeated, the remaining Vanir fled the realm as well. But, Njord's son, Brynjar Eindride remained, and he furtively took in his possession the tip of Odin's fabled scepter which, even in its fragmented condition, retained some of its enchanted power. Eindride carried with him Odin's relic evermore, riding upon his great steed with such celerity that gods and monsters alike couldn't catch him. He presents the Runkavle as a gift to men who have the forbearance to take it from him as he rides by on his agile steed. I view this gesture as the one benevolent remnant of a bygone era; Brynjar's decision to ride on tirelessly for man's sake. Furtively, he continues to help mankind, even if he might meet man but a few times per millennium.

"The Runkavle became a totem with which to aid man in his life, to help him when the Vanir had failed him. A single wish is to be granted to any man brave and powerful enough to retrieve the Runkavle from Brynjar. You see, man has long turned to gods and sorcery to cure his ills and mollify his woes, and through this method, Brynjar has surreptitiously been involved in man's prosperity for a great while.

"Think back in history, boy. Why do you think the Dark Ages came to an end at the close of the first millennium? Wherefore did the Bubonic Plague end, and how did the Age of Enlightenment come about? What influenced the great Arthurian tales of old; the venerable armored knights on steeds therein? What mystical relic inspired the creation of the legendary sword Excalibur itself; what relic inspired the sword in the stone, which might only be extricated by a person who proves worthy enough to wield it? Sound familiar to you? These tales are all based upon that very item that lingers in your robes, boy.

"History shows that man has forgotten him, and very few ever knew of him to begin with, but knowledge of Brynjar and the magic scepter of Odin have long inspired stories among men, and the wishes he has granted your kind has aided them in ineffable ways. As for Odin himself, the great Norse god whose spear was lost to him, they say he's back in his own realm, where he lies in wait for one to return the missing pieces of his scepter to him, thus fortifying him with the power to take back control of his realm, and rule over man and the Tree of Life once more.

"As the influence of Slavic all-god Perun and his fellow deities waned, this land plummeted into disarray, becoming poisoned with the unthinkable creatures and demons that now pervade Slavic folklore. People started to call it Drugoy Mir, or Otherworld.

"After the evil Muka Vechny became bound to Drugoy Mir by a powerful curse, his treacherous influence permeated the land. He began to use the humans who entered Drugoy Mir to his own advantage, stealing the very essence that the Vanir bestowed upon them and using it as sustenance while he searched evermore for one powerful enough to break him free of his curse.

"That is where you come in," the Leshy suggested. "That item in your cloak is new to you, is it not?" Koenig brandished the Runkavle, causing a sharp inhale from the creature. "I thought I would never look upon it with my own eyes," the Leshy exclaimed. "Some believe this is the missing piece that will hail the Ragnarök which, as I previously mentioned, results in the end of this desecrated world and the birth of a new cosmos. The vengeance of Odin shall be fulfilled. Look at it, young one. Even in its cleaved and mangled form, the Runkavle is such a sight. Those carvings on the blade and shaft aren't mere illustrations or adornments, they are from a lost language of ancient runes indecipherable to man. Runkavle was a name bestowed upon the device by men, but its real name is Gungnir, and it once housed within its slender metal frame much of Odin's power."

The word Gungnir reverberated around Koenig, and the trees shook as a great gust blew through them, as if the forest was showing that it remembered the name. "So how does the Runkavle, or Gungnir, create a portal between the real world and Drugoy Mir?" Koenig inquired.

"When the Vanir bestowed man with wisdom and knowledge, another belief system came into being that threatened the Vanir's influence upon man: Christianity. This form of monotheistic worship pervaded Europe and diminished the relevance of the traditional Northern teachings.

"In a cunning move, the Vanir used sacred Christian domains, such as local town parishes, as objects upon which man would gaze to receive visions of the future. In doing this, the Vanir encouraged non-believers to defy the Christian way, and solidified a level of influence and remembrance among communities for generations to come.

"Since the Runkavle was originally Odin's scepter, and he was the primary creator of this realm, the blade itself can act as a key, while the church serves as the door."

Daddy! Dalla's voice surged with a force that seemed to shake the surrounding trees. *They're searching Old Town for us. They'll be here soon!*

"You are running out of time," the Leshy appeared to be reading Koenig's mind. "I will take you to that which you seek."

"You can show me the way to Muka Vechny?" The languid creature stood upright and nodded to Koenig, its silvery skin shimmering in the moonlight. It turned and pushed through the thicket.

"Follow me," the Leshy said. Koenig slowly trailed the slender, silhouette-like creature through the woods and into a gulch where they became enveloped in a dewy mist. The walls of the narrow canyon were comprised of rock, and massive outcroppings spliced the canyons together overhead. A smattering of lichen coursed through the rock structures, and oddly shaped trees loomed in the darkness above.

"Why are you helping me?" he asked the Leshy.

"You are one worthy of my assistance," it hissed over a slim, gray shoulder. At the base of the gulch, the creature passed under the low hanging branch of a pine tree and paused. It craned its neck and, with a fervent passion that caused its arm to tremble, reached toward a string of sap that dangled from the branch.

"This land was once worth saving," the Leshy tenderly stated, more to itself than to Koenig. It dabbed the globule of sap on its finger and presented it to Koenig. Specks of grey dappled the congealed substance. The Leshy retracted its frail arm, sniffed the sap, and then noisily sucked it through its clumsy mouth.

"The vegetation here is withering away and rotting at the roots; like a plague spreading silently across a village," it said. "We're nearly there." He could see what the Leshy meant. All of the trees and shrubs appeared sickly. Thin black lines, like spider legs, needled up the trunks and disseminated into the leaves.

The clustered walls of the gulch unfurled and gave way to a brilliant hollow of skeletal trees. The atmosphere felt instantly heavy and stale upon entering, and Koenig found himself heaving and sputtering on the air. The silence of Drugoy Mir was magnified in this isolated pocket of land. The juicy throbbing of Koenig's heart the only sound, driving an underlying rhythm of dread.

The Leshy turned to Koenig with a look upon its silvery face that told him it would go no further. "You will find what you seek, Odinian," it said as it raised a brittle arm toward the trees. Koenig nodded. A breeze stirred and moaned, weaving a path amidst the desolate sentinels. The Leshy turned and hobbled back into the gulch.

A stream of leaves rattled on the ground and took flight, churning through the mist before him. He clutched the Runkavle under his robes and stepped forward.

Daddy! They're coming up the mountain! He closed his eyes and focused, smoothing out the tattered edges of his frayed mind.

I'm here, baby. Stay with Alistair, and I'll be back soon!

He watched as trees materialized ahead of him. At first they appeared as barely discernible outlines, then they came into focus and floated past, dissolving into the mouth of the mist behind him.

After passing several rows of trees, he saw a shadow poke through the haze. The thing looked minatory and dark, sitting squat on the ground. As he shuffled closer, he saw that the thing looked protracted, as if it was leaning back into the darkness and staring at the night sky. He saw a shiny object protruding from its surface, and discerned the gruff texture of wood. It was the door from the Fossegrim's illusion.

He walked beside the large door and gazed upon the frame. A

collection of stones bolstered the entrance in its semi-vertical state, and plunged at an angle into the ground. The structure looked nearly identical to the Tomb of the Irremediable's entrance.

Koenig thought back to when he entered Drugoy Mir and remembered seeing the church, which seemed to have made the journey through with him from the real world to this one. Perhaps Drugoy Mir was a like a ghostly illusion, a different dimension thrust over the real world, like a shade drawn over a baby's stroller, and all of the landmarks were still there, in some form or another. He remembered Darlene's description of the woman she had seen, the catatonic figure who was in the middle of a yearwalk.

Maybe one simply occupies both spaces at once.

He hesitated in front of the large oak door for a while. Whatever Muka Vechny was, whatever the future held for Koenig and his family, waited beyond that door. He could feel it. He reached for the handle with a steadiness and sureness that surprised him, and pulled the ponderous door open. It yawned and cracked, and fell upon its decrepit hinges, hitting the ground with a resonant thunder.

Chapter Fifteen
Deliverance

Please God let Eveline be in here, Koenig thought.

He stepped into a sheet of black and, one cautious foot at a time, wandered down the echoing stone steps. Clammy air collapsed on him and filled his nostrils with a stale scent. There was a dirty metallic tinge to it as well, like the putrefied smell that hung on the air the night he first saw Áki Koenig.

As he stepped into a hearth of black, blinding flashes of light erupted. All around him, torches inhaled life and licked striations of light along the ancient passage. Something, or someone, was waiting. He continued down the hall, nervously watching every nook and corner that was covered in shadow.

The narrow passage unfolded into what looked like the crypt where Zach's sister was killed. The walls were lined with archaic wooden caskets perched in large cutouts. The layout of the chamber was almost a facsimile of the Tomb of the Irremediable, save for a long mahogany table that lay to his left.

He stepped into the room and drew back his hood. Something shuffled in the darkness.

"Ed...Edward?" a familiar voice called. He scrambled to the center of the chamber. Veiled in shadow, he clutched intrepidly at the figure. He palmed long strings of matted hair that rested against a soft breast. His fingers danced upward and cupped a warm, soft cheek, the contours of which were instantly familiar.

"Eveline?" he cried.

"I can't...can't believe it's you. I thought you were another one of them." Her voice sounded tired and hoarse. He craned his head forward and nuzzled her cheek.

"Oh baby, I'm never going to leave you again," he said, feeling a tepid stream of tears trail down his face. "I'm so sorry, honey." He walked to a near wall, snatched a torch off its perch, and bathed his wife in the light. His heart plummeted at what he saw.

In a horrific semblance of Zach's sister, Eveline was tied fast to a tall wooden stake. She had on her coral nightgown, which she must have been wearing when the Vucari captured her. The material was tattered and blotched, and her frame underneath looked languid and malnourished. Her face was worn and bruised, and smattered with bits of days-old blood. On her countenance was a look of joy and hope, precariously hovering under eyes that showed horror and despair.

"What have they done to you?" he asked. "Oh Eveline, baby, I've got to get you out of here."

"He's here," she whispered. "You need to leave, Edward. Where's Dalla?"

"She's safe, baby." Koenig reached for her binds when he felt the tingling sensation of another presence lurking nearby. A shadow moved in his peripheral vision. He craned his neck to the left and gazed in horror upon the wretched sight.

Long, bubbling, hissing tendrils of black unfurled from the far corner of the room. Darker than the shadows that possessed it, the oscillating shape spread toward the long table and evanesced back into the darkness like an ill-mannered vapor, only to be replaced by more seething tentacles. A body of black, from which the tentacles appeared to spawn, wavered forward.

Inside the vacuous ether, a moon-white shape surfaced. Like the diffused beam of a lighthouse in a gale, the shape strengthened as it drew closer. A faint outline materialized as the pale silhouette unburied itself from the billowing curtains of smoke.

It was the figure of a man. He was large in stature and glowed an immense blue-white that was hellish to gaze at amidst the vaporous black that ensnared him. Bald and naked, the man stepped forth. The effervescent smog trailed after him, emanating from his figure like steam from a moving train.

The man's features were abominable. His face was a disjointed and mangled heap of tissue untenable for any normal human expression. His body was a contorted and deformed sprawl of muscle and bone. Koenig turned to face the figure, his very bones rattling.

"Acquirit qui tuetur," the thing said. "Do you know what it means?" Koenig said nothing. "It means, 'he who preserves something, will have something.' I have preserved but the stoutest of faith in the belief that, eventually, you would find me. Edward Tuija Koenig," the thing said, it's face rolling into a grotesque smile. "It has been a very long time."

"I...I've never met you before," Koenig replied. "But my father, Áki Koenig, has. You destroyed his life, Muka Vechny. You drove him to kill me, and to attempt to kill my sister. You spawned an army of followers from the seed of your evil, and have incarcerated my mother unjustly, leaving her to suffer and waste away in the Ambrose Asylum."

The glowing figure stepped forth and sank into a chair. He propped his elbow on the table, and continued to glare at Koenig with a voracious anticipation on his face. "The despondency of life stems from the indubitable and unshakable fact that it is fleeting. We cling helplessly to loved ones, pay our tithes at church, dither about in our daily toils...anything to forget our inevitable end.

"We look upon death with a tenacious fear. From our youth, we realize the tenuous frame upon which life is built. To most of us, life is but a candle in a maelstrom. However, somewhere in his rudimentary faculties, man manages to disregard the one true virtue of existence."

Muka Vechny gazed upward, the tendons in his neck bulging, and inhaled sharply into the thick, murky air. "The precarious balance in which it hangs is the quality of human life that makes it relevant. What I wouldn't give to possess the feeling; to lavish the taste of brevity." His glare returned to Koenig. "You shall be my succor, Edward."

"I don't owe you anything, you monster!" Koenig shouted, feeling a blazing swathe of resentment develop in his heart.

"Miserable wretch of a man! You know not the breadth of your transgressions!" The burbling cloud surrounding Muka Vechny bloomed outward as he bellowed, extinguishing the torches and wrapping the chamber in near total darkness. The only source of light that remained was the pale figure of Muka Vechny, which enlivened the chamber walls with a wavering resonance.

"Don't listen to him Edward, he's psychotic. You need to leave now!" Eveline pleaded through the darkness.

"I'm not going anywhere without you, baby." Koenig said.

"Allow me to impart my tale to you, Edward Koenig," Muka Vechny said, still seated imperiously at the table. "I have waited many long, arduous years to do so."

"Don't...don't listen to him, Edward," Eveline sounded desperate.

"You fucking demon! What did you do to my wife? Why is she tied up like this?" Koenig felt his anger reach a pinnacle, and subconsciously found himself grasping for the Runkavle. Muka Vechny seemed to notice and, with hideous agility and might, lunged forward. The black vapor that surrounded the monster gathered in a plume and then spiraled toward Koenig with ferocious speed. He could see it approaching through the ethereal glow of its master's body, but he dodged too late.

The vapor assaulted his body with tremendous force and threw him against the cold stone wall with a resounding crunch. Although her voice sounded as if it was a great distance away, Koenig could hear Eveline hollering his name. He raised his head and tried to shake off a cumbersome dizziness.

Before his eyes danced a pale white image that flowed from one side of his vision to the other in ghostly trails. The more he tried to focus on the image, the more his head swelled with a splitting pain. Muka Vechny was directly in front of him, merely a breath away. He could smell him.

"Oh Edward, your longanimity amazes me. What you had to do to get this far; the hurdles you've had to overcome. It's commendable, actually. All that was required of us was to uproot your wife and daughter from their cozy Chicago dwelling, and your true forbearance was revealed. Edward Koenig transformed from an unfaithful coward to the stalwart hero."

Koenig felt his equilibrium normalizing, but noticed a shooting pain emanating from his lower back. He began to fear that his spine was broken, and that he had suffered a concussion. Letting out a tortured grunt, he focused on the image in front of him.

The face of his enemy was clearer now. Hovering in a canvas of black, Muka Vechny was leering hungrily. Koenig's thoughts eked; his head, a threshold of pulsations and gyrating pains. The vaporous cloud was still folded tightly around him, keeping him flush against the wall. His feet were dangling above the ground, but he couldn't move them. He mustered an effort to free his arms, but they were inextricable from the stone wall. He was a hapless prisoner to a vengeful madman. Gradually, the pain from the collision attenuated and a lather of numbness began to spread from his head down. He noticed Muka Vechny's pale glow begin to surge and intensify, casting brilliant shards of light across the room.

Daddy, Dalla pierced into his mind. *They're close now. They'll find us soon.*

"Dalla," he said aloud, to which Muka Vechny retreated slightly.

"Dalla," Muka Vechny repeated. "Yes, the beloved daughter. The last Odinian."

Don't let him get in your mind, daddy. He's gonna try to hurt you.

A mild pressure gnawed at Koenig's head.

"Now that I have your undivided focus, my discourse can begin," said the monster. "You know me simply as Muka Vechny, which is appropriate, for it is the moniker that you gave me. Do you know what it means? It's Russian for eternal torment." The tension in Muka Vechny's face tapered and an ephemeral sadness swept over his visage, as if he was reliving an almost forgotten memory.

"In the early 8th century Ivan and Anya Petrov fled the Eastern Slavic state of Kievan Rus' during a brutal Mongol invasion. They came upon the beautiful and tranquil mountains of Sweden, where they and many other emigrating Slavs settled down and started a new, more auspicious life.

"The Petrovs lived amongst a sprawl of shambles outside the palace of Sigurd, King of Sweden. There, the necessitous couple birthed a son and named him Afonos Petrov. To their repugnance, the child was a miserable and unhealthy wretch, with such physical deformations that Ivan and Anya wanted naught to do with him.

"Living amongst the Scandinavian peoples, the Petrovs learned many customs foreign to their eastern norms. Among these was the wretched and inhuman custom of infanticide. If one was unable to provide for their child, or simply deigned not to care for it anymore, they would carry the baby deep into the forest, leaving it to perish in the elements.

"So, in the cold heart of winter, the abhorred couple carried the insalubrious boy deep inside the King's forest and abandoned him there with nothing but a thin blanket upon his person. Presently, a councilman to the king by the name of Edward Koenig ventured into the forest to hunt game with the king's brigade. He happened upon the pitiful, sobbing creature lying upon on a swathe of snowy ground.

"Koenig bade his king and his fellow councilmen to look upon the eerie sight. His highness became horrified by the repulsive thing, and instructed Koenig to terminate the child with the drawing of an arrow. Lord Sigurd then promptly retreated into the forest to gaze upon less unpleasant things, leaving the councilman to do his bidding.

"Koenig drew his arrow and aimed it at the wretch, but found he could not complete his task. The more he stared at the child languishing in the cold, the more he found that he felt an intoxicating sympathy for it. Dismissing the king's orders, he took the baby and raised it as his own in secrecy.

"The little boy's appearance caused his very own parents to estrange him at birth, and made him a social outcast in the noble society in which Edward Koenig raised him. But Koenig had the humanity to care for him. He was the single person who showed young Afonos affection and support, and he wouldn't allow the child into the city for fear that the king would have the boy killed, and have Koenig banished for directly dismissing an order. Afonos held his adoptive father in the highest regard, and depended on him for his guidance and education.

"By the time Afonos matured into a young man, Edward Koenig had become head of commerce for Lord Sigurd, and began making frequent trips outside the castle, leaving Afonos destitute and lonesome. Koenig traded goods with the villages surrounding the kingdom, and it was at the neighboring village of Dödkärr where he was taught the old Seidr tradition of yearwalking. And it was within the world of Drugoy Mir that he extricated the Runkavle from mighty Brynjar Eindride.

"Koenig returned home with the mystical item in his possession, but he kept the Runkavle away from young Afonos, frightened of its power, and afraid that the boy might hurt himself or someone else with it. One day, when Edward was in the next village over, Afonos's curiosity got the better of him; his heart burned with the desire to experience the world outside his little home. He dressed himself in his father's robes, throwing the hood over himself to conceal his appearance, and ventured out into the city for the first time. Alas, he took the mysterious Runkavle with him as a precaution against the dangers of the outside world.

"Young Afonos wandered over to the city market, in awe of all the new sights, sounds, and smells that tickled his nostrils. It was at the market that a group of four other boys approached him and, unlike the adults that littered the market, the children stood low enough to see what lay beneath his cowl. The boys mocked and jeered, and taunted poor Afonos, and began to beat him as if he was an old sack of potatoes. He was terrified, and needed to act to save his own life from the cruel and hateful boys. And so he brandished the Runkavle from within his garments and drove it through each of his assailants, leaving their bloody heaps upon the ground and fleeing back to the safety of his house.

"When Koenig returned from his travels, he heard of the four butchered boys, and noticed the Runkavle had a glistening of fresh blood upon its blade. Koenig became enraged at the atrocity, and feared that someone at the market would link the deformed boy to the killing, thus exposing Koenig's own transgression years before when he disobeyed the king's order to slay the baby in the wood. He feared that the king would order the boy killed, and himself banished from the land as a punitive measure.

"Clearly, the boy was not ready for society, or perhaps, society was not ready for him. Something needed to be done to keep the boy from being beheaded, and Koenig excommunicated. Koenig took the Runkavle and chanted in some foreign tongue unknown to Afonos. With some wicked and divine magic, he cast Afonos into Drugoy Mir, imprisoning the boy within its confines to save him from a dark fate. Little did he know, Koenig had created a fate for the boy far worse than death."

Muka Vechny paused to glance down at Koenig's robes.

"It's hiding on your person right now, isn't it? I can sense it," he said, sniffing the air like an animal and pawing at Koenig's robes with an icy hand. He relinquished the Runkavle and held it high. "Oh, device of treachery and torment! It is starkly as I remember it. The same device that imprisoned me here shall be my salvation." His gaze returned to Koenig.

"Yes, Edward, you were the first to snatch the Runkavle from Brynjar Eindride's grasp. Some before you attempted; they all failed. Some after you attempted, and most of them failed as well. It pains me greatly to admit that you are quite unique.

"When you snatched the Runkavle from Eindride, you became the first Odinian. You displayed the physical and mental prowess to obtain the mystical item, thus sealing an inextricable bond between yourself and the claimed weapon of Odin. Every member of your lineage henceforth was to be endowed with the same gift." A slithering line of black smoke embraced the Runkavle and whisked it away to the mahogany table, where it gently propped the device out of Koenig's reach.

"When Eindride offered to grant you a wish, you asked to live on long after a normal mortal would have perished. I speculate that this is the reason you were reborn to Áki and Mary Koenig many centuries later. It was Eindride's way of fulfilling your wish. Or, perhaps, your energies are a tenacious and unyielding lot which simply refuse to be snuffed out."

The pressure in Koenig's head raged and bloomed, leaving him nearly unable to process rational thought. "So…you've been in Drugoy Mir…the whole time?" he asked, wincing at the acuteness of the pain.

A tortured grimace entangled Muka Vechny's face. "Have you any idea what it is like to wander a desolate ghost land for centuries with naught but your own thoughts to comfort you? If I believed I led a sorrowful, lonesome existence on earth, I was but a fool awaiting his true condemnation."

"So you prey on the only victims you come across, yearwalkers?" Koenig asked.

"It is true that I became a creature of veritable bitterness and contempt in my isolation. Alas, over the years I developed ways in which to concentrate my will into the act of stealing another being's energy, their very life force. My only contact with your world became an interaction with the occasional wanderer who ventured into my prison, be them yearwalkers, or those who discovered the few other ways to enter this land.

"The energies I robbed these mortals of sated me. But was I different from any of the other beasts that roam this wicked land? Nay, had I not preyed on the living, something else would have taken my place to do so. Perhaps something far more treacherous."

"So what the Leshy told me wasn't true. It wasn't you who corrupted Drugoy Mir and drove it into a state of decay."

"Nay, my old friend. Daresay, my bitterness and malign heart merely complement the world in which you trapped me. And I finally have you. How effortless it was to render you immobile and defenseless." Muka Vechny clumsily licked his lips.

"So you discovered where I lived and kidnapped my family to lure me up here. Why didn't you just take me in the first place? And how did you know I would find Pinemist Bay?"

"Well my old friend, even if perchance you have retained just a shadow of your former self's might, I knew that you were still a powerful Odinian, and I knew it was imperative that I avoid rousing your true nature until the proper moment. Moreover, I divined that your daughter would be an Odinian same as you, and that she would connect with you telepathically if provoked.

"My theory came true. You followed the breadcrumb trail I laid before your feet, and here you are. The only miscalculation I made was in your daughter. She has proved a far more powerful, far more resilient and headstrong Odinian than I believed she would be. Her gift developed and matured at a very young age indeed, and she has been fouling my operations since the start."

"Now, I must satiate my other hunger; the singular thing that has kept me going in this miserable brothel of despair, and the final reason that I purloined your family that night, and not you. To see the look upon your visage as I destroy your world."

The crippling pressure in Koenig's head magnified. His cognizance was dwindling, but there was nothing he could do. His broken body lay splayed and stuck to the chamber wall while Muka Vechny drained him of his essence.

Muka Vechny slowly turned away from Koenig and stalked toward Eveline. Within the garish shroud of light that bloomed from his enemy, Koenig thought he could see the glimmer of something sharp. His arm was morphing into a weapon. Muka Vechny perched himself beside Eveline and leaned close enough to her that Koenig could see the despondence on her face as it glowed in his spectral light.

"Stay...stay away from her," Koenig said.

"Oh, Edward. All that Afonos Petrov ever asked of the world was to accept him as he was. Alas, Afonos Petrov is long dead, and the only thing remaining is the sallow image of a broken man that you condemned to a fate far worse than death."

"Please, I didn't do anything of the sort!" Koenig said. "Whether or not it's true, I have no recollection of that, it was another lifetime. I am a different man now, leave her out of it!" Muka Vechny raised his arm, unveiling the sword-like weapon it had transformed into. It hovered just below Eveline's face. Muka Vechny gripped her head with his other hand.

"Now, my old friend, I shall repay you for what you did to me all those years ago. Then you shall assist me, willing or not, in my deliverance from this wretched world."

"I'll never help you!" Koenig protested.

"Ah, but that is where you are wrong. Even as we speak, I am draining the essence right from your very veins. Since you possess a considerable essence, you will not die. Nay, you shall become my primary slave, brainwashed and begging to carry out my wishes." He raised his arm against Eveline's throat, her skin tenting against the sharp end of his fingers.

"Eveline, baby, look at me," Koenig cried. "Everything will be okay." The tip broke the surface of her skin, thimbles of blood dancing down her throat.

"Edward, please!" she screamed.

"I'm here, honey. Look into my eyes," he said. "God damn it, Afonos, stop this!"

Eveline's expression altered into a look that in his several years with her, he had never seen. "Look after our child, Edward." Her voice was faint as a whisper. With a thin gurgling sound, Muka Vechny's hand continued along her throat, drawing a curtain of blood and cleaving her neck wide open. Her face relaxed and her limp head slumped downward into the darkness.

An amalgam of despair, hatred, and anger jolted Koenig's mind, while a volatile surge of energy ignited every fiber in his exhausted body. With a resounding cry, he wrenched himself free of his bonds and crashed to the floor. Operating on instincts alone, he thrust his arm toward Gungnir, the fabled weapon of Odin. The device first flinched, then wobbled off the table and glided into his hand.

Muka Vechny made a guttural, shrieking ululation and flung himself toward Koenig. The brilliant raven-black vapor puckered into a clump and coiled forward in an inky stream. Koenig drove the Runkavle toward Muka Vechny as a burst of air shot out of the blade's tip. A loud crack reverberated as the stream of air from the Runkavle collided with the dark shroud, saturating the chamber in a maelstrom of energies. Fractured light flashed about the room, and a deluge of air crackled and whipped across Koenig's face.

Watching it knock about in the torrent, he was certain that his arm had broken during the collision. He didn't take heed. His singular focus, keeping the Runkavle pointed toward his enemy, allowing it to serve as an extension of his essence.

As he struggled against the might of Muka Vechny, he could feel that much of his own strength had been drained and assimilated by his enemy, fortifying his wicked powers and diminishing Koenig's. And even though his mind was a virulent storm of rage, and despite his arduous effort, he was losing ground.

Muka Vechny's twisted face peeled into a smile as the black shroud began to envelop Koenig. Just as his vision went dim and he felt his body collapsing, a small bud of pure, resplendent light pierced the dark vale. The light bloomed ferociously, and its centrifuge glared with a blinding immensity. A figure appeared inside, small and angelic amidst the glow. Her ashen hair floated weightlessly, her tiny frame hovering several feet above the ground.

The cold embrace of the vapor disappeared as if it was being siphoned away, and as the murk lessened, Koenig could see Muka Vechny.

He had recoiled in surprise and fear at the sight, making confused movements with his head. The tiny figure thrust her hands forward, and a brilliant white beam lashed out from her fingertips.

Muka Vechny let out a yelp and flung his misty shroud toward her. The energies collided and blasted Koenig backward several paces. He cradled his broken arm against his body and shielded his eyes with his other arm. The energies seethed and scintillated in the darkness, with neither side yielding to the other.

"Daddy!" the angelic figure called. "Do it now!" Muka Vechny craned his neck and glared at Koenig.

"Think...about it, Edward," he heaved. "If you kill me...you kill everyone whose essence is within me. Even your beloved father, Áki." Koenig clambered forward against the backsplash of energy. He raised the Runkavle with an unsteady hand.

"I have to stop you." Every laborious step he took toward his enemy felt like he was stumbling into a hurricane of energies. "The fabled weapon of Odin had the power to lock you in this world; maybe it has the power to drive you from it."

"What are you—what are you doing?" Muka Vechny spat.

"Dalla, I'm very proud of you," he said. "Please remember that you are the best thing that ever happened to me, and I love you very much." He smiled at his daughter, and her response caused a surge of warmth to flow through him.

I love you, daddy, she thought to him.

He pushed forward amidst tumbling energies and crackling torrents of blazing hot air. Virulent cascades of light emitted from the clashing powers, disorienting his every step. Within arm's reach now, Koenig raised the spear of Odin, feeling its energies vibrate and hum through the blade as it awaited his bidding.

He closed his eyes, inhaled, and thought of all those who had suffered at the hands of his enemy. From the sweet old, frizzy haired lady named Doris, to his father Áki and his sister Eva, to Adam Trevin and his sacrifice, to his late father George, and his birth mother Ella, and finally, the light of his life, Eveline.

He exhaled and drew the blade into his enemy with such force that it traveled clear through his back. Muka Vechny let out a tortured scream, his head cocking backward. A violent shudder pervaded the chamber, and he could see the stone walls begin to waver and crumble.

"Dalla, listen to me! You need to go now!" Koenig shouted above the cacophony of noises as the world dissolved around him.

"No daddy, I won't leave you!" As he wrenched his head to look upon his daughter, he saw that she was no longer bundled in an effulgent splendor of light; she was no longer hovering majestically in the air. Dalla simply stood upon the ground, pigeon-toed and innocently twisting her finger through her hair.

Seeing her now, the image reminded Koenig of all the times she would appear at his doorway in the middle of the night, the hallway light beaming over her diminutive frame. She would tell him that she had a bad dream, and he would cradle her in his arms and speak words of comfort and reassurance. He thought of how they would always whisper to avoid waking Eveline.

Realizing the innate and mystical bond he has always had with his little one, he imagined all the times he could have held her in his bed, singing her a lullaby through his mind instead of whispering in the dark. He wished he had known the true connection they shared.

"No baby, you have to go now!" he shouted, while Muka Vechny writhed and contorted in agony beside him. "This whole place is coming down. Daddy will follow you out, Dalla, but you need to leave now!"

"Okay daddy, but I'll wait right outside for you." The little girl turned and headed for the entrance, but just as she began to cross under, a chunk of ceiling crumbled and drove downwards.

"No!" Koenig cried.

In a visceral flash, he disinterred the Runkavle from his enemy and thrust it towards Dalla. A thread of air propelled from the blade's tip and caught the pulverulent mess of rock as it came within inches of his daughter's head.

"Go now, baby," he stammered, waiting to release the rubble until she had cleared the room.

"But daddy, you can't follow me if the wall closes!"

"Daddy can't hold it much longer Dalla, you have to get out of here!" The stinging heat of tears caressed his eyes, muddling his vision. "I need you to live your life, baby, your gift is too great to throw away."

With one final heave of Odin's spear, he pushed Dalla clear of the doorway and released the falling debris.

Muka Vechny shrieked in terror and defeat as he watched the passage crash to a close. Koenig wrapped his arms around his enemy, pinning him down as the room caved in about them. *I know you'll live a beautiful and dignified life, baby. Make your daddy proud.*

Everything faded to black.

****

He ascended from the bitter, dank chamber and into a rapturous light where an image shimmered before him. He was there on the day he met her. The girl was leaning on an old red Datsun at the only drive-in movie theater in Rochelle. Her hair was wild and long, and flowed down to the middle of her back. She had on jean shorts and knee-high leather boots, with one propped on the rear bumper of the car, the mud-caked soles smearing the chrome surface.

It was his first memory of her. A memory that he had once treasured, but in the last few years had become inhumed deeply within his guilty mind. For a moment that seemed impossibly drawn out, he lingered before her and breathed her in. He now understood why he had made the same detrimental choices over and over again. From the very moment he decided to approach her on that warm summer day, a part of him knew that he would never be good enough for her.

For the first time in his life, he dropped the burden of human emotion. He stopped trying to analyze his faults; why he stumbled time and time again. And that was when the girl on the Datsun turned to him, and smiled.

Epilogue

With the basket propped on her arm, the woman meandered down the aisle. She scrutinized the labels on several boxes and finally dropped a package of multivitamins into the basket. With a rattle, it settled in the grooves between a carton of eggs and a coffee tumbler labeled Blackrock Café.

The woman continued to the front of the store and stepped into the checkout line, giving a friendly smile to an old man in front of her. She gently placed her hand on her stomach and inhaled deeply. Still no movement.

"How far along are you, dearie?" a voice from behind startled her.

"Oh, I'm sorry. I didn't know anyone was behind me," the woman said. "About four months." The little old lady with wispy grey hair smiled. The woman smiled back and turned away.

"She'll be well off with your darling red locks, dearie," the little old lady said. "If your husband is anywhere near as special, she'll be a heart breaker."

"Oh, I'm not married." The woman smiled and turned away again.

"Oh. Where's her father, dearie?" the little old lady asked.

"He's, uh…he's no longer with us," the woman said.

"Well, I'm sorry to hear that," the little old lady said. "But I'm sure he's with us in spirit, or at least in essence." Startled by the comment, the woman turned around. But the little old lady was gone. In her place stood a young girl with ashen blonde hair flowing down over a battered nightgown. The girl smiled up at the woman and reached out her hand. She pressed it against the woman's belly, and closed her eyes. Beneath the girl's hand, the woman felt a kick.

About the Author

Alec Arbogast lives in Salt Lake City, Utah. When he's not deep in the world of writing, he's taking classes at the university, mulling over the next mod for his Mustang, reading way too many books at once, and incessantly drinking coffee. Before he discovered his love of writing, his passion for music led him to participate in a variety of ensembles, performing with rock groups at arts festivals and street fairs in his high school days. He doesn't play real guitar as much anymore, but his air-guitar is on point.

Alec appreciates all kinds of prose, but is continuously captivated by horror, mystery, crime thrillers, and historical fiction. In his own writing, he likes putting unlikely heroes in unusual circumstances, and he loves creating complex characters that quite frequently don't do the right thing. The Last Odinian is his debut novel.

You can reach him online at www.alec-arbogast.com, on Facebook as The Bumbling Odinian, or on Twitter @Alec_Arbogast.

CPSIA information can be obtained
at www.ICGtesting.com
Printed in the USA
FFOW02n1630031217
43814087-42745FF

9 781947 578012